Praise for *The Lightkeeper's Wife*

"*The Lightkeeper's Wife* is a beautiful, stirring novel full of captivating mystery and clear-eyed emotion. The luminous characters are beacons that guide the reader through a narrative as thrilling, expansive, and dangerous as the sea at night."

—Bret Anthony Johnston, author of *Remember Me Like This* and *Corpus Christi*

"In *The Lightkeeper's Wife*, Sarah Anne Johnson spins a riveting tale of piracy, shipwrecks, and 1800s New England life with an insightful and attentive eye on the roles of women so often overlooked by history. I was completely immersed in this world, and Hannah Snow's powerful journey is one I will long remember."

—Jill McCorkle, author of *Life After Life* and *Crash Diet*

D1111317

the

LIGHTKEEPER'S
WIFE

a novel

SARAH ANNE JOHNSON

sourcebooks
landmark

To Alice

Published by Sourcebooks Landmark, an imprint of Sourcebooks, Inc.
P.O. Box 4410, Naperville, Illinois 60567-4410
(630) 961-3900
Fax: (630) 961-2168
www.sourcebooks.com

Library of Congress Cataloging-in-Publication data is on file with the publisher.

Printed and bound in the United States of America.
VP 10 9 8 7 6 5 4 3 2 1

1

NEAR DAWN A LOUD CRACK CAME, LIKE A TREE FALLING. There were no trees near the house. Hannah reached quickly for a pair of John's work pants. She'd never worn pants before, but he wasn't here to stop her. Out the north-east window, the fog was so dense she could run her hands through it. Pants cinched in a rope knot at her waist, she stood at the kitchen counter eating a piece of salt beef. There was no pleasure in it. Outside, the wind had made the low-lying bushes tilt with a strange bend that made them yearn in the same direction rather than lean. The light, Dangerfield Light, flashed a steady pulse. There was nothing to see but more fog. No cries or calling out from below, only canvas sails snapping in the wind.

The familiar sound of a shipwreck.

From the top of the stairs that led down to the beach, the wreck was a veiled shadow some three hundred feet out from shore. She gazed toward the road, but there was no sign of her husband. John had been gone for a couple of days up Cape for supplies. She'd missed him in their bed, missed the size of him and his arms around her, but she wasn't going to wait for him, not with sailors struggling for safety. She followed the rickety staircase, down the two hundred and some odd steps that shivered beneath her footfall, easy for her heel to miss and send her to the bottom in a heap of broken bones.

The rain on the stairs sounded like pebbles pouring down, relentless. Rain trickled down the neck of her jacket, frozen until it warmed against her skin. Nearly one hundred and fifty feet she descended to the beach, where the surf frothed at her feet. She kept her eyes on the faint impression of the stranded ship. Wind lashed the covering over the rescue skiff until she got the canvas under control and shoved it beneath the stairs.

Make sure the lines are coiled. Keep the life ring at the ready. The thrill and shiver of the storm vibrated through her as she guided the skiff on rollers toward the surf. She rolled up the bottoms of her pants and waded into the icy cold, holding the boat steady as she pulled the oars from beneath the seat and climbed onboard. She'd promised not to go out alone, to stay ashore and keep the lights flashing, but there could be men aboard that ship about to drown. As she put her back into rowing, the beach faded in the fog behind her and the flash from the lighthouse grew dim. Over her shoulder was the looming architecture of the ship, sunk low in the water, the foremast shorn.

She kept a safe distance to avoid any wreckage, a falling mast or topsail spar. The skiff's seams creaked, the seat sagged beneath her as the waves knocked the little boat about, but she used the oars to steady it. The wind drummed at her ears, that hard rhythm the only sound now.

She rowed closer, until the ruin took shape. The ocean had poured into the hull from below. It had dismantled hatchways, bulwarks, cupboards, everything splintered apart and drifting. A froth of oil and something red and soupy floated across the water in a wide, reeking arc around the wreck. Seagulls dove into the slick, pecking at bits of bread and food, their cries piercing and debauched.

Hannah rowed to leeward, following the drift of debris, keeping her eyes sharp, glancing over her right shoulder, then her left, shifting her attention aft again. A clunk against the hull stopped her midstroke.

"Hello! Anyone there?"

The fog muffled her voice. Reaching into the water, she dislodged a six-foot piece of rail that rested against the skiff. She tried not to think about how many men had been onboard. Oars set and ready, she watched and searched, scanning the water in circles around the wreck. Minutes passed. Or was it longer?

"Hello!" Hannah called. Was that an arm reaching up from the water? Right there, a man clinging to a broken spar. The life ring was attached to a long rope, which she fastened to the back of the boat. She stood and shifted her weight in rhythm to the waves. She'd never saved a drowning man, but instinct took over, and with a heave, she flung the life ring toward him. *Grab it, you can do it.*

The man kicked toward the ring, but he wouldn't let go of the wood spar that kept him afloat. He rose and then dropped behind a wave, rose up, then down again. The wind billowed her oilskin jacket and chilled her. It dried the saltwater onto her skin in a thin crust. Waves splashed the wreck in a rhythmic blast as Hannah pulled the ring in. She tossed it closer to the man this time, intoxicated with the prospect of reeling him in. "Grab hold, man! Grab hold! You'll freeze out here." He lifted his head and slowly drifted toward the circle of bobbing cork. When he finally looped an arm through it and let go of the spar, she braced her foot against the stern seat and hauled until the sailor appeared, facedown, behind the skiff. She'd have to bring him over the transom. She pushed the life ring aside and grabbed him under the arms. His legs floated back so that she was able to use the rise of the waves to hook his elbows over the gunwale, then pull him up and tilt him into the boat. He landed in the bilge, a shrimplike curl. Frozen breath hovered by his mouth. She removed her jacket and draped it over him and pulled it to his chin to shelter him from the wind.

Hannah leaned in close to the man. "Was there anyone else? You've got to tell me now." The man groaned and pulled his arms in around his body. His eyes batted beneath the lids, thick eyebrows plastered to his skull, a blue vein marking the side of his face like a scar. She shook him hard. "Was there anyone else?" Hannah scanned the water in every direction. "Anyone out there?" She plunged the oars into the water and took another turn toward the wreck, but the debris had drifted off and there was nothing left to see.

The man didn't move or make a sound. She took notice of his gray undershirt and long johns, no other clothes. Sailors often removed layers in the water to stay afloat. *You're hardly blue at all. Sole survivor. That says something about a man.* She turned to get her bearings. *I'll get you ashore. You may be the first one I've rescued, but you'll not be the last.* The wind was dying off, the surf easier now, and the sailor wasn't jostled. The fog had lifted enough for her to see the beach. She ignored the ache in her arms and steered the skiff toward the lighthouse. If the sailor couldn't make it up, she'd have to haul him in the life cart. At least he was small. Some of the men John rescued were so big he had to wait while Hannah went for help to get the men up the dunes.

Blood ran from the sailor's forehead now, red streaks in the bilge water. Hannah crossed the oars in front of her and bent down for a look. A three-corner tear, but not to the bone. She quickly removed her woolen sweater, rolled it into a ball, and stuck it under his head.

When she turned to locate the lighthouse again—she wanted to land near the base of the stairs—there was Tom Atkins, John's best friend who lived next door, pacing the beach. Hannah recognized his willowy figure, one hand over his eyes to shield them from the hazy light. She didn't want to have to explain herself, or talk, or do anything but get the sailor up to the house. She'd known Tom since the day she moved to the lighthouse. The three of them—John, Hannah, and Tom—had sat around many fires and tended many half-drowned men. Once they got a man ashore, he was kept alive with heat from the fire, Hannah's chowder, and good conversation. The sound of people talking kept a fevered sailor attached to this world, Hannah was sure of it.

"Hey," Tom called, waving as if his worry could bring her in faster. Finally, he walked into the surf, boots, pants, and all. As the skiff lifted and rolled in on a breaker, he guided it onto the beach, eyeing the man in the bilge. "Hannah, Jesus Christ. You shouldn't be out in the boat alone."

"I'm not alone, am I?" she said.

"That was a brutal nor'easter, tore the corner of my barn roof off."

"Storm's over, Tom. Now, you want to help me or not?"

"It's just luck you're okay. You know that, don't you? It's pure luck." His long fingers felt along the man's neck to find a pulse. "He's alive, at least."

They lifted the sailor from the skiff and carried him up the beach. He groaned until they put him in the life cart and covered him with blankets. The life cart was nothing more than an old skiff with wheels on the bottom that John used for hauling injured survivors who couldn't climb the stairs, but it did the job.

"I went by the house to check on you after the storm, then saw the wreck and had a hunch you might be down here. This was the only one, then?"

Hannah nodded.

Blood from the sailor's forehead ran down the side of his face. Hannah wiped the blood with her shirtsleeve and took another look at the gash. "We've got to cover that," she said, "to stop the bleeding." She unsheathed the rigging knife from her belt.

"What are you doing?"

"You look at me like I'm going to kill him, Tom." She cut a strip of cotton from her shirttail, handed Tom the knife, and went to work bandaging the sailor's head, folding the strip of cotton in half and covering the wound.

Tom winced and stepped back when she tightened the bandage. "You'll need a shot of something to warm him up," he said, and searched through the gear beneath the stairs until he found the bottle. He held the man's head up and tipped the whiskey to his lips until he swallowed.

With the sailor in the cart, they worked fast to pull it onto the rollers, wooden logs shaved to be even all the way around, and then they maneuvered it back to the dunes.

"He's shivering near to death," Tom said.

"So, let's hurry up."

"I'll haul him up, just give me a few minutes," Tom said, heading for the stairs.

Hannah stared across the water, wondering how many men had been aboard the ship. Over a hundred ships wrecked along this coast every year—last year, 1842, had been particularly bad. And there was nothing anyone could do. No flashing light, no navigational chart could save them—the sandbars shifted during each storm and tides carried off parts of the beach so that the coast was always changing and impossible to chart. Experienced sea captains knew to stay offshore, but in a storm, the northeast wind forced ships onto the shoals where they ran aground and fell victim to the battering surf.

"Hello down there." Tom tugged on the line, and the front of the cart lifted. Hannah guided it up the dune, over brambles and sea grass until it was closer to Tom than to the beach. Then she trudged up the stairs, the wind at her back pushing her, nearly lifting her up.

Once they'd settled the sailor on a bedroll in front of the fire, Hannah tried to open his shirt so he could feel the heat, but he moaned and pulled away from her. She placed his arms by his sides, and when she unbuttoned his shirt, there were layers of bandages wrapped around his chest. "He's got some kind of injury," she said. "Broken ribs, maybe."

"Go on and change into some dry clothes yourself. I'll take care of him," Tom said.

In the bedroom, Hannah wrapped herself in a blanket and moved slowly to the closet to find another pair of John's trousers. As she stepped into them, she couldn't help expecting him to swing through the door, glance over at the man on the hearth, and say, "Hannah, you went out in the boat alone?" He'd be angry, but what she dreaded more was the look of hurt. They'd argued about it countless times, his need to protect her and her need to pursue her own inclination—she wanted to work in the boat, not stay ashore.

She'd been going out on practice runs in clear weather when John was gone, but she'd never faced the danger of a storm alone, never experienced the surge of energy that enabled her to act without thinking and gave her the strength to lift the weight of a water-soaked man over the transom. She'd never saved a drowning man until now.

With John's undershirt and a heavy shawl, she began to warm up. She ran her fingers through her tangled hair, and gave herself a quick look in the mirror, but there was no taming her dark, wavy hair. She closed the door behind her.

On the hearth lay the very proof of her ability. John couldn't argue with her now. When she lifted the sailor's head and tilted a cup of coffee to his lips, his eyes didn't open.

"Now that he's dry, you gotta roast the cold out of him," Tom said. "He's bleeding through that rag."

Hannah tossed a couple of logs onto the fire, and then leaned over the sailor to unwrap the bandage, clotted now with blood. "He let you change his clothes?" They kept a bag of odd clothes provided by the local church thrift for stranded sailors.

"Just his shirt. He seemed in pain if I moved him too much."

"And the bandage?"

"I left it."

"Bring me a bucket of water, Tom, and a clean cloth."

The cut was not deep and only required a good wash in warm water before she applied clean bandages. Tom made coffee in the kitchen, his back to the sight of blood, but Hannah wasn't afraid. She knew how to treat a wound, ease a fever, and clear a man's lungs of water.

Tom brought two cups of coffee to the table. "He'll make it?"

"If he doesn't, it won't be from the wound. He feels feverish. I'll have to watch him."

She sat at the table across from Tom, in the chair by the fire. Hands wrapped around a hot cup of coffee, she felt the blisters on her fingers. Her palms burned.

"What made you go out there, Hannah? What were you thinking?"

"I wasn't thinking. I just went."

"Just because you can handle a boat doesn't mean you should row headlong into a nor'easter."

"I thought John'd be back by now."

"You're changing the subject." Hannah shrugged. Tom leaned forward, elbows on the table. "Maybe he stayed over in Orleans to avoid the storm. He was going to bring me some roofing nails from Barnstable." Tom's talent was for making furniture, but he was an able carpenter, and if any of the widows in town needed help, he was quick to wrangle a group of men to lend their hammers.

If the shape of the Cape was a bent arm, Barnstable was the biceps, a long day's ride by horse and wagon, Orleans the elbow, and halfway home. Dangerfield was the wrist, exposed to the worst of the northeast storms that pounded its narrow shore.

The man in front of the fire hadn't opened his eyes. His chest rose and fell with his wheezing breath, so loud you could hear the rattle of it through his mouth. His lips were blue, the rims of his eyes swollen red. He mumbled blurred syllables, his head jerking from one side to another, and then resting as if defeated.

Tom watched him, then looked at Hannah, who was twirling her napkin into a tight rope. "I was planning on riding down to Orleans later if the wind lets up. You need anything?"

Hannah looked closely at Tom, reminded now of the world beyond Dangerfield. "No, I'm set," she said. He was handsome, with red hair that hung over his forehead and high cheekbones, a strong jaw, and soft chin. He didn't know his good looks and this made him more attractive.

"If I pass John on the road, I'll give him a shout." Tom took his coat from the hook by the door. "You okay with this stranger?" he asked, pointing to the sailor. "I can stay if you think—"

"No. I'll get him up before too long and send him on his way."

"Alrighty, then." Tom hesitated by the door.

"It's okay," Hannah said.

As much as she didn't want to explain the sailor on the hearth, Hannah comforted herself with the thought that John would be home soon, and the responsibility that sat on her shoulders would lift. Whenever he came home from his monthly trips, he rode his wagon straight into its stall, unloaded the supplies, and took Hannah's hand in his own. "Let's go up to the light-house," he'd say.

This time, before John left for Barnstable, he'd made her promise to record the passing ships she spotted each day. After his final scan of the horizon and careful notations in the logbook, he'd slung his carpetbag over his shoulder and gone to the barn to hitch up the wagon. But every few minutes, as Hannah stood in the kitchen washing vegetables or putting away the breakfast dishes, John hurried back inside to retrieve some forgotten item—his straight razor and strop, clean socks, his timepiece, which he finally found in his pocket.

"Just go, John. Whatever you don't have you can borrow."

"Right," he said, making an effort to laugh at himself as he swept the black curls back from his forehead and pulled his cap into place.

"I'll see you in a few days," she said, playfully pushing him through the door. She'd watched him steer the wagon, check-ing his pockets and looking back at the house as if willing it to remain attached to the lighthouse, so he could find it upon his return.

2

HANNAH AND JOHN HAD AMPLE ROOM IN THE lightkeeper's cottage, an open space except for their bedroom in the far right corner. A small kitchen to the right of the front door had three windows over the sink facing east, so that the lighthouse keeper had a clear view of the ocean. To the left sat a dining table, and in the farther left quadrant of the house, a sitting room with a large fireplace where the sailor now slept. A loft over the dining area offered a place for ship-wrecked sailors who needed time to recover. What had once been a borning room, they'd opened to create more space in the living area. Tom's two-story farmhouse down the road with its eight rooms was much more typical, but this layout made the house easier to heat by the single fireplace. South-facing front windows drew what heat and light could be gathered from the sun. The structure was built from rough-hewn boards, the beams beneath the house still covered with bark. The white plaster walls at night shined bright in the light of whale oil lanterns and the wood fire, another small mark upon the shore.

At the kitchen sink, Hannah stared out the window where the ship had gone down. She'd saved a man. She was thrilled and terrified and she wanted to do it again. Hadn't she been training for this since she was a young girl? Before she could walk, her father took her out on his boat, and he taught her to row as soon as she could hold an oar. She'd worked with him on his boat since she was seven years old, pulling lobsters from the traps and pegging the claws while her father did the heavier work of hauling the traps from the water. She didn't wear pants then, but a skirt that was the only one her mother would let her wear on the boat. Her father let her tuck the bottom into her waistband so that she could move around easier.

His sleeves rolled to the elbows had revealed his forearms, blue veins running through hard muscle that swelled with work. She loved how his hair curled at the ends in the salt air. He steered the boat up to a buoy, headed the boat into the wind and let the sails flap, fastened the buoy onto a hook and hauled away on the trap line until he got the trap alongside the hull. The sun glared across the water and his eyes reflected with light, his hair blown back in the wind, sideburns thick and long. He held the trap open for her small hand and taught her how to grab the lobster between the claws so it couldn't snap at her. Then she pegged it and dumped it in the bucket. "Thatta girl, Hannah," he said, and pulled out the flask he carried in his jacket to take a swig. He let her take celebratory sips and gave her a penny for every lobster she pegged.

Once Hannah turned fourteen, her mother forbade her to go out on the boat anymore. She was made to work in the store and wear a proper dress with a corset and baleen like a young lady. The dress nagged at her; it followed her around like a pesky dog. The corset pinched the skin on her ribs and she was always pulling at it.

"Hannah, stop it," was her mother's constant refrain.

She missed being on the boat. The sun taunted her through the front windows of the store while she counted money from the cash drawer and refused to smile at the customers. She yearned for one day on the water with her father, for the smell of fish and lobster, for her father's appreciation of her skills on the boat and his brief words of approval. "That's it, Hannah, good."

Her mother was nothing like him. Unlike any other woman in town, Nora Paine thrived on business. She rose at dawn to make breakfast, dressed in one of many fine skirts, with shirt-waists to match, corsets cinched tight, and then went straight to the shop to take a quick inventory. At the harbor she pushed her hat back to reveal eyes the color of the sky, whatever it was that particular day. Soft feathers of gray in her dark hair, long eyelashes, small pretty hands—these were the things the merchants noticed when she negotiated prices on corn meal, flour, coffee, bolts of fabric, and rope. Nora found a thrill when she talked the man down a penny on a pound of flour. The merchants knew she was shrewd and wanted to avoid her, but not only was she pretty, she ran the busiest store in town. They had to do business with her if they were going to move their goods, and conducting business with a woman was not a usual thing in 1843.

Nora feared poverty more than she feared anyone's opinion. A lobsterman's income was seasonal at best, and the sea had claimed many a husband. Without money a woman faced an awful fate. So Nora bought buckets made by a deaf man in town and sold them at a profit. She rented out a room over the barn to travelers, even baked pies over the holidays and took orders from the local men who had no one to cook for them.

If she worked hard and lived honestly, she believed God would protect her and her family from ruin.

The women in Dangerfield worried over every detail of a daily life centered around fishing—how many nets to mend, who was the best man to ask for help with the firewood. At least those worries they could do something about, unlike the larger worry of losing a loved one to the sea. No matter how much fish or money, journeys or adventure the ocean brought, she was a capricious friend. She could not to be trusted from one year to the next, and the women believed that to trust the sea, to believe that you would be spared, that your men would be spared, was to ensure disaster. If you remained frightened and humble, then God would watch over your family and protect their flimsy ships and precious lives, and if you lived in the midst of a volatile being such as the sea, God was your only hope. Hannah's mother believed that self-sufficiency was her only hope. Hannah didn't agree with any of them.

What difference does it make if I'm self-sufficient? With the sea as her only god, Hannah had no reason to be afraid. Whatever the tide carried in, it would eventually take out. Any bad weather would change to good weather, just as the good weather would turn bad. It was the nature of things. This was Hannah's faith.

And it had gotten this shipwrecked sailor ashore. There he slept, unmoving. As she looked at the frayed socks in the basket by her chair, she absently rolled a piece of thread between her fingers, sore from rowing. Is that faith, she wondered, to not be afraid? A shutter snapped in the wind; the storm door slammed hard in its frame, and she was up like a spark from the fire. She rushed to the window and pulled the curtain back.

She wanted to tell John about the wreck and how she'd managed to get the sailor onto the boat. Her eyes scanned the dark toward the barn. She waited several long seconds for the flash from the lighthouse to see what was out there, but there was nothing, only the barn door rocking in the wind.

Another two hours gone and it was time to trim the wicks and check the oil. Hannah followed the off-kilter passageway to the bottom of the lighthouse where she reached for the kerosene lantern. The light threw shadows against the brick walls that surrounded the spiral staircase. Huge casks of whale oil were stacked high against the walls. The metal grate of each step clanked beneath her boots, her hand sliding along the cool rail. Out the tiny window halfway up the stairs, the Atlantic sprawled. Hannah noted the position of two schooners and a brig. She would record her findings in the lighthouse logbook when she got downstairs, marking in pencil for each ship the direction in which it sailed, the approximate distance from the shore, and the type: brig, schooner, bark, or sloop. When John returned, he would review her findings, nodding his head at her meticulous entries.

Hannah continued up the stairs, her tired legs accustomed to the work. The wind had died off, but the upper windows still whistled with every blast of air that gusted up the dunes. She climbed into the thick scent of burning oil and lamp smoke. The top of the stairs spilled onto a round landing, and she stood in the tall windows and looked down the full forty-seven feet of the tower. Her eyes followed the path of crushed shells to the house, then eastward where Dangerfield rambled in narrow roads, occasional houses situated amid sweeping properties.

Dangerfield was a town of nearly eighteen hundred wind-blown residents. The Pilgrims had settled the town in the 1600s. John told her stories about how the Pilgrims took advantage of the native Payomet Indians, stealing the corn they'd stored in the dunes, bartering their land out from under them for nothing of value, and introducing them to alcohol, until all that remained of the tribe was their name, Anglicized to Pamet, given to the land they no longer owned.

Many of the town's men had drowned while fishing on George's Bank two years earlier during the October Gale of 1841, leaving behind scores of widows and fatherless children. The men who remained continued their lives on the sea—fishing, whaling, cargo hauling, and running passengers by sloop up Cape or to Boston. These men couldn't imagine their lives any other way, regardless of the pleading cries of mothers, wives, and sisters. Seamen came home and then went to sea for days or months or years at a time, their lives spent whaling or transporting cargo to foreign ports, while women waited at home for news, praying over every lost ship off their coast as if it held their own loved ones.

With only a thin sliver of light left in the sky, Hannah could see the sand dunes of Provincetown to the northwest. She turned to her work, holding her hair back with one hand as she checked the oil in each lamp. She trimmed the ends of wick by snipping off the charred bits with her fingernails, and pulled the wicks up to align the center of the flame with the center of the reflector. Then she struck a match and worked her way around to light each lantern, twenty-four in all. People didn't know that it wasn't one giant light, so powerful a glow did the separate flames create. When she'd first come to the lighthouse six years ago, John had taught her the everyday routine of checking the lamps for oil and trimming the wicks. He'd held her hand as she lit one of the lanterns for the first time, not because she needed him too, but for her initiation into his life, which became their life. She'd started on the opposite side of the light, trimming the wicks and filling the oil before lighting the lantern as he'd shown her, until they met in the middle and he grabbed her around the waist. She dropped the scissors on the floor and kissed him hard on the mouth until he let her gently onto the floor and they made love in the glare of the lanterns.

Every four hours during the night, one of them got up and filled the lanterns with oil. For months, when it was her turn, she felt the thrill of their lovemaking each time the light flashed in her face. When the sun rose each day, they doused the lights and readied them for the evening ritual to begin again.

The first night she'd arrived at the lighthouse, they had stood side by side atop the light. They watched the beam flash a path across the ocean and illuminate the waves and the narrow beach and the impossibly long set of stairs leading up to their yard. She knew then that she would love John forever no matter what came to pass. He had delivered her home. The sky was clear and black. She believed that together they would live this life, and if their love faltered or they encountered some failure between them, they would have their shared love of this place to hold them together.

She turned her gaze southwest where John should be traveling toward Dangerfield. There was no sign of him, but she
could see Sam Potts the peddler camped beneath a tarp near the
end of the lighthouse road. John always let him rest there if the
weather turned bad or his trip was too long. He always made a
point to buy something from Sam: an ounce of sage, a money
tin, a small cutting board.

She rubbed her char-stained fingertips together. The heat of
the lanterns penetrated her back, and exhaustion settled into her
like sand at the bottom of a barrel. Maybe she'd spend a couple
of pennies on that licorice John liked.

Early afternoon and the sailor still hadn't budged. At least he
was breathing, she told herself, and she left a hot cup of coffee
beside him before changing into her skirt to leave the house.
She wanted to think that she had good reason to go back down
to the beach, to take notes about the wreck, or to check for
more sailors, but neither was true. She wanted to see for herself
what had washed ashore since this morning, as if the flotsam
could contain some clue as to how many lives had been lost
and why. On her way around the lighthouse, she looked up the
road, but there was nothing to see. John should be home by
now, regardless of where he'd stayed the night. But she tried to
push the thought from her mind.

Now that the weather had cleared, onlookers from town
came to stand along the shore and set fires with driftwood to
stay warm and keep vigil where the ship had gone down. They

watched the ship tilt farther into the ocean and listened to the crack and yaw as the hull ruptured and seawater filled the last empty spaces to sink her. No matter how many ships went aground, there were always people fascinated and terrified and reverent of the sinking ship, and they watched with an attitude akin to prayer. Hannah walked the beach among them as they ventured guesses as to why the captain ran aground with the lighthouse so near. They speculated on the money lost and imagined the valuable cargo that could have been sold in town but now lay on the ocean floor.

"John find anyone after the storm, Hannah?"

"Damn near tore the shutters off my house."

"What'd he think of the wreck?"

"Hannah, where's John?"

"He's up Cape for supplies. He'll be back soon," she said, and she wanted to believe it.

"He'll be sorry he missed this one." They respected her distance, walking the beach, not talking much, as part of her job as the keeper's wife, figuring out how the wreck happened and how the next one might be prevented.

Hannah understood that they considered themselves lucky to be standing on the beach, but more than luck, they believed it was fate that drove a ship aground, it was fate that took a man's life. Fate created the storms and tides and determined where ships would be and who would be upon them when they drove themselves aground. Destiny was not something any human being could control. Humility and gratitude were their only hope, and once they'd spoken enough about the wreck to remember this simple truth, their talk faded into random remarks. Hannah tilted her head into the wind and let it blow her hair back from her face. The salty air filled her nostrils and lungs as she started up the stairs to the lighthouse. The town's voices hung about her ears. *Where's John?*

The first time John had come into her mother's store, nearly seven years ago, she hadn't looked up from where she stood at the cash register, running her finger through dust between the register keys.

"I need supplies for the light up at Dangerfield," he said. "Silas Gibbons finally retired. I've only been up there a couple of months, and the store down at the harbor doesn't have a lot to offer. I mean, it has enough for the day-to-day, but not much more." He wore a dark blue seaman's jacket, unbuttoned. A red handkerchief held his hair back under his black cap, tilted to shield his eyes from the weather, and dark curls sprang out in all directions. Baggy trousers and a loose linen shirt could not contain the energy of his limbs, as if all that fabric was there to make room for motion. "I need whitewash and staples for the kitchen."

"Hannah, give the man a hand," her mother said, waving her toward him.

Hannah led him across the floor to the whitewash. "You need any brushes?" she asked.

"No, just the whitewash, a hundred fifty feet of one-inch hemp rope, some potatoes, and smoked meat, whatever else you have. I'll trust your opinion on that."

"You have a stove up there?"

"Wood stove and a fire."

"Good," Hannah said, filling the wicker basket he'd brought with potatoes, carrots, green beans, a jar of blackberry preserves, a smoked ham.

"You ever seen the lighthouse?" he asked. "It's a beautiful spot out there, right on the edge of the dunes."

"Lots of wrecks, I hear. Ocean's Graveyard they call it." As she added up his order, she took in his long, lean body and hands thick with work, like her father's.

"You make it sound bad. That's not the only thing about it." She looked up at him then.

"My name's John Snow," he said. "I'll be down here pretty regular now. I was out on a whaler for a few years before I took this post. I'm not used to land living yet. I appreciate your help with the groceries."

Hannah nodded and placed the change in his open palm. He didn't bother to count it before folding it into his pocket. After loading boxes of groceries and supplies onto his wagon, he retrieved his last crate, and on his way out he stopped. "See you again," he said, smiling. His attention made her flush, but she refused to show it, and so bent down to reorganize a shelf.

Every few weeks John Snow came in for supplies, and their visits became friendlier. Hannah's mother began to notice her daughter's interest in the lightkeeper, and while she wasn't convinced that he was an appropriate suitor, he was the only man Hannah had ever paid any attention to. For this reason alone, she decided one morning to give him a good look. Under the guise of giving him two loaves of cranberry bread, she invited him to sit at the counter and drink a hot cup of coffee. John hung his jacket and hat on the rack. He wore a black wool sweater that exaggerated his dark features. "Those berries are harvested here in Barnstable," her mother said, pushing the cream and sugar in front of him.

"Thank you, ma'am. I don't get a lot of baked items up at the lights. I've no talent for it myself."

"Hannah can bake when she sets her mind to it," her mother said, wiping a clean rag over the varnished counter. Hannah ignored her and walked to the front window where she glanced up and down the road. She spotted Evan Pierce strolling by as if he didn't have a care in the world. Evan worked on his father's boat fishing for cod off George's Bank, and she'd come to know him on the docks working with her father. His eyes flitted just like a fish until he spotted her and stopped in front of the window. His brownish-red hair reflected the sun like fish scales, tiny rainbows of shimmering light. They spoke through the window.

"What're you doing in town?" she asked.

"Had to borrow some caulking for repairs."

Hannah gazed into her clasped hands and then back up through the streaked glass. Now that she was stuck in the store, there wasn't a lot for them to talk about. Evan looked up the street. He shrugged, then tossed a quick wave on his way toward the harbor.

Hannah sighed in as frustrated a tone as she could muster, picked up the duster from its hook, and began lifting items from the shelf and dusting, then slamming each item back down again.

"She doesn't like working indoors," Nora said. John smiled, his eyes on Hannah.

When Hannah invited him to go clamming out on the flats at the end of Wharf Road, her mother took her into the stockroom. "Couldn't you wait for him to ask you on a proper outing?"

"What difference does it make, Mother?"

"It's no way to win a man over."

"I don't want to win him over. I want to take him clamming."

She watched John work the clamming rake in the mud, scooping until he heard a solid clank against the metal, then he dunked the rake underwater to reveal the clams and drop them in the wire basket. Hannah carried the basket across the flats and instructed him on the finer points of using the rake. She refused to play coy with him, as her mother would have her do. "You look for the blowholes in the mud, then rake slowly, deeper and deeper, until you hit something. Hold the handle lower, so you get a better angle, right, that's it." The marsh grass, verdant and shimmering in the summer light, swayed in unpredictable patterns, and across the bay the sun flashed off the dunes of Sandy Neck. They walked along the flats barefoot, John shirtless and tanned, following the rippled edge of water, Hannah with her skirt rolled and tucked up into her waistband so that her ankles showed white as the underbelly of a fish. When the tide started back in, the clams spouted jets of water from under the wet sand, and John gathered as many clams as he could, until the basket was too heavy for Hannah, and he had to carry it while she raked. With the basket full, they worked their way back along the flats to the beach where they sat together on the edge of the water.

Hannah told him about her friends, the Coopers, whose father was on a whaler. They only saw him every three or four years. He sent money and paid for their house, and the kids grew up hardly knowing him. One winter he tried to stay on shore, and he spent all his time drinking and starting fights, until his wife begged him to go off to sea again.

John knew the type, the ones who had it in their blood. He was not that sort. He was not cut out for such a bloody business. Even stripping the whale was an ordeal for him. They pulled the whale alongside the ship and sawed off the strips of blubber, and the water filled with blood, and the sharks lurked all around, and the decks ran with blood. The blood and the smell and sight of the fish ripped up and desecrated drove him ashore.

While John talked, she became aware of his solid arms, his hands mapped with dried salt, gesticulating as he told his story. His feet dug into the sand, the tiny curls of dark hair on each toe pressed flat, and his sweaty smell mixed with the salty bay water.

"You've let me go on now. What about you, Hannah? It's clear to me that you don't like working in the store."

"I used to work with my father on his fishing boat, pulling in lobster traps, dragging for scallops. Sometimes we fished for cod or bass or whatever was running. I loved being on the boat with him and working outside, just the two of us. But my mother put me to work in the store like a prize heifer on display." Hannah scraped a stone into the boulder they sat on, then tossed the stone into shallow water. "If I could get away with it, I'd go out on a whaler, blood, guts, and all."

John laughed. "It can't be that bad."

"What do you know? You're up there at the end of the earth watching for ships from the lighthouse."

"True," he said. John stood up and extended a hand for Hannah. As they walked back to her house, he told her stories of shipwrecks and the men who'd washed ashore, men who'd sailed all over the world, men with stories of their own told around the fire over hot cups of coffee, and with the urgency and disbelief of eyes that had seen death up close. Hannah longed for contact with the world beyond her mother's store, for a life on the water like she'd known with her father. She resented her mother for bringing her ashore, and resented her father for not sticking up for her.

At the house, she lit a lantern in the barn and set to work shucking clams. She brought a bucket of clean water from the well, a wooden bowl from the house, and sat next to John on a narrow bench. The lantern cast their faces aglow and illuminated only a small circle around them, so that they appeared to be working in an orb of light.

"Watch now," Hannah said, holding a wood-handled, six-inch, flat blade in her right hand and the clam in her left, snout pointing right and the hinge away from her. "You slide the knife in here, aft of the siphon, then through the muscle like this." She pushed the steel blade into the crease between the shells and pulled back through the tight muscle. Then she ran the knife around the rim of the shell toward her body until the clam was open. With one quick motion she scooped the fleshy meat, making clean cuts across the last bits of muscle that clung to the shell. With the clam on the end of her knife, she pinched the stomach to release the guts. "Then you just peel this skin off the siphon," she said, and peeled back the black membrane. Hannah dunked the clam into the clean water to rinse the sand, then picked up the clam in her fingers and dropped it into John's waiting mouth. Her fingers brushed across his chapped lips, and he smiled and chewed the clam until she could smell the sea on his breath.

"Damn, that's good," he said. "But I know how to shuck a clam."

He grabbed a clam from the basket, positioned it in his large hand, and made fast work of shucking it.

"Not bad," she said, laughing. He delicately slid the clam onto the ends of his two fingers and lifted it toward Hannah's mouth. She waited, perched like a bird, her lips slightly parted, then she opened her mouth as his fingers swept nearer. He dropped the clam onto her tongue and slowly removed his fingers, letting them graze her open lips, then sweep across her suntanned cheek. When she swallowed the clam, she leaned in close, face upturned, and John kissed her, the taste of seawater in their mouths. When he stopped, she felt dizzy.

All that summer John's trips up to the store became more frequent, and Hannah took him to all her favorite places, rowing through the salt marsh near the bay, fishing off the Mill Bridge, clamming on the flats. They went out cod fishing with her father and came across a humpback whale sunning itself, its massive, sleek black body and ridged fins floating quietly. "I'm not a man who wants to harpoon that whale, Hannah. I'll never be rich."

Hannah ran her fingers along his neck, and she kissed his Adam's apple when her father wasn't looking. They stood together at the stern of the boat to watch the whale turn itself over in the sun, water running off its body, and the splash when the tail slapped the water and soaked the boat.

Oct 12: Winds > 30 NE, rain, 0 visibility

Oct 13: Ship aground, total wreck, one survivor, NE < 20

Over the logbook were pinned the torn pages from the almanac with the tide charts for each month. She checked the tide and filled in the events that she'd been too busy to record, right after John's notes from his last scan of the horizon that day he'd left for Barnstable. With the house restored to order, she sat by the shipwrecked sailor and watched him sleep. Then she was on her feet again and casting about for something to do. She ate a piece of toast standing at the kitchen counter. The humming through her body drove her outside to gather wood from the pile on the front porch. In between trips to the lights, heating the room became her focus, warming the sailor back to health, waiting for him to wake up and for John to come home.

She and John had been married for over six years now. The second summer of their marriage, when Hannah was twenty years old, they had their first real fight. John hadn't allowed her to row to a wreck, even though the storm had passed and there was no real hazard. Hannah couldn't accept his judgment that no wife of his would endanger herself on his behalf. "You want me to participate in your life here, to take on your responsibilities, but only those that you see fit."

"You do plenty, Hannah, more than your share. This is for your own safety." The calm in his voice was a counterpoint to her anger.

"I think I can judge what's safe for me and what's not. I've been in boats my whole life. It's torture for me to know there are men drowning with the lighthouse in view, and I'm stuck on shore. It makes no sense." Hannah paced behind him where he sat at the table, until he stood up and crossed the room to put his plate in the sink. She followed at his heel.

"You're in no position to judge what's safe, Hannah. You'd row to Nantucket in a snow squall if it suited you."

"That's ridiculous and you know it. I just want to help. Yet you want to keep me cooped up in the house like all the other wives."

John turned from the sink, face flushed, his voice angry but even. "I can't believe that you think I'm concerned with myself when it's *you* I'm concerned for."

"You're not concerned for me at all. You're concerned for your own pride. You don't want any wife of yours risking her life alongside you. What kind of a man would allow that? Not John Snow. What would people think?"

"Hannah, stop it." He stepped toward her. "You're being unreasonable."

"I am not unreasonable," she spat. "You're a coward."

He held her wrists down by her sides and wrapped his arms

around her to calm her, but she fought him, flailing with her torso and legs. She struggled to free her wrists and writhed against him. "Let me go, John. Let go." But he didn't let go until she'd worn herself out and collapsed against him, then he carried her to the bed and lay with her until she fell asleep.

Dusk settled over the house like a trance. Dusk fell across the fields and emptied the air of any promise save the light flashing every eight seconds, a steady pulse, as familiar to Hannah as her own breath. She kneeled down for a closer look at the sailor, then she nudged his shoulder until he opened his eyes for a moment and squinted at her.

"You're okay," she told him. "You're at Dangerfield Light."

He looked down the mummified length of his body, the layers of blankets and quilts.

"Your ship went aground," she told him. "You're injured, but you're safe now."

"You should've let me drown," he said, his voice scraping his throat, his eyes fierce now and fixed on her.

She sat upright in her chair. "You should've let yourself drown," she told him, startled. "When I found you, you were clinging to a spar. What's your name?"

"William Pike." He remembered clinging to the spar, his elbows hooked over on each side, his head resting like a child's while his legs drifted. Frigid with cold, he'd stopped caring whether he lived or died. Still, he didn't let go of the spar. It was the weakness in him, clinging to life.

"You cut your head. I've been changing the bandages so you don't get infected. It'll scar though. You'll be quite distinctive."

"I've got enough scars."

"And the name of your ship?"

"It wasn't my ship." He held his arm over his eyes. "*Cynthia Rose*. We went aground in the storm. The light was so close. I don't know how it happened."

He struggled to free himself from the blankets, took a quick look around the room, and then dropped his head back onto the bedroll.

"Where are the others?" he asked.

Hannah looked into the pattern of wear on the blanket, pilled and frayed on the edges. She picked at the torn edge and thought she should mend it, but the blanket was too old for mending.

He clamped his teeth down and turned his face away from her. "They're all drowned, aren't they?"

Hannah was silent, and he turned his face toward the fire. "You're the only one I found," she said.

He placed his hand to his forehead, as if remembering the pain. He let her hold a cup of broth to his mouth and drank a little before he slept again.

Hannah added wood to the fire, his rasping breath a lonely kind of solace as she waited for John.

3

WILLIAM PIKE PRETENDED TO SLEEP, BUT INSTEAD watched the woman mend a shirt, then get up and pace by the front window before she sat down and took up her mending again. She jabbed at the fabric, then pulled the thread taut with three sharp tugs. He kept his eyes partway open for minutes at a time. When she stood to press a damp cloth to his forehead, the gentle sound of her voice eased him as she said *fever, delirium*. The smell of chicken cooking in a pot that hung over the fire and the warmth of the room made him drowsy. When the woman found out who he was, she'd make him leave.

When he was awake, the overwhelming knowledge that he'd washed ashore with no place to go, no people, drove him to sleep again. Dreams swept through him, vivid as life. He tried to remember a time before he'd gone to sea, before the *Alice K* and the *Intrepid*, when he'd lived in Worcester and known his family. The last William heard about his own mother was that she worked as a laundress. His father had died in prison, where he was incarcerated for embezzling funds from his biggest client, a textile manufacturer who found him out when they hired another firm to audit the accounts. The lightkeeper's wife tugged the blankets tight around his neck, and as she leaned over him, he felt her breath on his face. Her careful attention frightened him in its intimacy. He couldn't move. She sat again in her chair and sighed, leaned back as if waiting for a cup of tea, but there was no one here to bring her one. He didn't deserve her kindness, born as he was from criminal blood and grown into the same stuff or worse. His father had always been setting up investment schemes that never paid out, or finding himself with another windfall that he couldn't explain. The man was a thief and a liar, and he died in jail. *And now look at me. No different. I turned out just like him.* But it wasn't until he'd gone to sea that he discovered his ruinous potential.

In his fevered state, he tried not to think about Annie, but she taunted him back to the ship *Intrepid*, where his misadventure had begun. He remembered the first signs of her pregnancy, her heightened sense of smell, or rather, her limited tolerance for foul odors, such as the fish guts flung into a bucket when one of the sailors caught and filleted dinner, or the stench of the men, or the putrid stink that rose from the livestock pen. He wanted to forget how the smell of Annie's own husband, who'd taken care to bathe in lavender and oil his skin, turned her stomach so that she heaved over the rail.

The lightkeeper's wife pressed her palm to his forehead, and for a moment she pulled him from the events that had led him to her house. Why she took him in he didn't understand, but she wasn't the only woman who'd shown him kindness on his way north. There had been women in Jamaica, women he'd never speak of, but Annie was the beginning, and when the lighthouse keeper left him alone, his mind drifted back to that ship.

It had only taken a few days for Annie to realize that her belly's bloating was not due to illness. She was with child, and when the blood didn't come, she told Daniel.

"A son," he said. "Wonderful."

"Or a little girl," Annie corrected.

"Ten fingers and ten toes, that's all I care about," Daniel assured her, patting her tenderly on the back. "You stay down here and rest. Are you warm enough?"

"It's stifling in here," she said.

"Would you like a cool cloth?"

"Oh, Daniel. You have better things to do. Send your cabin boy."

"I'll find you a nurse in the next port."

"The cabin boy will do for now."

Annie rolled to face the beadboard wall, counting the lines of white slats with her finger. Boy. Girl. Boy. Girl. Let's try it again. Boy. Girl. Boy. There was no telling the sex of the baby, and her mind filled with images of cherubic faces and big ears, or wide black eyes like her father. Would her child have Daniel's sparrow-hawk nose? Annie's blue-gray eyes? The possibilities ranged from the beautiful to the terrible, but the question that persisted was *who are you?* She dreamed of names—Adam, Jacob, or Elliot if it was a boy; Katy, Margaret, or Abigail if it was a girl—as if assigning this unformed creature a name would help her know him or her any better.

She hadn't wanted to get pregnant. Every time Daniel climbed on top of her, she resisted, physically willing her body not to conceive. She had no sexual desire for her husband and no longing for a child. When the baby started growing, her body grew strange and round, swelling into a monstrous shape that she did not recognize as her own. She felt overtaken by this thing growing inside her. Her muscles grew soft, her thighs softer. Then the baby kicked and the promise of a child surprised her. Someone to care for and fill the hours with this unexpected love. She would guard her baby against loneliness. No matter what happened, she would never leave the child. No matter what, she repeated like a mantra.

When Daniel told her that he was going to leave her in Jamaica in the care of the local midwife, she thought he was joking, until his silence confirmed that he meant these cruel words.

"How can you even consider leaving me alone to have your child? They don't have real medicine or—" She hadn't been able to think of what to say or how to describe her utter sense of abandonment. "They're strangers."

"It's perfectly safe," he consoled her. "The midwives are very good."

"I'm not going," she said.

"You can't stay on the ship, Annie. None of the men are prepared to deliver a baby. It's just not possible. And this is done all the time, believe me. It's for the best."

"Please, Daniel, don't make me go. I can't bear it."

"I have no choice."

"You're the captain. Of course you have a choice."

"You need a midwife."

"Then stay with me. Don't make me have this child alone.

Can't you see how frightened I am? Can't you imagine the things that can go wrong on that island?"

The *Intrepid* sailed into Negril, and one of the crew rowed Annie into the docks. Daniel said good-bye, but she couldn't look at him. She watched neither the ship disappearing behind her, nor the shore as it approached, only her bare feet in the bilge water stretched before the sphere of her belly.

The midwife who met her at the dock carried her by horse and wagon to a small hut near the beach. It was a rickety structure with one solid wooden wall that seemed to hold the whole thing up, and the other walls built from bamboo and palm fronds. Annie stood in the doorway but didn't step inside. A small bed with a night table, a basket for her clothing, and a single chair were all the comfort she could expect. "I can't stay here."

"I will take good care of you. You will be okay here, better than on that ship." Ishema fluffed the pillow on the bed and folded the blanket back. "Come, lie down now, rest." Five feet tall, a perfectly round head, and hair shorn close to her scalp, she was a sturdy woman with wide shoulders, no waistline, and flat feet that rooted her firmly to the ground.

"I'm not tired. I don't even know where I am."

Ishema looked Annie over, assessing her strength. "We'll take a walk; you'll see where you are." She left Annie's bags outside the cottage and led her along the beach, a scooped-out section of the island about two hundred yards wide with tall cliffs on the eastern edge. "This is the southern shore. We get the warm breezes. And these cliffs." She waved her hand to indicate the rock walls that protected the area. "They protect us from the weather, so you are safe here."

Daniel had told Annie that Ishema was well respected on the island and that she had delivered many sea captains' children. Once Annie settled into her temporary home, her fear began to subside. Local children ran by and stuck their heads in the window to see the white woman. Ishema's friend Therese came every day with a basket of mangoes, papayas, bananas, coconut, lime, roast chicken, or grilled fish. She wore her hair braided with multicolored shells and ceramic beads that rattled when she walked.

"Who is she?" Annie asked one evening. She and Ishema sat on woven mats outside the hut and watched the sun go down while they picked at chicken bones.

"She is my friend," Ishema said.

The birth had been difficult, the baby girl born two months early. Seeing her daughter was like seeing God. It filled her with hope. But in the first two days, the baby developed an infection in her lungs. Ishema nursed her with island herbs, and Therese brought medicinal remedies from the village, but the little girl stopped breathing in the middle of the night.

They buried Annie's daughter in a tiny grave beneath a wooden cross that existed as a blur across her mind. Did she throw herself on the grave, or had she dreamed that? Did the baby cry during the funeral? Did Daniel know?

When Annie refused to get out of bed after five days, Ishema threatened to pour the chamber pot on her. "You're not the only one to lose your baby. There's many ladies lose their baby."

She peeled a pineapple while she spoke. Her hands were always in motion. When Annie got up, Ishema brought in a basin and bathed her, lifted Annie's arms to scrub her armpits like she would a child's. "You stink," she said.

Annie pulled on the light cotton shift Ishema gave her and drank the glass of water forced upon her.

"Come now, outside."

Therese leaned against the curved trunk of a palm tree, her head tilted back in the shade of the fronds that sheltered her like an umbrella. A frayed end of rope held her braids back off her face so that they poured down her back like a dark waterfall. She followed them through the beach grass toward the village road. "You need to move your body to get your mind back," Ishema said, tossing the words over her shoulder.

Annie felt as if she was trying to walk underwater with the tide pushing against her. When was Daniel going to get her off this godforsaken island?

In the village, small huts constructed from palm fronds and vines served as storefronts for locals who sold fruit, soup, and brooms. The huts lined the road down to the harbor, where small skiffs splayed out from the long dock like fins. Several schooners and a brig swung on their moorings. Of course none of them was *Intrepid*. It wasn't her husband she longed for but escape from this place where her baby had been buried in the ground, escape from the strange sound of these women's voices telling her the names bougainvillea, jacaranda, pimento.

"The women in Jamaica don't have husbands to do all the work for them. Sometimes the husband is useless, and these women here"—Ishema waved her stout hand along the row of huts—"they provide for their families. No husband like yours to take care of them."

"But he left me here," Annie said.

"He'll be back, and we'll still be here working for ourselves. You count your blessings while you have them."

Therese stood to one side during this conversation. Somewhere along the road she'd picked up a cedar branch to use as a walking stick. Now it was propped at her left side, her long fingers wrapped intricately around the bark as if staking her claim to the soil she stood upon and to the league of women left to fend for themselves. Her lithe, strong body, upright and relaxed, seemed to embody the power of these women.

"Come now, let's go," Ishema said, and she pushed Annie along the road. They walked past the harbor into thick woods until the path ended.

"Now what?" Annie asked.

Therese climbed, catlike, the tendons in her calves taut like an animal's as she followed the trunk of a fallen palm tree. She walked along the trunk to another tree, where she climbed down the branches to a wooden plank that led deeper into the woods.

"You go," Ishema said, her finger poking Annie in the back. Annie stepped onto the tree trunk. As her legs found their strength, her balance came and she stepped easily onto the wooden plank. She lost herself to the rhythm of her huffing breath and the work of keeping up with Therese.

They followed a dirt path through boulders until they reached a lagoon, where light turquoise water reflected harsh light and burned the eyes. Cliffs rose a hundred feet on the western side of the lagoon. Behind a grove of coconut palms, away from the water, was a cluster of huts where women sat outside and wove blankets, mats, and baskets. Beyond the huts, closer to the water, four women were arranging and counting crates like the ones Daniel transported on his ship. As Therese led her toward a hut with a veranda and a room on each side of the front door, Annie began to sense in her reserve a leadership that came not from speaking but from knowing.

Annie sat across from her on a rattan mat backed with bright pillows while Ishema went inside to get them something to drink. She had questions but was afraid to speak.

Therese leaned back against the pillows. "So, you see. This is how our women work."

"You give them work," Annie said.

"We have sailors who come ashore often. They need to unload their goods, and visit with the women, and eat good food before they go back to sea."

"You help them sell their cargo?"

Therese nodded. "These men," she said. "They can't go to a buyer in the harbor. They need to sell through another means. Do you understand?"

"No."

"They are robbers."

"Pirates?"

"We break up the cargo and sell it off in pieces where it can't be traced. Coffee, spices, lumber, hemp—for everything there is a buyer."

"And these women, they…work with the men?"

Therese lit a hand-carved pipe and puffed it out the side of her mouth. "You can't judge us. We have to survive, like you. We all make arrangements to survive."

Ishema brought three glasses on a tray and sat beside Annie, her heft and her sweat overbearing at that moment.

"Drink," Therese said.

The liquor burned at first, then warmed her throat.

"Why don't they have husbands?" Annie asked.

"They don't want them or lost them or left one that was good for nothing. What does it matter? They are here now. We get paid to please these men. Nothing for free."

Annie leaned back into the pillows and finished her drink. The hot coil of her pain cooled in the relief of the liquor. "Do you never rest, Ishema?"

"Rest will come later."

"Do you miss your husband?" Therese asked.

"Not yet," Annie said.

Daniel didn't come back for another month, and after weeks spent with Therese and Ishema, Annie had no patience for his grief. She flailed between bouts of drinking and sleeping; she cried in her bed and cursed her husband. He should've been here. He'd arrived too late to console her, and she blamed him for leaving in the first place, for leaving her on this island where her baby had died.

"This is your fault, this infection. Some island disease! It could've been avoided!" She fought with him and accused him even when she didn't believe her own words. Annie's rage was forged in grief and only deepened as they sailed away from the island, away from her baby interred in dark soil.

4

TOM RAPPED HARD ON THE DOOR AND CALLED HANNAH'S name, scraped the mud from his boots on the edge of the porch before he stepped inside. No sign of her, only the sailor wrapped tight and dozing by the fire.

Tom ventured down the passageway and yelled up the lighthouse steps, "Hannah, you there?" But the echoes of his own voice were the only call back to him. He felt a terrible emptiness standing there.

When he ducked back through the passage into the house, the man by the fire looked over with startled eyes. "She went down to the beach," his voice rasped.

"You any better, friend?"

"I'm awake, aren't I?"

Tom pulled the door shut behind him and made his way to the stairs. Halfway down he spotted Hannah dragging a man out of the surf. She held him under his arms and carried him backward so his head bobbed side to side. When Tom's feet hit the sand, he hollered for her and waved until she looked up.

The body she dragged hung loose as a bag of rocks. Her wet hair whipped in the wind as she leaned forward and pulled harder on the man to get him up the beach.

"He's dead, Tom. Can you grab his feet? He washed up into

the shallows with the tide. Should've been carried out with the rest of them."

Tom took the man by his boots and watched Hannah's frenzied eyes dash back and forth from the dead man to the steps.

"Let's get him in the cart," she said.

They carried the waterlogged body across the beach and lifted the man into the life cart. "I was dousing the lights when I saw him," Hannah said. "At first I thought it was a seal, or a black fish, then I saw his legs knocked about in the waves and I knew."

"Maybe that other one up at the house knows something about him."

Hannah looked into the bloated face of the drowned man. A thin lace of light green seaweed stuck to his right cheek, and his fingernails had wood splinters under them, as if he'd clawed his way out of some airless place. His pants were shredded, one boot missing, and his foot was tangled in rope.

She and Tom strapped the dead sailor into the life cart and coiled the ropes and tucked the blankets in around him. Hannah fingered something along his chest that looked like a locket. She folded the blanket back and opened the man's shirt. Small black hairs curled delicately against his skin. No locket. Only a broken oyster shell pressed into his flesh. She left it there, a vestigial relic to mark these last hours.

"What are you going to do with him?" Tom asked. "If he's got no wallet or papers, you'll never find his people. I can send Billings over."

"He would've been better off swept away with his shipmates."

"Yep," Tom said.

They maneuvered the life cart with the dead man to the side of the stairs and out of the wind to wait until Billings the undertaker could come for him. "He'll be okay here," Hannah said, disturbed by the unmoving weight beneath the blankets.

"Crows," Tom said, and they took the canvas tarp from the skiff and draped it over the man, pulled it tight, and weighed it down with rocks.

Tom followed her up to the house, where Hannah went to the stove to heat a pot of water. She opened the cast-iron door and poked at the fire. She added one of the logs from the bin until the fire caught and she closed the door. Still in her jacket and boots, she asked, "You see John up Cape?"

"That's the thing," Tom said, looking tentatively into her face. "I didn't see him. Come sit down."

Hannah shook her head. She leaned over the sailor's disheveled sheets. "Looks like he was up earlier."

"I didn't think he could move," Tom said.

His rank, snorting breath disgusted Hannah as she tucked the blankets in around him. Finally she sat in the chair Tom held out for her. "Just tell me, Tom."

"Thing is, no one saw him coming back. Could be the last person to see him was your mother when he left the store two days ago."

"Well, where did he go?"

"I don't know, no one knows."

"A man doesn't disappear into thin air."

They both watched the sailor as he muttered and groaned in his fevered dreams.

"We could ride down there."

"Someone's got to watch the lights. I can't just up and leave," she said, pouring hot water into two cups. She knew from Tom's look that he thought she should leave the lighthouse to someone else to watch, one of the many able men from town. It wasn't any place for a woman, especially a woman as head-strong as she. But they'd never left anyone to tend the lights, and he knew better than to suggest it. As she swung the kettle toward the stove, she knocked one of the cups to the floor. Tom's eyes flashed and she saw then how absolutely green they were, and bright, like the fresh seaweed on the dead man's face. "Where on earth is he, Tom?"

"I'll go up Cape, see what's what," Tom said. "You write a note for your folks, see if we can figure how far he got on his way back."

Hannah sat at John's desk and found a piece of notepaper in the top drawer. She penned the following letter:

October 14, 1843
Dearest Mother & Father,

I'm writing to you in an urgent request to deter-mine the whereabouts of my John. He did not return from Barnstable as scheduled three days ago. I thought at first it was the storm that kept him overnight in Orleans, but he was not spotted in Orleans at all. I am wondering when he left you, and if he mentioned any plans or stops along the way. Such unpredictable behavior is unlike him, as you know, and so I find myself concerned,

unduly, I hope, but nonetheless. Perhaps you can
alert Sheriff Eldridge.

Please let me know anything you can as my ability
to wait patiently without word is eroding with each
hour.

Your loving daughter,
Hannah

The next day was a series of minutes that passed into hours, each ticking one into the next until Hannah begged them to stop. If time stopped there would be no bad news. She tried to find something to do that wasn't waiting. Even the steady tasks of keeping the lights did not release her from worry. Why had John resisted going to Barnstable, all that foolishness about a forgotten razor? She stood over the desk and opened the logbook to that day, but there was nothing out of the ordinary. His notations looked like all of the other notes made in his careful square script, counts of passing ships, wind direction and speed, visibility.

In the kitchen, she nudged the stove fire to life and heated the fish stew. She carried a steaming cup on a saucer and waved it in front of William's face until he rustled beneath the blankets and opened his eyes. "You're awake," she said.

"I wasn't sleeping," he told her. He tried to lift his head but couldn't, and so Hannah lifted him by the shoulders and slid another pillow beneath him. He pulled his arms loose from the blankets and turned them this way and that before stretching them out.

"This isn't my shirt," he said, and patted his hands down the front of the fabric.

"We had to change your clothes. You were soaking wet."

"Who changed me?"

"We didn't disturb your bandages, William. Were you injured before the wreck?"

"I have an old injury, ma'am. Billy's what I'm called." His words were cautious.

"How did you come to be sailing past Dangerfield, if you don't mind my asking?"

"That's a long story."

"I've nowhere else to be. My husband is the keeper here and he'll want to know where your ship was heading, and where from."

He sipped from the cup and licked the broth from his upper lip. Hannah kept her eyes on him in the most intimate way.

"You said earlier you were going to Portland."

"Yes, ma'am, from Jamaica. We stopped in Virginia to pick up cargo, but I don't know what it was. I didn't go ashore." He didn't look at her but stared straight ahead, his head resting on the pillow.

"Do you know who owned the ship?"

"It was owned by a company in New York. The captain was a Theodore Walker of New Bedford, been in the merchant marine for years but never owned his own ship. Guess he never will now, eh?"

"And how about you, where were you headed?"

He turned his cloudy eyes on her. "Anywhere north. I swore if I made it, I'd never get on another boat again. Now here I am, and all I can think about is signing myself aboard the first ship that crosses my path."

Hannah watched Billy poke at the logs with a broken twig. She'd never met a man who could be still in front of a fire. They had to adjust the lay of the logs with their boot, or add more wood, or bring out the bellows, or wonder about the draft of the flue and whether the wood had dried enough and if locust or oak was better for burning. "What is this place anyways?"

"Dangerfield Light, at the outermost edge of Cape Cod. Nor'easters drive more ships onto the shoals here than any-where else on the eastern seaboard. You're not alone in finding yourself stranded."

Hannah's wavy brown hair fell over her shoulders as she leaned down to loosen the laces on her boots. A single strand of gray hair. Her hazel eyes reflected the gray afternoon. She had a strong jaw and sultry lips, skin lightly freckled by the sun. She watched Billy notice her. She let him look.

"What drove you north?" Hannah asked.

"Many things," he said. "Lost my family, lost everything. Thought if I got back north, I could start over."

The wind shuddered against the house as if to remind them that it was there. She offered him another cup of broth, and when he refused, she left him to rest.

Billy's cough was the first thing she heard in the morning now. Not John's boots scuffing the passageway from the lights. Not his distracted whistle as he fried some eggs. Not his voice whispering in her ear to wake her for breakfast, even though he knew she was already awake and enjoying the remnants of his heat in the bed. The lights kept flashing and she wanted to get up and douse them to save oil, but she couldn't rouse herself. She wanted to stay in bed, but she couldn't give in.

She pulled herself from the sheets and made her way to her feet. The kitchen held no promise. Eggs, she needed eggs, and so filled the pail with chicken seed. The sound of bickering and feathers beating back reached her before she saw the chickens in the coop. The egg hens perched in the cubbies John had built. Others clustered near the wire gate as she approached and fought over the arcs of seed she cast. A hole in the wall let them go outside to a larger pen. John kept a pig and cow before they married, but with his pay from the lighthouse, and the expense and work of keeping the animals, it was better to barter for their provisions or buy them outright.

Outside, Hannah walked along the edge of the vegetable garden, covered in sea hay. She grew turnips, sweet potatoes, onions, and squash in the sandy soil. The best soil blew away in the stormy winds. Root vegetables kept all winter in the dirt cellar. They still ate salt pork and salt beef that Hannah had brined six months ago. Hannah's mother had taught her well how to survive the winter months.

If the vegetables are sprouting or decaying, spread them to a drier place. Keep the beef and pork under brine that is sweet and clean.

Lamps will have a less disagreeable smell if you dip your wick yarn in strong, hot vinegar and dry it.

Then it occurred to her. Her mother's remedy, equal parts camphor and hartshorn spread along the throat, could cure a hard cough. "So simple," she muttered on her way back to the house.

Four days since the wreck and Hannah cursed another day of not knowing where her husband was. With John's trousers drawn up around her, she knotted the waist with a piece of rope and left her upper body bare. The cold water in the basin was clean. She thought of heating it but didn't want to go into the front room where Billy slept. As she opened one of the curtains, her bedroom took on an amber hue. She touched a water-soaked cloth to her skin, scrubbed under her arms and all over her torso and the parts of her back that she could reach, working as fast as she could. When John was home and he came upon her washing, he stepped up behind her and wrapped his arms around to cup her breasts. She would lean back against him and feel the length of him along her body. He'd be home soon, she told herself.

She dressed in a long-sleeved shirt and a sweater from John's closet. Wearing his clothes was the closest she'd been to him in six days. What had started as a practicality had become her only intimacy with her husband. She favored clothes that he'd already worn, clothes that still carried his distinct smell of sweat, salt, and sex. Without him here, she didn't care how she looked. She tried to push her fear away, but he was due four days ago, and it was only a day's ride from Barnstable to the lighthouse. There was no reason he wouldn't be home by now. She brushed out her hair and tied it back, pulling all the loose strands off her face. Anyone who saw her would think she'd lost her mind. Never mind that she wasn't properly corseted, but wearing men's clothes!

On her way into the kitchen, she turned to the hearth to make sure the fire hadn't gone out. Billy was gone, the blankets heaped like discarded clothing. "Billy!" she called. She fumbled through his blankets as if they contained some clue. There was nothing but the odor of his sweat, fever, and camphor. The cure must've worked. She followed the passageway to the bottom of the lighthouse and called his name, but only the cold sound of her voice called back to her. "Where on earth are you, you stupid fool," she muttered. He was too weak to go anywhere, and why would he bother? She was insulted one minute that he had the nerve to leave, and relieved the next that she wouldn't have to explain him to John or deal with him anymore. But he didn't have the money or means to go anywhere. She grabbed her jacket from the back of the chair and pulled the front door shut behind her. The brown fields roved toward a line of beech trees sketched against a metal gray sky, white fog drifted over the fields and showed the speed of the wind, faster than a man could walk.

She circled the house by the outhouse, peered over the edge of the dunes and down the long staircase to the beach. Then she started across the yard toward the barn. The worn cedar shingles and high barn door were painted green, but chipped and peeling like so many of the barns in Dangerfield. The heavy door slid back along its track, leaking afternoon light into the barn. "I know you're in here, Billy," she said. "There's nowhere else you could be."

Her voice echoed, and Nellie stomped the hay in her stall, and the chickens flapped their useless wings.

"You should've let me drown." His voice wavered and slurred, and he couldn't get hold of it.

Hannah walked toward the sound. "Where are you? What are you doing out here?" She inched her way toward the back of the barn where she thought he was hiding in one of the stalls. Then she spoke in a gentle voice, as if coaxing a skittish dog. "Come on out of there now, Billy. It's not good for you to be out in this cold air."

As she stepped forward, a cluster of barn swallows swept down from a railing over the loft and performed an uncanny display of acrobatics as they darted around her.

Billy dragged himself out from the stall at the end of the barn and staggered toward Hannah with his head in his hands, the smell of whiskey emanating from his every pore. When he lifted his face, his eyes were rimmed in red, bloodshot, and wet. "You don't even know me. I could be anyone," he said.

"You're drunk." Hannah stood with her hands on her hips, the sharp edge of her anger rising. "I risked my own life to save you, and now you're out here drinking and feeling sorry for yourself? You think I don't know you're hiding things? You think I've never met a liar? I'm not afraid of you."

He didn't say anything.

"If you're drinking and acting like a fool, I can't do my job." Her voice was angry now, and she couldn't stop. "My job as keeper here is more important than you. Do you understand?"

Billy's emotions shifted across his face like weather: angry at first, then startled and contrite.

"We've got weather coming in. You can leave here if you want to, or else you can go inside and sleep it off so you can help me later on. Looks like you're strong enough to make yourself useful. You can start by closing that door," Hannah said. "I'll be up at the lights."

"Yes, ma'am," Billy said quietly. He fastened the barn door by swinging the wooden boom down into the clamp, and then he walked unsteadily back to the house.

Hannah's livid energy carried her swiftly up the lighthouse stairs. He had no business drinking the liquor she kept on hand, no business wasting her time. Who did he think he was? By the time she reached the landing atop the lighthouse, her duties took her attention off her anger. She took her time filling the oil lanterns, trimming the wicks, and wiping the windows. No dousing the lights this morning, not with this fog.

She didn't want to go back to the house. Who was to say what this William Pike was capable of? Her father's drinking had never frightened her, but she'd seen other men become dangerous. Once when she went fishing with Tom, they were approached by a group of drunken men swaggering down the beach. It was during the end of her first year at the lighthouse. She and Tom carried rods and some live eels in a wicker basket and walked north where the wind was at their backs and they could cast over the outgoing tide.

As the men neared she saw them handing a bottle back and forth.

"Hey, you catch anything? We seen you casting," one of the men called out. The others laughed, snickered, and did not meet her eyes.

"What's in the basket?" A face that caved in on itself, rheumy eyes and drooping eyelids, seemed no match for the man's broad shoulders and legs strong as stanchions.

"What do you want?" Tom asked.

"Maybe we just want to talk to your woman. I want to see her catch something." The man moved toward Hannah, an eye on Tom, watchful. "Go ahead, little miss."

"No thank you," Hannah said, her words dry like salt on her tongue. His eyes taunted her. She wanted to beat him back like a dog, but that would only satisfy him.

"Listen to her. *No thank you*," he said, mocking her. "Who do you think you are?"

"I'm the lightkeeper's wife at Dangerfield."

"So you think you're somebody. That it?"

"And who are you? What brings you to this coast?"

"You got no place asking me nothing," he said, and thrust his hand toward her throat as if that's where it had been headed all along. Hannah stepped aside, and in one fluid motion Tom had his fishing knife unsheathed and held firmly across the man's neck, the glinting blade scraping black whiskers.

"Don't think I won't do it. I've killed men like you for less. I'd be happy to do it again and let the tide get rid of you for good."

The man searched his gang for help, but they stood mute as children.

"Go back north from wherever you came and keep walking. I don't want to see you here again. Next time I'll be down here with a gun, you hear me?"

The man nodded.

"You hear me?" Tom said.

The man's shoulders hunched and he said, "Couldn't help but hear ya. You're screaming in my goddamned ear. Now, soon as you get your knife off my throat, we'll head on out."

Tom slid his knife across the man's throat so that it left a thin scratch, then shoved the man away from him. Without stopping or looking back, the man led his gang away. Tom vibrated with energy and fear. He had been ready to kill, and for her. She saw it in him and was overcome with her own fear and relief. She collapsed against him, his arms around her so different from John's in their longing. His heart was a solid force against her cheek and when she tilted her face up, his passion was fierce and she received his kiss willingly, felt it through her body like wind. When he pulled away from her, they were both embarrassed and stared down the beach after the men.

"Have you really?" Hannah asked. "Killed someone, I mean."

"I never have, but I would've just then. I would've cut his throat."

She felt safe with him, with John's best friend. He would look out for her. They never spoke of the kiss again.

5

BILLY PUT HIMSELF TO WORK STACKING WOOD ON the front porch and closing the storm windows. He carried wood inside and stoked the fire, put water on for coffee and swept the kitchen floor. If Hannah kicked him out, where would he go? He had no money, no strength. He felt trapped in her house as Annie had been trapped aboard the *Intrepid*. After losing the baby, Annie was no longer content to sit belowdecks mending or stitching samplers, reading or writing letters for Daniel. The confines of the captain's quarters, the grief and loneliness that resided there, drove her mad. He remembered her frenzy as she fetched a bucket of hot water and lye soap and set to scrubbing the floors and walls of the small berth until there wasn't a particle of the cabin board she hadn't cleansed.

He'd do the same for Hannah. He couldn't lie in bed knowing all his shipmates had perished. He couldn't rest. Why was he the one to survive? After everything he'd done. On his knees, he ran a wet rag over the floorboards, scrubbing at the day's grime while Annie's faraway world drew him back.

During her years at sea with Daniel, Annie had collected small dolls from every port. It was customary to give a gift upon boarding another captain's ship, and she usually brought small drawings she made of islands they'd visited, or a handkerchief with a border of yellow daisies. She received gifts from other captains' wives in return.

She gathered her collection of dolls and dropped them into a canvas sack, and she remembered the dolls the island women had brought to her for luck, small wooden totems painted bright colors. With the sack over her shoulder she stepped up to the deck. At the ship's transom, the wake rippled behind them, indicating their progress across the expanse of sea. Annie leaned against the aft rail and dumped the sack of dolls into the water. Then she watched them bob in the ship's wake and drift like buoys. When she dropped the sack in after them, it caught the wind like a sail and drifted up and swirled before falling into the sea.

Day in and day out the sailors ran up the rigging to carry out the first mate's order to trim the topsail, or raise the main to flatten the sails. They maneuvered rigging, spars, and sails in easy, fluid motions, bending their bodies into the work so that they became part of the system of wind, water, and sail. Annie watched one sailor make a halyard fast around a belaying pin with several quick flicks of his wrist. "What's your name?"

"Robinson, ma'am," the sailor stuttered, surprised to find the captain's wife speaking directly to him. He was no more than a boy, the stubble on his chin barely grown.

"Robinson, I want you to show me how to do that."

"Yes, ma'am." He responded as if given a direct order. The belaying pin was a large wooden peg stuck down through a hole in the ship's rail so that there were two vertical sections of peg exposed. "Okay, ma'am, you wrap the end of the line around the top part, like this, then take it down and cross it over and around behind the bottom part like this, then around front and cross over again to go behind the top part. You make figure eights around the pin like that," he said, pulling on the loose end of rope to show how it held. "There you have it."

Annie waited while he unfastened the rope, then she made awkward figure eights around the peg as instructed and pulled on the rope to test her knot.

"It only takes practice, ma'am."

With Daniel, Annie maintained a distracted silence. There was nothing to say. For all his authority with the crew, Daniel appeared to be at a loss as to how to reach her. To humor her, he encouraged her curiosity about the boat. At least it created conversation between them.

Once she spent more time on deck, she began eating again, and the color came back to her cheeks. She sat across the table from Daniel in his cabin and asked endless questions. "I'd like to learn to steer the ship," she told him one afternoon. "I sailed a small boat as a girl. The principle's the same, isn't it?"

The whale oil lanterns flickered across the beadboard walls and left a slight stink in the small quarters. But the light was soft, and the food was good, and they ate hungrily after a day's hard work. Daniel wiped his bread across his plate, then looked up at her, surprised. "Yes, it is, but this is not a small boat. There are twenty-three sails to watch and keep trim, not to mention the weight on the helm. It's no easy task."

"Let me try taking the wheel, Daniel. With you alongside," she said.

Daniel shook his head and put down the bread. His voice rose with authority. "You don't understand, Annie. I've a reputation to uphold in front of my men. If you gallivant around the ship doing as you please, the crew loses faith in me as captain of this vessel. I must maintain my authority at all costs. I cannot have you manning the helm. It's just not done. There's many a sailor on this ship that objects to a woman aboard at all. Women are considered bad luck. You know that, Annie."

"That's rubbish, Daniel. I've been sailing with you for years. If you believed in that nonsense, you wouldn't have allowed me to come in the first place." Annie dropped her utensils across her plate with a violent clatter. She fixed her eyes on Daniel. He wasn't handsome, but he wasn't unattractive either, tall and lean, with broad shoulders, olive complexion, and dark close-cropped hair.

He reached for her hand. "I must ask you to respect my decision," he said, his words gentle now.

She pulled her hand from his. *And if I cannot?*

Daniel stood. "I don't understand your reckless mood." He tossed his linen napkin onto the table and stormed from the cabin.

The wind blew steady from the northwest, and *Intrepid* sailed close-hauled, the sails trimmed and full. Annie stood with the first mate, Donovan, a freckled Irishman. He was compliant and followed orders in a way that made him invisible, like part of the ship that functioned so well one barely noticed it. His red hair curled up in the back as if caught by the wind, and he always tried to flatten it with spit on the tips of his fingers, trying to rid himself of his one distinctive feature. Daniel was belowdecks, scanning the blue-backed sea charts. "The captain has said you could explain to me how to read the compass and hold the ship's heading."

"He did, did he, ma'am?"

"Yes," Annie said. "Do you question it, Donovan? Because I can have him deliver the order himself, if you like."

"No, no, no. That's okay, ma'am. I can teach you. It's just... never mind. Come stand over here by the binnacle compass."

The compass was situated by the helm in a housing three and a half feet off the deck and protected beneath a glass globe. From the wheel the ship's heading could easily be read. Annie took her position beside Donovan and awaited instructions.

"If you want to head down a few points east, you steer toward east on the compass." He demonstrated, tilting the wheel slightly to change the ship's course. "Give it a try, ma'am. Take the helm and hold your course."

At first, standing behind the huge wheel with her skirts billowing in the wind and her body braced against the lean of the boat, Annie was surprised by the weight of water against the ship's rudder.

"You steer with your whole body, ma'am, like this," Donovan said, leaning his weight in the direction he wanted the wheel to turn, using his legs and arms and torso to guide the vessel through the wind. "Now take us two points into the wind and keep her as close to the wind as you can get her," he said, relinquishing the wheel.

Annie took the steering pegs in her hands, braced her legs, and leaned her body into the wheel, her eyes shifting from the compass, up to the sail to check for a luff, back and forth, until she held the ship's position as Donovan had requested.

"Fine job, ma'am," he said.

"You get the heading from the navigator, who gets it off the charts, is that right?"

"Yes, ma'am," he said.

Annie learned to handle the sextant, how to balance it against the horizon and take a mark, how to look up the figures in the tables and locate the ship's position on the chart. When Daniel ventured belowdecks one afternoon, he discovered her bent over a book containing columns of numbers, her finger running up and down the page as she wrote on a piece of scrap paper. "What have we here?" Daniel asked. "I've not allowed you to steer the ship, so you've found another way to direct our course?"

"I thought I could teach myself some navigation to pass the time, Daniel, then we could talk about it over dinner. You could instruct me."

"I've told you how I feel about you working on the ship. It undermines my authority with the men. I'll not have it."

"What are you so afraid of? That I might be good at this?" she asked, glaring at Daniel, her eyes a hot beam of light. Then they heard the noise overhead, a scuffling on deck as a group of eavesdroppers dispersed.

"There, now you've done it," Daniel said. "I'll not have you talk to me like that again!"

Daniel's anger didn't discourage Annie from steering the ship and watching the crew in the rigging as they tied a yardarm off in rough weather. She asked the men questions about the rigging and learned which line hauled which sail. After mastering the differences, she watched the sailors on deck and bribed them with Daniel's money into teaching her how to tie a square knot, sheet bend, bowline, and to tell her what each knot was for. It was clear that some members of the crew resented her presence among them.

"That was my wife I'd swat her right back into the kitchen. She don't like her fancy cabin, I'd put her to work scrubbing the decks. Who does she think she is?"

"Nothing but bad luck."

"Ladies on ships always are. I'll not go near her for any price."

Annie stepped out from behind the foremast where she'd been eyeing the halyards and glowered down at the two men weaving monkey's fists into the ends of frayed lines. "I could have you cowards banished to the bilge to sleep with the rats for the rest of this journey. You dislike my being on this ship and trying to make myself useful, then speak to me directly."

One of the sailors, a man named O'Malley, leaned back to take in the length of her. He was a tall Irishman from Dublin, freckled and weathered by thirty-one years of life, nineteen of them at sea. She knew from Daniel that he was discontented with his position among the crew and wanted a promotion with higher pay, but he wasn't going to get either. Daniel had taken a natural disliking to the man, and there was nothing to be done about it. "We're not to speak to the captain's wife."

"She just gave you permission," Annie said.

"We're hired men, ma'am, paid to do our job, nothing else," the other, called Nickerson, said. She knew he was respected among the crew. His opinion carried weight. He often sat on the bulwark dressing the men down for lazy seamanship, or rallying them to change sails in rough seas.

"It's wrong for a woman to be working on a ship," O'Malley said, meeting her eye. "It ain't done, and the men don't like it."

Annie listened without interrupting.

"With you roaming around we have to watch our language and worry you're going to see something or report back to the captain. If you were one of the crew, that's one thing, but you're not. You're the captain's wife."

"I'll not report anyone, if you'll agree not to report me. In fact, I'll pay each of you to persuade the men that I'm one of you, not against you, but with you."

The sailors looked back and forth between each other. "With us how?"

"I intend to sail this ship."

"How do we know we can trust you?"

"I care more about learning to sail this ship than I do about whatever trouble you and your mates manage to get yourselves into. You've seen me take the helm. You know I'm serious."

O'Malley had an odd habit of pinching his cheek when he was thinking or bothered by something, and he went at it good and hard now. Annie wasn't sure how to assuage him. "I'll bring the coins after your dinner this evening."

O'Malley smiled and nodded, as if she'd solved a puzzle he'd been trying to figure.

"How do I know I can trust you?" Annie said.

"We'll get the men to come around, ma'am. We can help them see things different. Will that prove it to you?"

She looked at the men, their eager eyes and serious faces. "All right, then we have a deal?"

The men nodded. "Yes, ma'am."

On a bright, nearly windless afternoon Annie announced to Donovan, "I want to go up into the rigging."

"That's taking it too far. You have to talk to the captain about that, ma'am. I couldn't allow it. It's dangerous up there, even for a man, with the waves tossing the spars back and forth and the swing of the mast. You have to be strong to hold on. The captain wouldn't allow it. I'm sorry."

"I'll talk to him." Annie disappeared belowdecks and reappeared sometime later with Daniel's old breeches pulled on beneath her calico dress. Her loose skirts swelled in the air around her and she let them fly. With the ocean in her lungs, she grabbed the ship's rigging and swung her weight around to climb the rope ladder. There was no reason she couldn't make it to the crow's nest. At first, she gripped the ropes so hard that her knuckles went white, but then she got her footing and kept her weight on her feet, using her hands for balance. Her legs did the work of climbing up, up, over the decks and the sea and the men. The air was silent except for the sound of the wind against the sails. No voices, no boots scuffing the decks, no hammers pounding or hatch covers slamming. Just air and sky. As she climbed, she felt herself entering another world entirely, as if she could become part of the sky to look across at flying birds and see their wings and fine heads cutting the wind instead of looking up to see their bellies and feet pressed flat against their white breasts. She ducked under the rim of the crow's nest and sat against the mast, her arms draped over the rim.

A crowd of sailors gathered below to watch. Daniel had

been called topside. He was a speck down there, indistinguishable from the other men. Had she ever loved him, or had
she loved the idea of sailing around the world and living at
sea? Whatever it was in her that had cared for Daniel had died
when the baby died. She couldn't stand the sight of him as
he stood below staring at the bottoms of her boots. His arms
beat the air, sending a signal she chose to ignore. As the wind
picked up, the mast rocked to and fro in great sweeping arcs,
and Annie gave herself over to the motion. She focused her
eyes on the steady line of the horizon, and then she climbed
down, one foot first, then the next foot feeling for the ratline.
With each step into the world of the ship, the air closed in
around her. The expansive silence of wind and sky atop the
mast shrank to the noise of the crew shouting up at her and
Daniel cussing out Donovan, whom he blamed for Annie's
trespassing on the ship's rigging.

Some of the men gathered by the bowsprit, snickering loud
enough for the captain to hear. They scattered when she swung
herself from the rigging onto the deck, landing with her knees
bent, using her legs like springs to break her fall. She gazed at
Daniel triumphantly.

"I will speak to you in my quarters," he said, teeth clenched,
and turned a dismissive shoulder to her.

Annie sat at the table in the captain's quarters, tapping her
fingers restlessly, as if he'd kept her waiting. He flung himself
through the cabin door and unbuttoned his coat, threw his
shoulders back as if he could bolster himself for the conversation, drawing upon his authority as captain of the ship since she
didn't respect his authority as her husband.

"You're making me look ridiculous in front of my crew, Annie. You can't dress up in my clothes and climb the rigging like a man. It's simply not acceptable!" He sputtered these last words and wiped his sleeve across his mouth. "It's practically immoral," he said, calmer now and seemingly convinced of the validity of his argument.

Annie stared into his bloodshot eyes and wondered what she'd seen in him that made her marry him. He'd seemed courageous to her four years ago, a man who sailed around the world conducting his business, buying and selling goods to make a profit.

Daniel cleared his throat. "It was a reckless thing to do. I'll not have it happen again. Not on my ship. I'll put you off at the next port and you'll not sail with me again. I can't be concerned about you putting yourself in danger when there are real dangers to consider. Do you understand?"

Annie sat up straight now. She blew across her red, burning palms, chafed from holding on to the rigging, and looked into his face. "It's no more dangerous for me to go aloft than for one of your men, Daniel, and I'll do it again."

"Since that baby died, you've done nothing but try to humiliate me. You've embarrassed me in front of my men and eroded my authority. You'll not climb the rigging again."

"I've embarrassed you, that's all you have to say?" she stood and yelled back at him.

"I've been a much better husband to you than you've been a wife to me. At least I've tried, Annie."

"You left me alone to lose our baby," she said, bitter and disgusted.

"You'll never forgive me. If I'd been there, the baby still would've died."

"But you would've been there! You fool!"

The cabin door slammed behind her. It rattled the brass lanterns in her wake. On deck, she felt free of him. He might be captain of the ship, but she was in charge of herself, and he could not take that away from her.

The next morning she was in the cabin when Daniel ran down the steps to tell her that they'd been boarded by pirates. His voice was fused with authority and fear. She heard a scuffle on deck, strange men barking orders.

"They're onboard?"

"They said if I turned over the cargo and supplies they'd leave us with our lives. I don't see any choice. I don't have the manpower or weapons to fight them."

"You can't let them take the cargo," she said. "If you don't fight, we'll lose everything."

"We'll let them take what they want and hope they don't notice you. No telling what they'll do with a woman," he said. "You've got to hide."

The sound of Daniel's voice infuriated her. "You need to gather the men. You let our daughter die, now you're going to give up without a fight?"

"Stop it, Annie." The conviction of her rage caused him to doubt himself, not as a ship's captain, but as a man—had he let his daughter die?—and this was where she found her stronghold.

She took the pistol he kept beneath the foot of the mattress ticking, and she tossed the machete hanging from a sling by the doorway directly at him so that he caught it by the handle.

"This is not a fighting ship," he said, but once armed with Daniel's pistol, Annie shoved past him.

On deck, she found O'Malley. "Go below, get arms. You'll take your orders from me, not the captain. Do you understand?"

O'Malley eyed the pistol and hesitated.

"Are you in, O'Malley?"

"Yes, ma'am."

Annie hid behind the bulwark to watch the pirates work with a frenzied sense of purpose, unloading crates of cargo one after another and loading them onto their own ship. They wore guns, machetes, hammers. Fear broke through her resolve, but she realized that she wasn't afraid of being robbed. She was afraid of dying. She didn't want to die, and she wasn't going to let her husband's cowardice cost her her life.

When Donovan, Nickerson, and O'Malley appeared from below, armed with pistols, she said, "We can protect our ship, or we can roll over like dogs. What'll it be?"

O'Malley scanned the deck for Daniel, then eyed Annie. He looked from one of his fellows to the next. "We'll fight, ma'am." O'Malley spoke for the lot of them. A few more men came up from belowdecks, armed and cautious.

"All right, then."

"If we go at them from the stern, we'll surprise them. That's our only chance. Wait until most of them are on their own ship stowing the cargo. When they come back across the gangplank we can shoot them one at a time," O'Malley said.

"Where's the captain, ma'am?"

"Gathering ammunition, and getting the rest of the men in formation. He wants to try to reason with them, but there's no reasoning with men like this." Her lie came easily. She didn't want to tell them that he was hiding.

She ventured up the ladder to peer across the deck. "You'll wait for my signal," she said. When one of the pirate crew, a thin man in oversize trousers held about his waist with a rope—he looked more like a pauper than a pirate—caught her eye, she fired and hit him in the leg.

"That's her signal," one of the men said, and they ran up the ladder on either side of her.

She aimed again and got the man in the shoulder. Shots rang out until three pirates lay on the deck near the hold, blood pooling around them. Annie loaded her gun and readied herself for the attack. She positioned herself aft of the helm so that she had a clear shot to the gate where the pirates boarded, and when they began running across, guns and cutlasses raised high, she and the crew fired. The flinty smell of gunpowder and smoke filled the air. Daniel was a fool. "The worst kind of fool," she muttered.

The *Intrepid*'s crew picked up arms from the fallen pirates and fought the men coming at them from the other ship. They took orders from Annie, and she led them into surrounding the pirates, and shooting at them from behind cabins, and distracting them with stray shots from the foredeck while a group of sailors attacked from behind.

The danger heightened her senses so that she could feel and hear an approach from behind or the backward swing of a cutlass or a pistol's cock in time to react. The motion of her body felt separate from herself, as if her physicality had a mind of its own, her body driven by instinct rather than reason. Annie strode across the deck until she heard the words, "Stop. Don't move. Not a muscle, or I'll take your head off right here." Her body froze and her senses took in the sound of a man's heavy breathing. He stepped closer, nearly pressed himself against her back but did not touch her. His heat radiated through her jacket. "Turn around slowly," he said, and she followed his orders. "A wench who thought she could save her ship. Well, I'll be." He seemed pleased with himself to have captured her. "You could be very useful to me," he said, and turned her by the shoulders to face him. "If you're willing to fight like that."

She considered the man in front of her, thick arms and menacing eyes. He was taller and wider and certainly stronger than her, his gun pointed at her ribs. Thick black hair rolled in waves to his whiskered jaw, and sideburns tapered to a fine point near his chin.

"I'm the captain here, Jack Hawkins. I'll sign you onto my crew. How would you like that? The wayward life of a pirate? It's so easy even a woman could do it," he said, rubbing his closed fist over his mouth. "It's that or else I'll kill you where you stand. Or keep you for my own use. I haven't decided which."

She couldn't speak.

"I got plenty of bullets. I can put one in you right now. I saw you kill perfectly good men, and now you will replace them. First you'll have to prove you're up to the task," he said, grabbing her by the elbow and shoving her aft toward the captain's quarters, his pistol pressed hard into her ribs, while her own gun dangled from her hand. There was something utterly masculine about his odor and his gait and his brutality that intrigued her as much as it repulsed her. He stood atop the companionway and pulled her closer. "Go down there and finish the job."

He searched her eyes for signs of fear, but she wouldn't reveal herself. She shook her elbow loose and climbed down the steps into the cabin. Daniel sat on the edge of his bunk worrying the button of his waistcoat, twirling it around as if it would deliver answers from its shining brass surface. When he saw her, he turned to slap her, but he couldn't reach.

"You've ruined us," he said. "If we'd let them take what they wanted, they would have left us alone. How many of my men are dead? What in God's name are you doing? Have you gone completely mad?"

"Shut up." She stood back, held the gun with both hands, and tried to level it at his head. She wanted to remember why she hated him or if she ever loved him, but rage shook her—she would not die for Daniel. Her certainty coalesced in a cold and thoughtless will to carry this out.

"Think for a minute, Annie. What are you doing?" When she didn't release her focus, he said, "You are utterly lost. You are not my wife."

The gun shook violently in her hands. She pushed the muzzle into his chest to steady it.

"That's my gun," he said.

"Finish it, or I'll kill the both of you myself," Jack said, leaning down the hatch, his voice a serrated edge.

"You'll not be the end of me," Annie said.

Daniel shoved her back against the wall. He lunged at her

and struggled to reach the gun, but she moved her arm back and forth, dodging his reach. She had to get him off her, but he was taller, stronger. She drove her knee into his groin, and when he doubled over, she swung the gun at his head. Then he was on top of her, trying to pin her right arm to the deck. His breath on her face infuriated her, and she shook herself loose. The strength she'd gained over the last months of working on the ship drove her into a frenzy of activity, and she swung the gun at his head again. The crew's attention on the fight only heightened Annie's focus. She wasn't going to die, but she started losing track of herself. She was tired. They struggled back and forth amid the hollering crowd of sailors. When the gun went off, the sound ricocheted in the cabin, loud enough to burst the wooden boards.

Jack climbed down the stairs, his buttons rattling like coins in a pocket. He stood over the pair and watched as blood ran across the floor. Daniel lay on top of Annie, and Jack kicked him off with the heel of his boot, so that he fell onto his back, blood pooling from the hole in his stomach.

"You did good," Jack said. "Now get up and make yourself useful. Get me a sack or a sea bag."

Annie stared at the blood, the gun hanging from her hand as thoughtlessly as a child might hold a rag doll.

"Move it!"

Once she handed over Daniel's sea bag, Jack went to work ransacking the drawers. He took a watch engraved from her father as a gift, Daniel's gold cuff links, and a pair of sailing pants, whatever he could find of any value.

Annie headed for the ladder to get out of the stuffy room

where it reeked of blood and gunpowder. Her legs swayed beneath her.

"You're not going anywhere. Where's he keep the money?"

"Under there." She swung the gun toward the drawer beneath the mattress. "That should be enough to buy my freedom," Annie said.

"Your freedom's not for sale. You'll fight with us to replace the men you killed, and we'll need some of the ship's crew to replace the others. Which are worthy?"

Annie let her face reveal nothing while a typhoon of emotions swept through. Sheer terror at the prospect of the pirates, rage at Daniel for not fighting. "They're all useless. Not a fighter in the lot of them. You've seen for yourself." She grabbed the trousers back from him, and a red jacket. "I'm keeping these. I'm going to need them," she said.

"Keep your pistol, too. Johnson, take her aboard while I collect what's mine."

Johnson walked her to the break in the rail that opened onto the pirate ship. Her stomach lurched and she leaned over the side to puke into the sea, and then wiped her mouth on her shirtsleeve. Johnson laughed.

The two ships bobbed together in the swells amid wafting clouds of gun smoke. When her boot struck the unfamiliar deck and she caught her balance, she saw two cabins with round portholes and the helm and binnacle positioned at the stern and the same rigging, masts, and sails that she'd learned aboard *Intrepid*. The only difference in this ship was the guns loaded into holes cut in the bulwarks. She stood clear of the gate and watched the men loading crates down into the hold. When Jack crossed onto the ship, the sailors cast off the lines, and Annie watched as they drifted clear of *Intrepid*. Daniel lay dead in the captain's quarters. She wanted to feel regret or remorse, but she didn't feel anything at all.

The wind had come up now and the captain spoke loud enough to sound like he was dressing the men down, but he was only talking, his stentorian voice a roar in the sea air.

"I'm the captain of this crew in battle and you'll follow my orders when that time comes. In all else we're a democracy. You'll get equal shares of any booty, and food and drink and a say in what happens on this ship. You being a woman makes no difference. You could be a goddamned duck for all we care, as long as you fight like a man. You hear?"

"I hear."

"You didn't tell me your name," Jack said.

She hesitated. "Blue," she said. It was what her father had called her as a child, Blue for the color of her eyes. Blue for the sullen disposition he could not cheer. And wasn't that appropriate since her father was a kind of pirate himself?

"Go down the fo'c'sle and find an empty bunk, get the lay of the ship. You know how to fight, but can you sail?"

"Yes," she said. "And I can navigate to true course."

"So you're good for more than murdering my men. I'll make use of you then," Jack said.

Blue stood at the rail holding on to the clothing she'd taken from Daniel. She stared blankly into the heaving ocean, letting the spray wet her face and hair. This was as close to tears as she could come. When the ship's rocking motion broke her gaze, she headed to the hatch that led down to the crew's quarters. Each step into the bowels of the ship carried her into an underworld that bristled the fine hairs along the back of her neck and made her muscles twitch. The fo'c'sle smelled of stagnant bilge water, sweaty men, unwashed clothes, and rum. It was the odor of oblivion. Under the low ceiling, Blue inhabited a limbo between the woman she had been and the woman she would become. She dropped the armful of clothing onto the aft-most bunk on the starboard side. She quickly undressed. Daniel's cotton trousers hung loose from her hips. She rolled the waist down and cuffed the hems. She felt safer in men's attire. The bunks were built two high into the hull on either side of the ship. Blue, satisfied that her bunk on the end offered easy escape and sufficient space from the other sailors, stuffed her clothes in the wooden chest beneath and lay back, her pistol in her right hand, her arm crossed over her chest so that the pistol rested on her heart.

6

By the time Hannah came down from the lighthouse, Billy had stoked the fire and boiled water for coffee. He'd filled the lanterns and lit the candles and brought in extra firewood. Hannah slid a pile of root vegetables from beneath the sink into a scooped-out wooden bowl and placed it alongside a cutting board and a knife on the dining table.

"Peel and chop these," she said.

Billy shook his head. "I can't cook."

"I've yet to meet a sailor didn't know his way around a knife. All you have to do is peel and chop."

Billy scooted his chair up to the table and peered into the bowl. He was handsome, blond hair and gray-blue eyes startling in the way they looked right at you, then looked away as if that moment of seeing was too much to bear. Fearful as a kicked dog, she thought, and smelled nearly as bad.

"How big do you want them?" He sat at the table with his head resting on one hand, exhausted, as he would be for a while. How long was she going to be stuck with him?

"However you like," she said curtly. "I'm making a soup that has to last us through the storm. We'll have no time to cook once it hits."

They worked with their backs to each other, silent but for

the wind shaking the chimney and the strike of the knife on the cutting board. Hannah wouldn't tolerate disobedience, Billy realized. There was no room for stepping out of line. He needed to get a hold of himself, but he'd learned from Annie that recklessness was not a thing you could overcome.

After supper, Billy finished with the dishes and wiped his hands on the seat of his pants. "Galley duty's over." He leaned back against the counter, one foot crossed over the other. The hollows of his hips showed through his low-slung pants. She needed to fatten him up so he could leave.

He pulled a rigging knife from his pocket and began to run it along the underside of his fingernails.

"That's a disgusting habit. I'll thank you not to do it in my kitchen."

"Yes, ma'am," he said, holding his hands up. He sheathed the knife, lifted his pant leg, and slid it into his sock so that it rested along his calf. "So where's this husband of yours?" he asked.

"You should be in bed," Hannah said, annoyed. "You've still got a fever."

Billy swaggered to the bedroll where he lay back against the pillows and stared into the fire. "Not many people come out here." He leaned on his side now and looked up at her.

She didn't want to answer him. Still, there he was, waiting for her to respond. What was his point? Was he trying to frighten her? Because she wasn't afraid. He was too weak to do anything foolish.

"Tom comes regularly, as you know. You'll meet others." The truth was that other than John, she had the company of Tom and shipwrecked sailors and travelers passing through who saw the light and sought refuge—mostly men.

"I never heard of a lady lightkeeper."

"My husband's the lightkeeper, I told you that."

"Still, it's strange, and you wear pants." He laughed.

"Aren't you tired?"

"I'm glad it was you here when our boat when down. I bet he doesn't go out there like you do. I never heard of a light-keeper doing that," Billy said.

Hannah went to bed early to get away from him and his questions. She dreamed of water running so heavily that it filled the ocean and ponds and lakes in Barnstable to over-flowing; it ran down the roads and turned them into rivers, it lifted John from his horse and carried him downstream, shattering his wooden wagon to bits. Torrents of water carried him off, and he couldn't rescue himself because he was too far from home and the lighthouse and his rescue boat and his tools were off in the distance. He needed a rope thrown to him, or a tree branch stretched low over the road, but there was nothing. If only she could reach into her dream and pluck him free, pull him under the covers where she could feel his heat, but he drifted farther and farther out of sight.

She woke crying, reaching for him on the other side of the bed. The empty space where John slept was cold. She stretched herself across it, hoping that he would climb in next to her, and say, "I'll explain in the morning."

A loud knock on the front door drove Hannah up from the bed. She looked around her room, disoriented. She'd been up and down all night, climbing the lighthouse stairs to check the flames, and then back to bed, up the stairs, then back to bed. The instinct that drove her up to check the lights was heightened in John's absence—there was no one to rely on but herself. At four in the morning, she'd stood with her back to the flames, her eyes toward Barnstable where John had spent the night with her parents, spent the night in her childhood bed, but all she saw was her own reflection staring back at her, and a look in her eyes that said, *You are alone*.

Now it was dawn, and she was exhausted.

The knocking was louder now. Hannah pulled a wool sweater on over her nightdress. "I'm coming," she said, and she splashed cold water on her face, glimpsed her startled expression in the glass. She looked tired, her eyes red and irritated from not sleeping well. When she rounded the corner into the kitchen, Tom stood holding his hat against his chest. Billy had opened the door and stood by the fire to see what was going to happen, but when Hannah appeared, he ducked out the passageway to the barn.

"I got news, Hannah. You better sit down."

"I can hear it standing."

"I just rode back from Yarmouth. They found John's horse, wandering loose down by Dennis Pond. There was no sign of John."

"What happened? Where is he?" She held her stomach, as if she'd been kicked.

"They don't know. Search parties have gone out but they found nothing so far. They're still looking."

"What do you mean they don't know? Someone had to see him."

"Your mother said good-bye to him near daybreak the day of the storm. Wilbur Dickinson saw him pass by the post office soon after that, and his trail stops there. Next sign of him is his horse found down by the pond. We didn't find any of his cargo or any indication of where he could be."

"I don't understand. What could've happened?" Her voice rose in pitch, her words came out in a stream of grief. "If it wasn't the storm, what was it?"

Tom hesitated. "Well, there's been speculation, of course. He could've been robbed or thrown from his wagon. There's no way of knowing until we find him."

"You think he's dead?" Hannah held her fists clenched at her sides, her body rigid. All color had drained from her face, as if she was the corpse they'd been looking for.

Tom looked down. "There was a lot of blood, Hannah. I didn't want to say, but you might as well know."

Hannah fell into the nearest chair, her legs weak. Her head swam with possibilities, all of them accompanied by an overwhelming grief that set her adrift in the soft cushioned chair. "You've been searching for his body," she said, the fact like a rock dropped into the room.

Tom fell into a chair and landed, elbows on the table, the weight of his head in his hands.

"He could've been taken off, you know, kidnapped or something," Billy said. Hannah turned to see him standing in the doorway.

"How long have you been standing there?"

"Not long," Billy said.

Tom interrupted him. "Are you in the habit of listening to people's conversations?"

Tom tried to reassure Hannah, but he couldn't overcome the despair in his voice. "Your father went out on the search team. Half the mid-Cape men are searching day and night, but so far they've come up with nothing. Your parents want you to come home. They don't want you here alone."

"I'm not alone, Tom. I'm keeping the lights while John is gone, just like I always do."

Tom looked at Billy. No one spoke.

That night, Hannah slid the fireplace grate into place and doused the candles one at a time. Her body felt as if it were filled with sand that shifted and dragged with each step across floor. If only the floor tilted toward the bedroom, she'd have an easier time getting there. It was easy to let herself drop into the chair by the fire. She wanted to feel something, to cry or scream or wail, but her mind worked hard to leave no room for grief. She searched for explanations that would mean John was alive. He could've been robbed, beaten, and left in the woods while the criminals got away. Maybe he fell from the wagon and wandered off, disoriented. Any number of things could happen to a man traveling alone, even in a small place like this, she told herself.

She had to see for herself the place where he'd gone missing. If anyone could find him, it would be her. She'd know where he was by instinct. Tom would watch the lighthouse. At the front window, she looked toward the road, but it promised nothing.

7

THE MUSTY AIR HIT HER ALL AT ONCE WITH A memory that was not a picture in her mind but an ocean swell of feeling. It was a lifetime of days spent stepping over this threshold through the smells of tobacco, human dirt, and earth brought in on the bottoms of boots, mildew, damp wool, whale oil, and spilled beer, all the meals they'd ever eaten, every fish cooked, every pine wreath hung, every bayberry candle burned. All of these odors seeped and layered into the shifting floors and in between walls, smells that could not be kept back with daily cleaning.

"Hannah, is that you? Come here, come in. I'm so sorry, dear." Her mother pulled her by the elbow into the front hall. There was her father's pipe spattered with paint, propped on a sack of tobacco, his boots kicked off by the door.

Hannah let her hat drop to the floor and stepped into her mother's fleshy arms, into the scent of rose water and fresh linen and cooking smells from the kitchen. That's when her tears came heavy and hard.

"Oh, dear, dear. We'll do our best to find him. You're home now. I'll take care of you." Her mother helped Hannah out of her coat and hung it on a peg by the door. She faced Hannah and looked at her squarely from the top of her hair to her bootlaces and nodded. Nora had gained weight, but she carried herself with dignity and purpose.

"You can go on upstairs, freshen up. Dinner will be ready in a few minutes. We'll fatten you up while you're here."

Hannah glanced up the darkened stairway toward her old bedroom, the last place where John had slept, the last place she wanted to go. Her father nudged her mother aside and kissed Hannah on the cheek, took her by the shoulders as if to feel her strength, and then, satisfied, stepped back and let her mother take the lead.

Hannah stood in the hallway, not wanting to step in any direction. As she looked toward the kitchen, she saw John frying a fresh fillet of sole as he'd done the night he'd spent here. Or when she looked toward the living room, there he was with his boots kicked off by the fire, talking with her father about his catch.

"Why don't you relax with your father while I finish getting dinner ready?" Nora said.

Her father led her into the parlor at the front of the house where he'd set a fire going. The room was warm, and Hannah fell into a chair and stared into the flames, suddenly tired. Her father sighed over his newspaper and she turned to him, but he did not look up. She had never considered the fact that he would age, but there he was, stooped a bit at the shoulders, a soft belly pressing out against his sweater. Still, he was a handsome man with a swath of dark hair and brown eyes, a heavy jaw that strengthened his round, poutish face.

They sat for some time in silence. Theirs was normally a conversation of dropping a trap off the side of the boat and a wave signaling the buoy's rise to the surface. It was watching a squall blow in from the horizon, battening down the boat, and racing for the harbor with hardly a word spoken. But this silence was something else.

He sat with the newspaper across his lap, his spectacles balanced near the end of his nose. "When did you get those?" Hannah asked.

He looked up, pulled from thoughts deeper than the news. "They're just for reading." He folded the paper and slapped it against his knee. "You must have questions, Hannah."

"I want to see the place tomorrow."

"We'll go, then."

Hannah stood and gazed out the front windows, imagining herself into the distances beyond the dark. The men John had rescued walked through their lives with a scant memory of him or no thought at all. He'd ridden away from here and into his absence, which only seemed broader and deeper now.

"Been awhile since you stood right there," he said. He took his glasses off and dropped them onto the side table. He asked Hannah to help him get some firewood and groaned as he stood up and stretched his back. "I'm no good at getting old. No good at all."

He led her out the side door into the yard where moonlight lit the side of the house. Alongside the barn, the cords of wood he'd stacked rose near as tall as him. He reached behind the woodpile, wiggled his arm back there, and came up with a bottle. He drank and dabbed his mouth with his shirtsleeve. "You want some?"

"No thanks."

"I hurt my back pulling traps. This relaxes the muscles or makes me too drunk to care. I don't know which." He drank, leaning back against the woodpile, his head tilted to look into the sky. The moon cast the woods into an otherworldly glow and they could see the yard, the broken traps and boat parts and mangled nets.

"If there's anything you can't do—"

"Forget it," he said.

"Why hide the bottle?"

"Your mother doesn't want to know about it, but if I need it for the pain, she'll ignore it. It's just her way." He sat on the chopping block, and with his hands on his knees, he leaned forward and spoke as if he meant to be heard.

"I heard about that rescue of yours."

"You know better than to listen. People like to hear themselves talk."

"Sure, but I know you, so when I hear something like that and weigh it against what I know about you, there's not a lot left to question. I'm no fool. I know what you're capable of doing in a boat."

"There's nothing wrong with what I did."

"You think you're so goddamned invincible," he said. "You always have." He spat at the ground. "I taught you good but everyone is susceptible. I'm not saying this because I doubt you. You know I don't, but you can't control everything that happens out there, no matter how strong or good you are. You can't control an ocean."

He sloshed the liquor around in the bottle and took another sip. "I wish you'd just *think*, Hannah. Stop and *think*. That's what scares me. You're so full of passion you don't stop to consider the consequences."

"You believe some thirdhand story, but you've never once come up to Dangerfield to see what I do."

"I guess we've both been remiss."

They sat for a while watching the dark. From this part of the yard Hannah could see the bedroom window she'd stared out of for years as a younger girl. The bedroom where she'd spent her first night with John. The bedroom where he may have spent his last night.

"Mother's heard about the rescue too?" Hannah asked.

"Not from me." He rocked himself forward and stood from the chopping block, slid the bottle back behind the woodpile. He loaded Hannah's arms with wood, then his own, steady as if he hadn't taken a drink. They stacked a couple loads of maple by the fire and went outside again to brush wood shavings from their clothes.

In the dining room, the table was set with everyday dishes, scratched and worn with years of use, while the good china remained in the cabinet on display. Hannah's mother swept from the kitchen to the dining room and back again, placing serving dishes around the table.

"Christ, Nora, would you come in and sit down? We're half starved."

"You've never been starved in your life," she said, untying her apron and hanging it on a peg behind the door.

Her father didn't look up from his meal. The food seized his attention, and he worked his way around the plate as if finishing was another task in life.

Now Hannah's grief took a turn, and she found herself chattering as if the silence would destroy them. She spoke frantically, afraid that if she stopped, the heavy oak table would crack down the middle in the face of John's absence and her father's drinking and the years not spent sitting together around a good meal. "I haven't had a roast like this since the last time I sat right here. I just can't seem to get it to cook for the right amount of time. Father, pass the salt, would you? I love how the potatoes are crunchy on the bottom. Did you roast them in the same pan with the meat?"

"There's plenty more," her mother said, nudging the potatoes toward Hannah.

"Father, what do you think? Is this the best dinner you've ever had?"

He looked up from his plate as if caught in the act. "What? Yes, yes, it's good, real good."

When her mother finished eating, she folded her napkin and placed it beside her plate. She leaned back and considered her husband before speaking. "Edward, those traps have been piled out back for months. I'm not saying you should move them on your own, but now that Hannah's here—"

"I told you I'd take care of that," he said.

"He won't admit he needs help, Hannah. Maybe you can talk some sense into him. We can afford to get someone to help him out, but he won't allow it. He's too stubborn." Her mother leaned forward in her chair. "It wouldn't kill you to get a little help, Ed."

"I'm fine," he said. He pushed himself up from the table.

"Where are you going now?"

"I'll be outside."

"Getting some more wood from the pile?" Nora asked, her voice a sarcastic snap.

The sound of the kitchen door slamming shut was answer enough.

In the morning, when Hannah was making coffee, she watched the fog drift past the kitchen window. An off-kilter formation of geese flew over the trees, their call growing distant and marking the immensity of the world beyond their yard. She'd woken several times during the night to check the lights, but the lighthouse beam didn't interrupt the dark and she felt her childhood bed beneath her. There in the shadows her dresser settled into the floor, the washbasin right where it had always been, and the night table by the bed. She'd thought of lighting the candle, but the darkness softened. What a blank and sprawling enormity—nighttime without the regularity of the light flashing, the four-hour check for oil, the threat of bad weather that would call her out onto the beach.

She drifted back to sleep and found herself alone in her dreams wandering the woods behind the barn, running along the trail toward Dennis Pond, through the thick patch of spruce that thinned to pine, an occasional birch tree and then a green field and brambles and there was the pond. Still and flat as the beginning of time. *Did you take him?* The place where they'd found his horse wandering was less than a mile east of where she stood. In her dream the water smelled like rain and mildew, and when she turned toward where his horse would've been, her feet froze and she couldn't move. She tried to speak, to scream. *Where is John?* But her throat didn't work and she had to pantomime the words, holding her hands out and stabbing the pond with her questioning glare, as if to say, *Where, where, where?*

The next morning, she stared into the fog from the kitchen window and tried not to think about John, but his absence took up space and had weight. If he'd been here to spend the night with her, they would have fallen asleep wrapped around each other and would have woke to make love. He'd cover her mouth to keep her from making noise, and when they fell away from each other, they'd lie back in bed and talk about the lighthouse like it was a child they'd left behind.

When she heard her mother's firm foot on the back stairs, she poured a cup of coffee for her and cut thick slices of bread for toast, relieved by the simple act of placing her hand on a loaf of bread.

"You're up early," Nora said. "Aren't you tired from your trip?"

"Habit. The lights," Hannah said.

Nora arranged the butter dish and the jam pot on the table and set two places. "This is strawberry, but there's beach plum, too, if you'd rather."

Hannah felt her mother holding back the one thing she wanted to talk about. "Strawberry's fine."

Nora carried her coffee to the small table by the window. Hannah took the toast from the stove, tossed it on a plate, and brought it to the table.

"Did you sleep well?" Nora eyed her cautiously, stirring her coffee, the spoon against the cup an annoying tinkle in the air.

"He didn't want to leave that last day. He kept forgetting things and coming back to the house. I just wanted him to leave so I could get on with my day. I thought he'd be back in a couple of days. He always came right back."

"I know."

"And then there was the storm. I thought for a while he stayed in Orleans to get out of the rain, or was injured." Hannah scraped her knife around the rim of the jam jar, over and over, and then dropped the knife.

Nora opened the window a crack and let the cold air into the room. "You'll have to get on with things at some point," Nora said. "Do you think it's practical to stay in Dangerfield? You could have a good life here, find a husband when you're ready."

"I have to stay. It's my home now, Mother."

That afternoon, Hannah rode alongside her father, who was in a bad humor but determined to take her to the place where John had gone missing.

"It's hard on your mother," he said, rocking with the stride of his horse. He could've been talking about his drinking or losing John or just about anything. He spat into the bushes and scratched his whiskers. "There's things you lose that don't come back."

She felt him trying to right himself like a man holding on for his life to a capsized dinghy. Only he couldn't get hold. His thoughts ran scattershot, careening in one direction, distracted by the sound of a dog barking—"Don't know whose dog that is, but if it was mine, I'd whack it good and hard"—then taking off in another direction that led to a place of dumb silence. He shook his head, repentant about things that were not his fault— John gone missing, Hannah's refusal to stay ashore, his disabled back—when so many things were his fault.

On Summer Street, loose rocks and tree roots upended the road. They passed the old graveyard in silence and then onward through the pines. The smell of pond scum reached them first, a smell that Hannah remembered from childhood.

"It was over near here." Her father pointed. "The horse was just wandering, like it was waiting for him to come back."

Hannah stared at the ground where he pointed. Nothing but dirt and dried pine needles. If the horse had been waiting for him to come back, John must have stood right there, but the ground showed nothing. She followed a trail into the woods, casting her eyes into the bushes, looking for…*what?*

When Hannah had exhausted herself searching through the woods for any sign at all of her husband, when her eyes grew tired and common sense told her to stop, she stood by her father and looked across the pond. What had she expected? This place meant nothing. It was a spot in the woods, unchanged by whatever had happened here.

"There were marks from different hooves, marks from wagon wheels going in both directions up the road. One line of thinking says he was ransacked and carried off around the back of the pond along that skimpy bit of road. Another theory is they sunk him out in the pond, but you know how far you have to go out there to hit any deep water. We went out in rowboats with tall branches, poking them all around down there. We did that for six days. Men traveled along the main road with a sketch of John and talked to anyone who would listen. We tore this place up, Hannah. There was nothing. It's like he was standing right there." He tapped his foot on the ground in front of him where two stones rested side by side. This was his offering, his uncertain knowledge. "Right there," he said, "and then he just disappeared."

Grief was like a wave cresting, gathering size and velocity. Hannah braced herself against it. Isn't this what she'd wanted—to know?

On the ride back to the house, her father didn't know what to say or how to console her, and she couldn't find the words to express her distress. A woman standing on her porch watched them pass. Hannah felt the woman's eyes on her, thanking fate for sparing her own husband and sending a prayer out for Hannah, as if this act of goodwill would spare her. Hannah didn't want her prayers. It was too late for that. The sun became a sliver on the sky, the cold a slap on her face that said, *Wake up! Wake up! Don't you see what's going on? Your life is not here. It is gone, like your husband is gone, and you are left, Hannah, left.*

Back at the house, Hannah went to her room and lay across the bed until her tears became sobs she couldn't control. John was torn from her, one rip at a time. She was relieved to let go, and then stricken once again by the thought of a life without him.

The sound of his voice, the weight of him in the bed beside her, or waiting for him to return from the beach during a storm. For over six years, she'd feared it would be the sea that would take him, never the road. Not once had she imagined danger on the road, and for this she blamed herself. If only she'd thought to worry about the road, this never would've happened. If only she'd held him back from leaving with one more thing. *John, you forgot your…* Was it the weight of the wagon that had slowed him down enough to run into whatever had killed him? Or had he left her parents' house too early, or too late? *Why? Why?* At the window she watched the road. The evil, darkening road. Never again would she trust it. She'd ride home alone in spite of it.

Her father's shadow by the woodpile. How much time did he spend out there? The sound of her mother downstairs, a storm of domestic activity that started in the front parlor and worked its way down the hall toward the kitchen. She saw how they rattled around in their own pain. No one was exempt.

Hannah wiped her face, swollen from crying. She pulled back her hair and went downstairs.

Her mother placed an apple tart on the cooling rack by the window. "Did you get any rest?" she asked. She ran a cloth under cold water and folded it neatly, then held it out to Hannah to place over her swollen eyes.

"Not really," Hannah said.

"It's going to take time."

"I don't think we're going to find him," Hannah said.

"I know, I mean to grieve. For all of us, but for you, dear—"

Hannah removed the cloth from her eyes. "When did his drinking get this bad?"

"Oh, Hannah, stop it. You need to think about what you're going to do."

"I'm serious—when?"

Her mother went to the window for the tart. "You've got to try this. I rolled the dough out thinner, which makes the crust a bit crispy."

Hannah watched her wipe down the counter and put the dishes away. She bent to pick up crumbs that had strayed from their proper place atop the pie and brushed them into the sink. Nora worked hard to keep back her waves of anger, all the things she did not want to say. The disappointments and devastations that coursed through her over the years took shape in her stooped shoulder, the rolls of fat around her waist and gathered at her ankles, the squint of her right eye that held some essential part of herself back, as if she'd given everything she had to her husband and her child and her store, and this one thing, hidden, she would keep for herself. Hannah saw it glittering beyond the dark reaches of her mother's pupils.

"It's only because of his back," she said finally, then took out the trash herself. "You're grieving your husband, Hannah. You don't need to worry about me."

That night was her last night in Barnstable, and her mother roasted a chicken. The three of them gathered around the table staring into the candles, grief palpable like ocean waves they had to walk through. Her mother carved the bird, her face bowed and in shadow. She looked beautiful right then, the strong lines of her cheekbones, her eyes focused on her work, but her mind was somewhere else as she lifted generous portions onto each plate.

"I wish you'd stay," her father said. "I don't know how you're going to get along out there by yourself."

"A young grieving widow should be with her family," Nora said. "We can take care of you and help you get the rest you need. You're going to kill yourself up at that lighthouse. And for what?"

"She's right, you know. Now that John's gone—"

"Just stop, both of you. I'm not helpless, and I need to work if I'm going to get through this."

"The man you rescued. What's his name?" Nora asked.

"Billy," Hannah said.

"It's not right, him still there with you," her mother said. "I know you're alone, but—"

"You might want to chastise her about the thing that could actually kill her, Nora."

"Yes, of course. I just…I don't know what to say about that. I can't believe it, and yet I do. Then I ask myself why? But I know why. We raised you, didn't we?"

Hannah saw then that her mother knew better than her father that Hannah couldn't stay ashore in a storm. If she'd been able to stop herself, she never would've gone out in the boat alone. Whatever pulled her was a thing beyond reason, and it would keep her going back. Her mother's efforts to guide Hannah into moving home were like trying to steer her to safe harbor.

"I could ask you to stop, I suppose," her mother said. Her father watched, dumbfounded. "But you wouldn't listen."

"By God, she will listen." He slammed his fist on the table, by now an impotent gesture.

"Oh, just eat your dinner, Ed," her mother said.

8

Upon her return to Dangerfield, and in the days that followed, what had started with a storm of activity and talk from Dangerfield to Barnstable had become a quiet resignation that settled like fog. She'd decided against a funeral. Without John's body, she couldn't bear it. She'd mourn her husband in private, the same way they'd lived their life together. Still, she wanted to shake herself loose from grief the same way she shook herself from sleep in the morning, but all she could do was brace herself for another day and try not to think about the morning John left, the way he'd looked back as if to secure the place in memory, where he could not lose it. *Just go, John.*

She stared blankly out the kitchen window toward the water, clouds like steam drifting then gone, the sky a darkness like foreboding. Billy came in from the barn covered with chicken seed. Two days ago, she'd ridden John's horse straight through Orleans to Dangerfield, until the lighthouse flashed from the road, and there was Billy standing on the porch, as if he knew Hannah would appear at that moment and had stepped outside to watch her ride into the yard. His cough had lessened now, and he was able to stay awake most of the day. "Mr. Billings still hasn't come. I can see the body down there in the life cart and there's crows swooping over it."

"Billings hasn't come? Aren't you angry? That man was your shipmate."

Billy walked to the table as if he was crossing a ship's deck, his swagger accounting for any fluctuations in the ground beneath his feet. He rubbed his hands across the tops of his pants and stared at his place setting as if a plate of eggs would appear any minute.

"You look like a dog waiting to be fed. Put the water on for coffee, and get the stove fire going."

He did what he was told. Since she'd been gone, he'd taken to cleaning the chicken coop and feeding the chickens, cleaning the stalls and feeding the horses. He repaired the broken catch on the front door and nailed down the loose barn boards. Tom must've gotten him started on one task after another until he could move through the work on his own.

When the kettle poured steam into the room, Hannah poured water over the coffee grounds, but she was distracted. The coffeepot spilled across the counter and boiling water dripped down the front of her clothes. She slammed the kettle down and lifted her shirt to keep the boiling water from her skin. Her eyes roved feverishly across the mess. She swept her hand across the counter and in one swift motion sent everything flying onto the floor. Broken bits of glass and shards of clay cracked beneath her boots. Coffee seeped into the floorboards, and the kettle rolled across the floor and settled under the stove.

"I'll get the broom," Billy said quietly.

The women of Dangerfield knew about loss as surely as they knew how to fillet and fry a strip of cod. Women gathered around the bereaved like a covey of quail and suffered as if their own loved one had passed into the next life or into no life at all. They offered consolation, knowing that their presence was the only consolation they had to offer. Mourners came by in twos, as if grief were a storm that required reinforcements. They carried baskets of pies, preserves, cooked chicken, bowls of potatoes, all in an attempt to stem the loss.

"Eat. It will help you sleep," Ruth Miller said, sliding a hot plate of chicken and potatoes in front of Hannah.

Hannah wasn't friendly with these women on a regular basis, but they shared camaraderie as they shared the risks of living in Dangerfield. The women discussed which men had been lost that year and how the widows were faring, which whalers had been heard from after rounding Cape Horn, and who they expected to come in off the banks with the most cod. In their small town with its small economy, the news affected everyone, and the women talked and talked as if talking could save them.

When Billy stuck his head into the room from the barn passageway and saw the women, he retreated like a scared rabbit.

"Will they look for a new lighthouse keeper?" Mary Hopkins asked. She was the wife of Everett Hopkins, a sturdy and well-liked man, known for his inventive ship designs. Mary was Everett's opposite, nervous, slight, and predictable down to the dish she brought a grieving widow: chicken potpie, which could be heated up and eaten without a lot of fuss. "I'm sure you will want to leave before winter."

Hannah hadn't thought beyond the simple structure of her

tasks, the steady reliance of the light. It was the physical work of getting up and down the lighthouse stairs, firing up the lamps, checking the whale oil, noting passing ships in the log, that anchored her to each day. She was not going to leave the lighthouse. She would not go back to her family in Barnstable and work with her mother in the store. She hadn't married John and moved to the lighthouse and established her life here only to go back.

"I'll remain here to take care of the light," she said.

"But—"

"I'm not leaving," Hannah said, slamming her words like a fist on the table. Without a body, no one could prove that John was dead.

Ruth and Mary looked at each other and gave Hannah a sympathetic stare.

"You don't have to decide right now, dear," Mary said. "But you'll want to send that sailor on his way."

"He's a ruffian," one of the women said. "I don't understand why he's still here."

Hannah didn't answer, and they covered the bowl of potatoes and combined the chicken dishes in an impressive display of domestic efficiency. "Just make sure you eat something," Ruth said, pulling on her gloves and buttoning her coat against the wind.

Hannah felt them wanting to offer a comfort more than food, and since they couldn't, Hannah felt obliged to receive the food more wholeheartedly. "I'm going to eat the entire chicken when you're gone," she told them, holding the door while they stepped into the cold.

On the beach, the breakers rolled low and wide. Billy helped Hannah get the corpse onto a board and fasten it with canvas straps. On the count of three they lifted the board into the back of the skiff so that it tilted from beneath the middle seat up over the transom. All Hannah had to do was tip him into the sea and it would be over.

"It's what should've happened in the first place," Hannah said, setting the oars, while Billy walked the skiff into the surf. "No man should have to rot on the beach. It's a disgrace."

"He was the ship's cook, Brennan Jones. Knew his way around the galley, but could barely bring himself to look at the ocean. He paid the first mate McNealy to write letters to his sister. We all used to listen because he had a nice way of talking and describing things."

Hannah nodded.

"Okay, you're off, ma'am," Billy said, giving the skiff a good shove.

Hannah dug in with the oars, working against the extra weight in the boat. She wanted to get out far enough into the tide where he would be carried off to sea with his shipmates. With the board wedged beneath her seat, she had to straddle the corpse to row. Even though the man's face was covered, the smell of his decay and his inert form beneath the blankets filled the skiff with death. She rowed harder, until she felt the tide's northbound pull. Here she drew the oars in and made them fast. She loosened the board from beneath her seat and maneuvered the weight of the corpse. A couple of flicks of the clasps and the canvas straps fell loose. The body jostled as the boat rocked in the swells. She wanted to say something. She folded the blanket back from the man's face and touched his forehead. Then she tilted the board to let him slide into the water. The body bobbed for a moment before thrusting up once then dropping below the surface. Hannah whispered, "Good-bye."

She thought of John and the troubled look on his face when he'd left that day, the worry she didn't want to see as she'd rushed him out the door. "John," she said, watching the shadowed form disappear below the surface. He'd been at her mother's. Then Wilbur Dickinson saw him heading for home with the wagon loaded down. Then gone.

"John! John!" She screamed until her throat couldn't make sound, then sat down hard and sobbed, the boat drifting. If she'd known she wouldn't see him again, would she have done things differently? If she hadn't gone out in the boat alone, would he have come home? Could she go back and do it again, stay ashore and wait for him? Then would he walk through the door, soaking wet from the storm, and shake himself dry?

Light drained from the sky, and she couldn't bring herself to set the oars. What had she said to him? *Just go, John.*

The next morning a cold wind crept in around the door frame. When Hannah saw that she'd run out of split wood for the fire, she almost called for John. How many times a day did she nearly speak to him? How many times a day did his absence confront her anew? With months of winter ahead, she was afraid of the storms that would heave ships onto the shoals. She imagined countless trips up and down the lighthouse stairs, endless barn chores, and the small garden needing to be turned and planted in the spring. With her boots in the wood chips and her nightgown billowing around her in the morning air, she knew that she must face her fear before it took hold.

Hannah reached for the ax, right where John had left it leaning against a log. The handle, worn smooth, had taken on a patina from the oil in John's hands. She felt the ax's weight and heft, then lifted it over her head and let it fall forward in a practice stroke. It couldn't be that hard. She'd seen John do it a hundred times. She tipped a log on end and stood with her legs hips' width apart. Then she swung the ax forward into the wood. The log didn't split. It only gave the ax a place to lodge itself. After wriggling the ax loose, she tried again, aiming for the outer edge of the log. This time, the log split. Encouraged, she swung the ax one more time, and the log fell into pieces. Sweat dripped from Hannah's brow and collected under her arms, but she couldn't stop. It was hit-and-miss at first, but after a while she split the log more often than she missed.

"What do you think of that, Johnny? I'll bet you never thought I could do it, did you?" she yelled into the wind, tears filling the creases by her eyes. Exhausted and spent, she turned toward the house. Billy was there in the window, watching.

9

~~~~~~~~~~

THE SHABBY, MISMATCHED CREW TAUGHT BLUE how to fling a buck knife at a target nailed to the mast, how to shoot at rotten pineapples, shells, and pieces of wood from the rail, and later, the finer points of punching, choking, tripping, and slitting an enemy's throat. Daniel and the death of her baby became distant memories that she folded into drawers in the back of her memory. Every loss fueled her rage, until Annie was replaced with blind fury. She fought the men until she beat them as much as she lost to them. She fought as if she was fighting for her life.

One afternoon, as she dumped the slosh bucket over the transom, she looked up and spotted a three-masted schooner, a merchant runner. Blue stared until she was sure, until she saw the bowsprit bob on a wave and the steady progress to windward, then called, "There's a ship out there!"

The call echoed among the pirates as she ran belowdecks and rushed to the fo'c'sle for her gun and her knife, fumbling among the others. Johnson slung one cutlass across either side of his belt, loaded his musket with one round, and filled his pockets with lead. Jack stood amidship to eye their prey. Spyglass to one eye, he gestured Donovan to hold his course.

"Looks like we got work to do. Get some loot and head to

shore for a fuck." The sailor called Rusty spat the words at
Blue. He was a short, broad man with a wide, concave face
like a shovel, his square nose flat as his chin, his green eyes
tarnished. His vein-splattered skin was bloated with liquor.

"Leave her alone," the one called Donegan said, a pistol
tucked under the belt that he wore high on his waist. He held
his right hand on the pistol butt and shoved past Rusty with
one shoulder.

"You can fuck all you want," Blue said, her hand on her
knife. "But you're going to need a pile of gold to convince any
woman to take that shriveled little prick into her twat."

Rusty lunged toward her, and she unsheathed her knife and
held it pointed outward so that if he advanced his stomach
would puncture on the fine tip she'd sharpened every day since
her arrival on the *Alice K.* She couldn't give in or show weakness; it would be the end of her.

Rusty saw the knife and stepped aside. "Fucking whore,
you'll be the one to die in this. You!"

Blue grabbed him by the shoulder and, catching him off his
guard, swung his great weight around, slammed him into the
wall, and knocked the wind out of him. She stepped forward
and grabbed his windpipe with a thumb and forefinger on
either side. Her heart knocked loud in her chest. "I'm nobody's
whore," she said, tightening her grasp. "You understand? I'm
here to fight and get my money just like you. You hear me?"

Rusty spat at her, and when she loosened her hold on his
throat, he jerked himself free and shoved her back, adjusting
the weapons hanging in disarray from his holsters. He pulled his
shirt down over his waist and spat again into the bilge.

On deck, blood still throbbed in her head. Jack stood at the helm and barked orders to the crew to hold the ship on course toward the merchant runner. They would pretend to be convening for a gam, as ships often met at sea to trade mail and news of other boats. "Take 'em off guard. Don't even give 'em time to think anything's wrong or pick up their arms."

Blue walked back to the quarterdeck so that she could be closer to Jack. His tactics appeared simple enough, sailing up to windward of the merchant ship and calling out for a meeting. When the *Alice K* sailed alongside the schooner, the crew threw ropes across to the merchant runner and the ships were tied together. The captain of each vessel stood amidships, and a plank was run from one ship to the other.

That was when Jack leaned in toward Blue and said, "You'll follow the men and try not to get yourself killed."

Jack stepped across to the other ship and spoke for a moment with the captain. He seemed to vibrate with authority, the fiend in him conveying orders by the sheer force of his energy as he handed the captain over to Rusty, who led him to the mast and held him there with the point of his musket. With Jack's signal, the men rushed across the plank. One of the pirates carried an iron spear; others carried hatchets and wooden clubs with nails protruding from the ends, pistols slung around their shoulders, and a variety of swords and knives swinging from belts. The men crossed the plank in a clatter of brass and boots, some of them barefoot and hollering obscenities. As the pirates boarded, the schooner's crew scattered and the captain's eyes darted about the decks. In a desperate attempt to escape, he kneed Rusty in the groin. Rusty bent over and the captain delivered an uppercut to his chin that Rusty seemed to barely notice. He grabbed the captain by the throat and pinned him to the mast. "You'll stay right here. You'll not move a muscle!"

The merchant ship's crew reached for any makeshift weapons: belaying pins, buckets, ropes. They fought for any hope of survival. Blue followed Jack toward the hold to take stock. When a young sailor swung a knife at Jack, Jack caught him by the wrist and bent his arm back to shake the knife loose.

"That's your one chance." Jack spat in the sailor's face. "Get moving."

The hold was full of coffee, salt beef, jute, sugar, rum, and other goods they couldn't identify without unpacking. "We'll take what we can use," Jack said. "And those extra sails, and any ammunition or weapons onboard. You got it?"

"Okay, okay," Blue said, counting the sail bags. She followed Jack to the captain's quarters, where Rusty held the captain on the floor with his boot pressed into the man's neck. Jack tilted his head in the direction of the open trunk, which held gold coins and bills, and then nodded and swept his hands around the room in a gesture that said, *Take all of it.* Blue filled the captain's own rucksack with the gold and cash and emptied the captain's jewelry box—a gold pocket watch, cuff links, buttons—and took socks and trousers as well as a sextant, a brass telescope, and a small box compass.

When the room was cleared of all valuables, Blue went into the passageway and heard a single shot that rang from the captain's quarters. *He's killed the captain,* she thought. The captain's murder unleashed whatever fight the crew had left in them— part fear of the same thing happening to them, and part rage at the unfairness of the attack, the sheer bad luck of crossing paths with the pirates.

Blue stuck her head above the hatch cover and saw men lunge across the deck only to be struck down by the pirates, who swung their weapons at anyone in striking distance. Blue unsheathed her cutlass and stepped into the foray. A tall sailor raised his machete over one shoulder, and she swung her blade across the front of his legs, not to kill him, but to disable him. He buckled onto the floor and dropped his weapon, which she kicked away from him. The smoke-filled air was infused with fear and the pirates used that fear to defeat the ship's crew. Blue came up behind a crewman, held her blade at his throat. His fear surprised her and she led him to the rail, where she tied his hands and left him.

She gathered as many sailors as she could until the merchant ship's crew was either dead or crawling on all fours toward the rail. The work was easy until she approached an able-bodied crewman from behind, her blade to his throat, and he started to fight her off. She kicked him in the stomach and knocked him back, but he came at her again, wielding a heavy oak board. Blue sliced him across the belly and shoved him onto the floor. His blood pooled at her feet, and he groaned as he took his last breath. She felt nothing, and this frightened her. She'd saved herself. "Any one of you care to fight, come fight, I'm right here!" But the few men remaining held their hands in the air and walked, heads down, to the rail.

The pirates worked in a long, slow procession, carrying boxes and crates of cargo, lumber, and sail bags and heaving with sighs and expelled breath as their reverent march continued. Blue lost herself in the work: carry one end of a swinging crate, pass over the water to the *Alice K*—until she was nothing more than the motion of her body. Without Annie to go back to, she only had this moment, this life, following the plank from one ship to another. By the time they'd stripped the ship of everything useful, the sun had started to sink and two of the injured men had died in pools of their own blood. When all of the pirates had disembarked, and only Blue and Jack remained on the schooner with the surrendered men, Jack paced the deck along the rail and spoke.

"You'll stay here for three days, then head on to wherever it is you're going. Understood?" One or two murmured in agreement. Jack spun on one boot, strode across the deck with Blue at his side, and led her across the plank. When they were safely onboard the *Alice K*, he ordered the plank retrieved and the sails trimmed. The ship drifted back and headed across the wind while the schooner floundered in a haze of smoke, men still tied at the rail. Sailing away on a strong wind, Blue felt her body warm from the hard work of battle.

"Come with me," Jack said, leading her down into his quarters, and pointing to a chair. She was too fired up to sit still, and she poured them each a mug of rum in the dead captain's pewter cups. Jack sat on the edge of his berth and rocked back and forth waiting for his rum, then drank it down and held his mug out for another. "Takes hours to ease off a fight. You'll get used to it. First raid's the hardest."

Blue filled both cups again. "Those weren't men. We hardly had any challenge in 'em at all. We could've done better, wasted less time, less ammunition."

"You did good. You're not dead."

The air inside the cabin felt close and hot. Blue removed her waistcoat and unbuttoned the top of her linen blouse and untied her blond hair so that it hung down. She shook her hair out as if she could free her mind.

"You're something to behold," Jack said.

Blue stepped across the small space, straddled Jack where he sat, and inhaled the musky salt stench of him, smelling her own odor against him and kissing his rum-soaked mouth until he lifted her up and dropped her back onto the table and removed her trousers. Freeing himself from his own trousers, he jerked himself into her and she wanted him to use her hard. He tore open her blouse so buttons scattered on the floor and he pressed against her. She locked her legs around him to pull him against her, away and across the water so that all she had was the sensation between her legs and the feeling of the boat rocking in the ocean, him rocking on top of her with a warm pulse inside her and his stinking breath matching with her own muffled groan, a voice not entirely hers but hers nonetheless. Before he came he finished her off and she let go into the heat that spread through her belly and a convulsion of limbs.

Then it was over. She was just back where she started on the table and he was riding her while she stared at the slatted ceiling and the whorled knot in the wood that shone through the varnish until his final heaving jolt and groan, then the wet suck as he pulled out of her, his body relaxed. He stepped back and turned for the rum. There sat Blue on the edge of the table with her pants at her ankles and the whirling rush of the battle now mixed with the rum and a feeling of climax. She stood to pull up and fasten her trousers and reached for the cup of rum that Jack held out for her, drinking it down hard.

"You killed again today. How did it feel?"

"He would've killed me. What was I supposed to do?"

Jack didn't answer, but she eyed him without flinching. "You're one of us now."

"I don't know what that means."

"You will." Jack leaned back on his bunk, his body nearly steaming with the release of tension.

"What brought you to this life?" Blue asked.

"I sailed on a merchant ship, like your husband's, but I couldn't take orders. I only lasted three months before I jumped ship in Barbados. I sailed on small fishing boats and did odd jobs, then one night in a bar I met a sailor who told me about a pirate ship on the other side of the island that was looking for men."

"You wanted to be a criminal?"

"No, I wanted the life. The freedom, the money."

"And are you glad of it?"

"Glad enough."

Blue took her leave and went up into the dark on deck. On this ship there were no rules, no morals, nothing to hold her back or discourage her from anything she wanted to do, and she wanted to do everything. She'd killed a man today, without thinking. Not like killing her husband, under duress, to prove some point or take some punishment. She killed to save her own life. The rush of fighting for her life made her feel more alive than any safe haven she'd ever known. Fighting made fear drift into the dark corners of her awareness. What did she have to be afraid of when she could fight like that? She wanted to forget the life she'd known before with its stuffy little corners and women's work and men telling her what to do, all of that expectation that brought no promise, no insurance, no guarantee of a safe life after all.

10

H ER FIRST YEAR AND A HALF ABOARD THE *ALICE K*
passed in weeks and months of waiting, then two or
three raids at a time followed by a month of debauchery. Blue
had proven herself an equal fighter and earned her share of the
money they stole and cash earned from selling stolen goods. She
made friends with the crew as she pulled her weight in battle
and didn't back down in the face of an enemy. She'd learned
to forget everything but the moment she was in. Annie existed
in her mind like the memory of a friend lost long ago. There
was no Annie anymore. Only this ship with the stink of liquor
and unwashed men. Nothing to look forward to but a drink
or a fuck or a fight. And she looked forward to these things
ravenously, for each brought with it a blissful oblivion.

The *Alice K* lifted and dropped, as Blue strode toward the rail,
accommodating the lurch of the ship with her own swinging
motion. The crew worked to raise the mainsail. Standing along
the ratlines, sailors loosened the reef, until the sail filled into
a smooth, billowing curve. Blue wished that she could unfurl
herself like that, but she was wound tight as a monkey's fist.

She lent a hand and hauled on the halyards with the other sailors,
heaving the sail with its great wooden boom. The strain in her
arms and in her back sent a familiar burn through her body, and

she pulled with her legs braced against a cleat until the expanse of canvas caught a gust of wind and the ship rushed forward.

Johnson made the halyard fast. He was a wiry little man with coffee-colored hair, his face ravaged by pockmarks and roped scars that disguised any youth or innocence that might have remained in him, though he was only seventeen. He was quick to offer help but rarely followed through, often leaving a pile of lumber half stacked or a length of sail unfastened to the boom.

As he coiled the ends of the halyards, he let one fly in his haste. When it whipped Blue across the face, she lunged at him. "You filthy little swine." She grabbed him by the throat with one hand.

"It got loose on me!"

Blue stared into every crater, every filthy crease of skin and purple vein pressing against the surface of his skin. She tightened her grip. Cords of muscle and tendon vibrated beneath her fingers. Johnson's cries sounded muffled and distant, as if it was him and not him whose veins rose beneath her fingers.

"You've gone round the bend," Johnson said.

"I'll kill you," Blue said, but she hesitated long enough for Briggs to grab her by the wrist. She shook herself loose from his fat hand. Briggs was a son of a bitch with ruddy skin and black hair cut close to his scalp, so that in the sun it shone like a helmet. He hovered six feet tall and over two hundred pounds. Blue knew better than to cross him.

Johnson sat down hard on the deck, his shoulders hunched forward, his head bent low to avoid further blows as he tried to catch his breath, careful not to look anywhere but at the deck by his feet.

"He'll live," Blue said.

"No thanks to you."

Blue spat over the side of the boat. She felt Briggs's eyes on her as she strode the planks aft to the wheel, where the first mate maneuvered the ship. The ship's wheel rocked back and forth with the force of the waves against the rudder. The rhythm located her as she rode the waves in her legs, feeling the boat fight the swells.

"Bit of a sea," she said, the rush of the fight singing through her.

"She's let up quite a bit," Nate said. His nose scanned the air like a dog's, as if he could read the news on the wind and smell the oncoming weather. Blue wanted to be able to sense something more than weather, but all she could see were lofty clouds and endless stretches of sea. She left Nate and stepped down the hatch to the captain's room. The cabin stank of whale oil from the lanterns, damp wood, and unwashed clothes. The pirates were a democracy, but Jack was their captain in any raid, and for this reason, and for the respect his authority and charisma commanded, he was given the best quarters. He lay back in his bed, smiling, bushy black eyebrows twitching as he watched her. Blue reached into the cupboard for the bottle, poured the dark liquid into a tin cup, and drank it down before she poured a second cup. She drank without speaking. Jack rolled over and propped his head on one hand to watch her in the dim light.

His square whiskered jaw lent his face a seriousness that belied his cynical amusement. When Blue finished the second cup of rum, she sat on the edge of the bunk beside him. He pulled her down to him. "I knew you'd come back," he said.

"I'm not back," she said. "I'm just here."

Blue found herself pressed into the corner between the bedding and the wall of Jack's bunk as if she'd tried to burrow through to another world in her sleep. She struggled to her feet and was shaking off the first sleep she'd had in days when the voices fell from above. "Look there! A stranded vessel four points off the starboard bow!"

She stuck her head up through the hatch. Fresh air assaulted her, the sun and wind an affront. On the near horizon a small whaleboat drifted. Two sailors pulled on the oars and the sails fluttered in the morning air. The sea spread around the tiny craft as if it would swallow them in one gulp. One rogue wave or fleeting squall could send the small boat to the bottom faster than a rock dropped in the water.

"There's enough of us already," she said, climbing up from below, shielding her eyes. "Let them save themselves."

But it wasn't long before the *Alice K* headed into the wind so that the sailors could row alongside. Blue avoided the sunlight and activity. She lowered herself into the fo'c'sle. She lay in her hammock, listening to the commotion of lifting sailors onboard, stowing the whaleboat atop the deck, and the murmurs of the crew as they listened to the sailors' tale of survival. Shipwrecks and stove boats, lives lost to drowning and sharks. She fingered her pistol, and the cold metal titillated her skin. These times in between raids, when all they did was sail and watch the empty sea, left her feeling raw and anxious. She wanted to peel her skin from her face, expose bone. She wanted to drink herself into an oblivion deeper than drowning. But for now she busied herself cleaning her gun, wiping down the barrel with oil, removing the cylinder and pushing the cloth inside with her finger, rubbing it around until she was satisfied. She was always alert, ready.

On a sunny afternoon between raids, Jack and Blue drank rum on the quarterdeck and looked forward along the deck as it stretched before them. Jack told her about the *Alice K*, a merchant runner the pirate crew had acquired west of Jamaica, leaving the original captain and crew on an old brig not worth the cost of the wood it was built from.

He drank straight from the bottle and carried on, telling her how the *Alice K*'s narrow hull and vast sail area made for fast sailing, which was essential for getting away from the ships they raided.

She'd learned from her own experience that the pirates lived according to their own sets of rules. They conducted business through an intricate system of underground networks developed among a group of Jamaicans eager for a share of the pirates' cargo. After a raid, the band laid up in a tiny bay in Jamaica where they sold or bartered their loot and replenished the galley with live goats and chickens, potatoes, bananas, mangoes, and anything of substance they could find on the island through the channels and networks that Jack had established. The islanders worked the pirates, maneuvering to get as much of the goods they wanted for as little in return as possible. The pirates were there to trade their stolen goods for money and supplies.

The islanders wanted access to the pirates' wealth and the opportunity to turn their knowledge of the island into money.

Blue hadn't gone ashore since she'd been taken onboard the *Alice K*. Nobody questioned her reasons. The first time Jack's island connection came to the ship to examine the cargo, Blue had been sleeping in a hammock on the foredeck. It was the slow lilt of the woman's voice that woke her. Even from behind, Blue recognized her stance. Blue watched from behind the mast, fascinated by the familiar confidence with which Therese conducted business. Therese was Jack's woman on shore, and she handled the distribution of the loot and the collection of supplies and money. She offered herself to Jack in return for a share of the take. Whether in the form of food, tradable goods, or money, it didn't matter. Therese knew how to get what she wanted. When Therese stood on shore waiting for the crew to come in, her body bent like a palm in the wind, a smooth curving arch. Blue waited to reveal herself until Therese came to the ship without Jack. She came on deck as Therese disembarked from her canoe, and when Therese saw her, she nodded. "Now you know," Blue said.

When Jack and the crew enjoyed the women ashore, Therese's crew rowed out in canoes to retrieve the goods and carry them to shore. They worked in the hot sun until the hold was empty, and in five days they returned with the supplies the pirates needed to go back to sea. Therese informed Jack of the planned routes of merchant runners and the occasional bounty hunters around the island. While the rest of the crew went ashore to spend their money on drinking and women, Blue still remained onboard. She occupied herself studying charts, examined the rigging for worn lines or frayed ends that needed splicing. Oftentimes she sketched the ship's rigging with charcoal that Jack had given her. She'd learned to draw as a girl, and found solace in rendering the Jamaican women who came aboard and the cliffs that hid the ship from the island cove that she remembered with its palm trees, huts, and overturned skiffs. It was a relief to be alone without the crude clamor of the men around her. At the end of the day, she wore only bloomers and a torn blouse and dove off the transom into the impossibly blue water, so clear and deep that she could see the coral and sea grass, red and orange and green and black, shaped like hands, fingers and thumbs askew. Schools of tropical fish drifted like clouds of color through the water. Blue swam hard against the currents to wear herself out, and when night came, she drank herself into a stupor to escape the undertow of her dreams.

The shipwrecked sailors had been onboard for only a few hours when Blue ducked into the mess quarters. Abbott, the cook, ladled soup into wooden bowls and handed over chunks of bread to the men. He had a habit of ingratiating himself by telling jokes that ranged from declaring the stale bread "fresh baked this afternoon" or the three-month-old salt beef "slaughtered today" to long-winded tales of drunken Irishmen, which as an Englishman he relished, pulling on his mustache harder and harder until he reached the punch line. He would've been a handsome man, a round face and huge green eyes, full lips and an eagerness to please, but the birthmark on the lower left quadrant of his face marred his features, and his passion for whiskey further drove his skin into an irritation of red splotches that caused Blue to look away. The hungry crew and rescued sailors sopped at fish stew with bread and ate until there was nothing left to eat. Mark, the taller of the two sailors, sat across from Blue, while Jeb, who was pale, small, wraithlike, sat in Mark's shadow. Mark's face had a hollow look. He reached for more bread. "Such good food," he said.

"This is a pirate ship, fool. We eat like kings so long as it lasts," Briggs told him.

"Too bad it doesn't last long," Rusty said.

Jeb didn't speak and Mark took an extra chunk of bread and put it on his plate.

"I've nothing against good food," Mark said.

The *Alice K* sailed the shipping lanes, tacking across the wind for weeks in search of plunder, and as food supplies dwindled to nothing but hardtack and limes, they searched for sea turtles. The giant turtles were easy prey as they swam or floated along the surface of the water. It was afternoon when the crew pulled one alongside, shot it in the head, and hauled it up onto the decks using a block and tackle. Briggs cut away the meat with his machete. Then he stood back to let another sailor labor among the flesh and blood of the animal. After they'd scavenged every scrap and packed the meat in a barrel for the cook, the men heaved the shell over the side and flushed the deck with buckets of seawater. Blue stood near the bow and watched the empty shell float into the distance. Eventually the shell would fill with water and sink, but at that moment it drifted lightly over the waves like an open palm.

She heard his footsteps behind her, knew they were Mark's because they didn't belong to any of the crew and the other survivor limped. He leaned his back against the foremast to watch the turtle shell bob across the water. When the shell was out of sight, Mark said, "You don't take sport in hunting turtles?"

Blue turned to size up this stranger, with his skinny arms and soft flesh. He was no fighter, even if he recovered his strength. "You'll not survive the next raid," she said.

"I'm good with a cutlass, and not a bad shot with a pistol."

Blue turned her attention aft, down the length of the ship, past the masts and cabins, over the stern bulwarks toward the frothing wake fanning out from the transom.

"Can I show you something?" Mark sat down with his back against the mast and unfolded a worn piece of paper, which held a few bits of wood and string. His weatherworn good looks and the gentleness in his voice pried something loose in her. She didn't want to talk to him.

"It's a model of the *Alice K*," he said. "I'm working on the hull. When I finish, I'll give it to the captain for saving us."

Blue laughed bitterly. "You think you've been saved?" She took the model and eyed the lines in all directions. "The stern comes in here," she said.

Mark took the model back and continued to work with his rigging knife.

"What happened to the other whaleboats?"

"Two others set out when we got stove by the whale, but

that's all that made it off the ship. Rest of the men went down.
That whale came up fast. Those cast into the water swam for
the whaleboats. Those other two boats, I don't know if they're
dead or alive. Could be floating in circles for all I know."
When Mark relaxed into his craft, his voice softened. "At least
that's what I hope."

"Hope's a fool's dream," Blue said.

"You're a cynic, but hope is in my nature."

"There's nature and there's will. I strive to let my will rule
my foolish nature. It's the only way to survive."

"Well said. You've been on this ship awhile?"

"Awhile," Blue said.

"And wearing men's clothes?" Mark asked, but Blue ignored
him and he wasn't bold enough to ask again. Blue watched his
arm shifting as he worked the knife, his energy focused and
intent. His wavy brown hair pressed flat against his head, shone
under the sun. A small black mole beneath his right ear looked
like a jewel set against his tanned skin. Mark turned from the
model to face her, his dark eyes a question she couldn't read.
She left without a word.

Her nightmares were the same every night: her hands soaked in
water as she tried to scrape away the dried blood caked in her
palms. "You can't get rid of a stain like that," Mark said. Blue
sat up in her hammock and searched the dark, but there was no
one there. Since Mark came onboard, he'd started appearing in
her dreams. Weeks of bad dreams, long days without another

ship in sight, pulled at the careful knots Blue had tied around herself. She made drawings of her dreams: sea chests stacked by her hammock so that she couldn't get out, Jack standing over her, his cutlass drawn across her throat.

When another week passed without sight of a merchant runner, fights began to break out along the deck, and the crew turned on each other, fists flying, over things as foolish as who got first pick from the basket of bread at supper.

The more Blue tried to sleep, the more sleep eluded her, and when she slept, she woke with her hands in pain from trying to scrape the blood away. One night, she flung herself out of her hammock and stormed up to the deck in frustration. She stood by the whaleboat, stored upside down near one of the cabins, and ran her hand along the smooth curve of the hull, then bent to take a look underneath. It was too dark to see anything. She squatted down and crawled underneath the boat, a small cave that would protect her from the night and the crew and her own bad dreams. Under the boat the air was close and quiet. She leaned her back against the hull and let go a heavy sigh.

"Who's there?" a voice said, not far from her.

Blue instinctively put her right hand on her cutlass and tried to distinguish the voice. "It's Blue."

"Do you ever sleep?" Mark asked. Blue didn't answer. "Well, if you're going to stay here, you can at least talk to me."

Blue couldn't see him in the dark. The cocoon of the boat surrounded them in a hushed privacy.

"Tell me how you came to be on this ship, and I'll tell you a secret."

"What do I care about your secret? You're nobody. You're lucky you're not dead. If you hadn't agreed to join the crew, you would've been fed to the sharks. There's time to get rid of you yet."

Mark listened to her rant and didn't speak.

"Maybe I should cut your throat now." Blue pulled her cutlass from the leather sheath halfheartedly, then let it fall onto the deck. She leaned back against the hull, knees drawn up. Nothing felt right, not the cutlass in her hand, or the slow progress of the ship, or the strange lure of this man's voice. "I've been onboard this ship nearly two years," she said.

"And before that?"

"I sailed with my husband off the coast of Jamaica on a merchant runner."

"This crew raided your husband's ship?" Mark asked. "They killed him?"

"If my husband had fought like a man, he wouldn't have died like a dog."

Mark was quiet. Blue tried to see his face in the dark, but beneath the whaleboat she could only make out shadows. She let her head fall back against the hull.

"So Jack spared your life for your service on the *Alice K*," Mark said.

Blue regretted the conversation already. "You don't know a damn thing about me." She jerked forward to leave, but Mark grabbed her by the elbow, and she shook herself loose.

"Wait."

Blue leaned away from him, as if to take in the length of him. She hated the way his voice worked on her.

"Give me your hand," he said, holding his out for her.

"What for?"

"Trust me," Mark said, his palm upturned, waiting. She didn't have to trust him—if he pulled anything, she could slice him up quicker than filleting a grouper.

Mark drew Blue's hand toward his chest and slipped her fingers beneath the folds of his linen shirt. He undid one button, then another.

"That's all you want? Why didn't you just say so?" Sex was nothing more to Blue than an itch to scratch, a way to pass the time. The physical rush of sex had the same effect on her as taking over a ship. A man was only something to conquer or climb onto. But there was a charge between them that made her uneasy. She wanted to make him stop.

"It's not what you think," he said, his sour breath mixed with the close sea air under the boat.

A voice scratched the air. "Watch that topsail, don't strain the mast in this wind. If it picks up at all, I want that topsail down, you hear me?" Jack was patrolling the deck in a jangle of buttons and knives and the assortment of gear he saw fit to carry around on the bulk of his body. That was one of the things that had intrigued Blue in the beginning. Jack was ready for anything, war or sex or eating—it didn't matter. He took it all in. His hunger was vast.

"He'll kill you if I don't do it first," Blue said, crawling out from under the whaleboat. She looked around and skulked through the shadows along the rail and down into the fo'c'sle among the snores and rumblings of the crew. She lay back in her hammock, her body pulsing, and fell asleep with the sound of Mark's voice running through her. She wanted to kill him. Or lie down and sleep beside him.

11

〰〰〰〰〰〰

EVERETT HOPKINS LEANED INTO THE STIFF BREEZE. He sat atop a wooden wagon, his black seaman's hat pulled down over his ears, the collar on his seaman's jacket flapped up against his neck. Hannah watched as he slowed the two horses and made the final turn onto the driveway. It had been weeks since a man had pulled up on a wagon. At the first sound of the horses on the road, she'd dipped her head to peer out the window with the old expectation, and then caught herself. Her life with John still pulsed through places inside her that had not yet heard the news.

Everett pulled back on the reins until the horses tossed their heads, letting go their cloudy breath. Hannah met him on the edge of the lawn, John's coat covering her down to her knees.

"What're you doing out in this cold?" he said. Everett was Dangerfield's shipbuilder, known all along the New England coast and even farther south for the merchant boats he launched out of his barn on the Pamet River.

"I could ask you the same, Everett." She saw then that his niece, Sylvie Avery, sat on the other side of him, hands tucked into the opposite sleeves of her black coat, as if it were a muff. Her black hair fell in wisps around the bottom of her gray scarf, and large green eyes lit the delicate structure of her face. She'd been widowed in the October Gale of 1841, her husband Job never heard from again along with fifty-six other men from town. These were young and middle-aged fishermen at work hauling in their catch on George's Bank when the gale struck. They sailed for Dangerfield Light, but the high winds carried them off to the southeast where they were wrecked on the Nantucket shoals.

Since Job's death, Sylvie had been helping Everett at the ship-yard, first on the books, then offering suggestions on designs. She'd even been known to pick up a caulking bag when they were late launching a ship. Hannah knew for herself that work was an antidote to loss—providing a momentum to carry her through grief. She imagined it was the same for Sylvie.

Everett coiled the reins at his feet and descended from the wagon, his legs supporting the barrel of his body.

"Come inside and warm yourselves up for a few minutes."

"No, no. That's not why we've come." His voice was warm, fatherly. Hannah wanted to swim into that voice and let it buoy her. "I've come to show you this boat."

The boat rested in the back of the wagon; the white lines of the hull and the full, swollen arc of the skiff's body loomed by Hannah's head. She ran her hand along the curve of wood and held her head close to the hull, as if she could hear the quality of the boat humming through its carefully constructed seams.

"I saw your hired man out on the fence. He's a good worker from the looks of it. Is it true what the missus said? He'll be leaving you soon?" Everett leaned against the boat, stretched an arm along the gunwale.

Looking up, she could see Billy making repairs along the

farthest length of fence, his posture akin to prayer. "I imagine so, now that he's got his strength back."

"I was in your shoes, I'd ask him to stay on a while. Couldn't hurt to have a little help through the winter."

"I'm sure he's got better things on offer."

"Worth asking," Everett said, scratching at the silver whiskers along his jaw.

"What'll people say, me having a strange man here and John just gone?"

"They'll say the usual rubbish, that you shouldn't be at the lighthouse for starters, that you should live with your parents until you find a man." Everett laughed. "Lord knows what they'll think of you keeping a man around the house. But don't let that stop you, Hannah. The old biddies will talk about anything, especially things they know nothing about."

"Leave her alone, uncle," Sylvie said.

"It's 1843. If they can talk about freeing the coloreds we can talk about our women surviving widowhood, especially in a town like this."

"You sound like a revolutionary, Everett."

"This Billy, he give you any trouble?"

Hannah stood back from the boat, arms crossed. "Some trouble."

"Enough to send him away?"

"Not yet."

"Well, you know where to find me, and you got Tom close by," Everett said, as if that settled it. He leaned away from the boat where Hannah brushed her fingers absently along the hull.

"It's beautiful, Everett. Did you build it?"

"The cedar and white oak's from my own land. She's nearly fifteen feet long, and look how she's tapered at stem and stern for riding through the surf. That was Sylvie's idea, there." Sylvie nodded and looked away toward Billy while Everett traced the curved lines of the hull with thick fingers. "I built air chambers in each end and added cork fenders here on the outer rails to protect her from bumping against sinking ships. And it'll help keep her afloat. You got your righting lines, here, in case you capsize, and she's light and maneuverable."

"She'll carry six or eight men," Sylvie said. "Depending on their size of course, and your own strength, but you don't seem to be lacking strength."

Hannah stepped back to create distance between herself and the skiff. "Are you offering her for sale, Everett? I could never afford a boat like this."

"I know, I know. But I heard about your rescue. It got me thinking, and once I'm thinking, then I'm building, and once I'm building, I can't stop. Your situation, what with you going out in a storm, and possibly not being as strong as a man…" He spoke these words delicately so as not to offend her. "You need a skiff you can maneuver through the surf. Well, it presented an interesting problem. I figured if you had the right boat, more might survive."

"Well, I suppose that's all true. But I still—"

"John helped me a considerable amount on that last schooner. He worked hard and didn't ask a penny in return. That's just the kind of friend he—" Everett said, but he stopped himself. "Consider this payment, if that's how you need to think of it. If it works out for you, you'll let me know. It's my first surfboat, and you're going to test her out for me. There's no one else who would do it. Now where do you want her, 'cause I'm not for arguing. I get enough of that at home." Everett leaned under the boat and unfastened the ropes that held the skiff in place. "You want me to leave her right here in the road? That won't do you much good, will it?"

"No, it won't," she said softly.

"All right then."

Half an hour later, the sound of Everett's horses clomping into the distance rose on the wind and settled somewhere out beyond the fields. She wanted to run inside, tell John about the boat, and make him come outside now and take a look. He'd go over every detail until he understood the boat beyond its practical use to a deeper beauty, where the clean lines and fine craftsmanship, hand-hewn boards and rigorous design came together in a boat that moved with a dancer's grace through the water. A boat that could perform rescues with unsurpassed safety and efficiency. *What do you think of that, John? I bet you never thought you'd see something like that.* The southwest wind came up sudden and cold, and loneliness swooped down on Hannah. If she went back to bed, she might never climb out again. The white bottom of the surfboat beckoned her from the beach.

That afternoon, William Pike searched for the lightkeeper's wife in the barn behind the hay bales, in the root cellar among bushels of potatoes and jars of beach plum and blueberries, but not until he climbed the lighthouse did he see the surfboat heading into the waves. Hannah used her body as if she had something to prove, when anyone could see what she was capable of in a boat. He climbed down the circle of the lighthouse stairs, and from atop the dunes, he watched her: a small white mark moving south along the shore. When the craft blurred with the white, foam crests of the waves, he squinted and held his breath until he saw her again. Hannah's life here felt familiar to him in a way he wanted to flee, but he had nowhere else to go, nor the strength to go there. Hannah's wholesome beauty and the swift regard with which she dispatched her duties accentuated his wretchedness and everything that had sent him running away from the Caribbean: the terrible things he'd seen there, the terrible things he'd done. He didn't want to return to that life. He wanted to use himself up with work and let sleep take him at the end of each day so that he could wake up and do it again. He was grateful for work and someone to feed him. Grateful to let each day pass. Grateful until he started seeing her in his half sleep. A woman whose attention he didn't deserve. Her long hair falling over her shoulders when she'd tended him by the fire in those first days of his recovery, the fierce gleam in her eyes when she confronted him about his drinking. She knew her own mind and it frightened him and snapped him awake.

He watched as she surfed the boat toward the beach, then veered off before she reached the shore and rowed again into the waves. He wanted to stop watching her, but didn't she need someone to safeguard her?

"What're you doing out here?" Tom asked.

Billy stared at Tom, wondering where he'd come from and why he'd come. "She's out in the waves in that boat." Billy pointed.

The itch in his body for physical work drove him down the stairs to the beach. He didn't care if Tom followed him or not.

"You can't stop her," Tom said, following too close.

"I can help her if she needs it."

"But she won't. You oughtta know that."

The skiff she'd used to rescue him was still nestled against the dune, the life ring and the oars tucked beneath the stairs should they need them. Billy kept her in sight now with the relief of proximity. Tom stood beside him and watched Hannah work the boat.

Hannah pressed her water-soaked boots to the floorboards for balance and hoped the boat would take her shape the way a new pair of boots got worn to her tread. She rowed through the breakers, the surfboat buoyant, light in the water. Each drop of the skiff off the crest of a wave she felt in the hard wood seat. Overhead, seagulls dipped and rose on the air, gliding over waves, then tilting to catch a draft into the sky. They cried a dull, complaining encouragement, their white underbellies lost in the glare as the bow of the surfboat lifted in the waves. She wanted to become one with the boat as the boat became one with her. With her weight to starboard, she held the right oar firm to veer the boat around, feeling in its light swinging motion the beginnings of an intimacy. They were developing their own language.

The icy wind pricked her cheeks and whipped her hair loose

so that it wrapped around her head in wet strands. Muscles trembling, her back a vicious knot, she drove herself through the pain as if there was no pain.

In a trough, she spun the skiff around, pushing first on the right oar, then pulling on the left. She caught the next wave, the boat rode high and fast, lifting up on a swell of water and surging forward. Hannah used the oars to hold her course as she surfed the boat in. *That's it, stay on top, surf in just like that.* She balanced across the tops of the waves, maneuvering the boat as if it were a part of her body, tilting her weight on the seat and leaning into the surf until she rode into shallow water.

Tom knew enough to hang back while Billy waded into the water. Hannah climbed over the side of the boat and lost her balance. When Billy grabbed her by the elbow, she felt the strength of his hand around her upper arm, the push of his body shoving her up from the waves. He knew how to move in the surf, how to accommodate the rush of water.

"Did you see how I rode those waves? Did you see how fast the boat was? I've never handled a boat so well in my life. I can do any—"

"You shouldn't be risking life and limb for the sport of it."

"If I'd had this boat to rescue you, it would've gone so much easier. I can assure you of that," Hannah said, and she shook herself free of him.

Tom stood on the beach, shaking his head, as if to say, *It's no use. She'll never listen.* Hannah respected him for his silence as she brushed by him on her way out of the water. She didn't need them here.

Sylvie's scarf trailed in the wind as she rode toward the light-house on a dark brown horse nearly the same color as her own hair. Hannah stood near the top of the stairs from the beach, exhilarated from her excursion in the surfboat, and watched Sylvie approach the house. She rode upright, confident, but in a loose and comfortable way as if she were as accustomed to riding the horse as to hanging a sheet on the clothesline or stepping over a pile of sea hay to reach the summer vegetables.

She swung herself from the horse and waited for Hannah to approach from across the yard.

"You have great timing. I just got in. First trial for the surfboat. Amazing. So buoyant and light. It's really going to make a difference." Hannah was still out of breath as she pushed through the front door and led Sylvie into the house.

"I hope you don't mind my visit," Sylvie said. "After we dropped off the boat, I thought—"

"No, I'm glad you're here."

Hannah pointed to the rack where Sylvie could hang her coat, and dropped her own coat on the floor, stepping out of it like a shed skin. While Hannah made tea, she answered Sylvie's questions about the workings of the light, what kind of oil they used, and how often she had to fill the lanterns.

When they finally made themselves comfortable at the table, Sylvie said, "Have you asked that sailor to stay on?"

"I haven't decided."

"He appears to be a hard worker, and a nice sort."

A nice sort, ha! They were quiet for a while, feeling their way around the silence that was filled with the fact of their lost husbands. Hannah's hands ached from rowing, and she opened and closed them into fists to stretch the muscles. John used to massage her hands, and the memory drew her eye to the veined ridges, her thick fingers and broad knuckles. Hers were hands meant to work, and now they closed themselves around the hot cup of tea with the memory of John's bigger hands holding hers and rubbing out the muscles as if to squeeze out the pain, a sea of memory: the day he took her out in the skiff to watch a squall blow across the water in a dark mass, the night they ate bread and cheese in front of the fire and fell asleep on the floor, curled around each other for warmth after the fire went out.

"You must miss him terribly," Sylvie said. "I try to keep busy with my uncle's business, and still, in the evening after dinner when the house is quiet, I fret over Job's last moments, the terror he must have suffered. He was a brave man, but how brave can a man be when he knows he's drowning?"

Billy had clung to the spar that kept him afloat after the wreck, even when Hannah tried to pull him to safety. Fear had kept him holding on until she arrived. Fear wasn't going to let him give up. "I'm sure he fought for his life with his last breath."

"So many men were lost, who am I to feel sorry for myself, and yet—"

"You've a right to your grief."

Sylvie stood and warmed her back by the fire. She eyed John's image in the daguerreotype on the mantel, touched her fingers to the glass before she turned to get her coat.

"So, this Billy, where's he from?"

"I only know that he was sailing north toward Portland."

"No family?"

"Not that he's mentioned."

"Well, you'll need help this winter. Maybe you should ask him to stay on." She pulled on her coat, wrapped her scarf around her neck, and tucked it down beneath her lapels.

"I've got Tom. He's always about, and he's just up the road."

"You should get someone who can help around the house with the chores and even the rescues, if you're determined to continue."

Hannah walked her to the door, and they stood in a moment of silence, before Sylvie said, "About the boat, what shall I tell my uncle?"

"It's a wonderful success. You tell him I'm eager to put it to work. And you come again, won't you?" Hannah didn't usually enjoy other women from town, but Sylvie with her boat designs and her bookkeeping interested her.

"I enjoyed our visit very much. I'll come back soon," Sylvie said, and stepped out into the cold, greeting Billy shyly as he passed her on his way into the house.

When Billy came in, he draped his coat across a chair, stepped out of his boots, and bent his lithe body before the fire. He worked hard, wore himself out most days.

"Come here for a minute, sit down."

Hannah gathered him to the dining table with a flick of her hand. She had to make use of him or he'd drive her crazy with his skulking around. He'd taken on chores in the barn, tending the chickens and horses, and he did his share around the house, but he still had too much time to waste brooding. "I have a proposition for you, if you're interested."

He dragged himself across the room with the resistance of a man walking through water.

"Do you enter every conversation with that look of dread?" He hardened himself at her words as if struck by an open hand. "I only want to ask you a question. I'm wondering if there's a way we can get a lifeline out to a shipwreck. Can I bring the crew ashore that way?"

"A lifeline?" Billy thought of all the ways the pirates had conceived of killing shiploads of sailors. He'd never heard one idea for saving a single life.

"Yes, it makes sense, don't you think?"

"No one could haul himself in on a rope. Not in the cold, and possibly injured." Billy pulled out one of the mismatched wooden chairs and sat.

"What if I rowed a lifeline out to the ship, and a sailor made it fast around the mast? Then would there be a way to bring them in?"

"Maybe you could use the old skiff and fill it with men, and run it back and forth from ship to shore with a block and tackle."

The haze of his mood lifted and began to clear. Sometimes at night his dreams woke him to the sounds of a raid, and he smelled gunpowder that wasn't there, heard shouts that didn't exist. Then he was brought back to the hushed closeness of these rooms.

"Most times the sea's too rough for that," Billy said. "I'm thinking about times it's near too rough to take them in the surfboat. You need some kind of bosun's chair or something you could jerry-rig like a swing to carry 'em in. But you got the wind to think about, then try convincing anyone to climb into something like that."

"What if it's either that or drown?" Hannah's face flushed and she swept her hair back, her eyes on Billy as he absorbed what she said.

"There's something else I need to ask you," Hannah said, her voice more serious than she'd intended.

Billy unsheathed his knife and started scraping beneath his fingernails, his sullen mood an undertow carrying him back to the depths. Hannah wanted to untie the knot of him and lay him out in a long, straight line, or smack him until he sat up straight and paid attention to her. He was nothing like John, who said what he felt and didn't withdraw into his own silence. She stared at him until he sheathed his knife. "Well, I notice that your strength is back, and I'm concerned you may want to be getting on now that you're feeling better."

Billy winced and stared at his boots.

"The thing is, with John gone, and winter coming, I wonder if you'd consider staying. I can't pay you, but you've got a roof over your head and plenty of food. You can work same as you do now. Nothing different."

Billy laughed, nervous as he looked up at her. "I thought you were going to ask me to leave."

"You're a good worker. You've made yourself useful."

"That's what I wanted to do."

"So, it's settled then?"

He nodded, trying to smile, but it looked to hurt him. "How

about a drink to celebrate? We got that bourbon you use to heat up the sailors."

"That's for emergencies." Hannah had noticed the amber liquid diminishing since she'd found Billy drunk in the barn, and then lightening in color as he added water to compensate for his theft. "I know you've been going at it. You can't drink and take care of the lights. Can't run the risk of passing out or falling asleep."

"One belt won't kill you," he said.

"How long have you been a drinker, Billy?"

His eyes swooped toward the bottle on the mantel. Hannah realized that he could've spent the change from his trips to the grocery on a bottle from Millie Bragg, who worked the cod flakes down at the harbor, or maybe he found a bottle that John kept hidden in the barn.

"If you stay here, you have to stop."

"I'm going to quit after tonight. I promise."

"How do I know I can trust you?"

Billy gazed unflinchingly into her face. Rather than bear the intimacy of that look, she took the bottle from the mantel and poured a small amount into the bottom of a mug. "Here you are. I know you've got your own somewhere."

"What makes you think that?"

"Just because I live out here in the middle of nowhere doesn't mean I don't know a few things. You think I haven't met Millie myself? Isn't a soul in this town hasn't made use of her at one time or another."

Billy took the mug and swallowed his drink in one good gulp. He wiped his mouth and rubbed his fingers together, as if pressing whatever remained of the liquor into his skin. "I'll need one more."

Hannah nodded toward the bottle and let him pour his own drink. Now that he'd agreed to stay, she was relieved.

"Do you have charcoal and paper by chance?"

"In the desk, bottom drawer on the right," she said.

He wiggled the drawer along its runner until it opened. Then he set himself up at the table, pulling the candle closer, shifting the slant of light across the room. "I'm gonna draw you," he said, his head tilted back to take her in.

"You're going to draw me?"

"Just stay as you are. Pretend I'm not here."

Billy worked fast, the charcoal scratching the paper. She tried to glimpse his work, but his body protected the page. There was something possessed in the way his drawing overtook him, his hands animated with new life as he worked the charcoal across the paper with his right, and made rubbing or smudging motions with his left. His rough fingers worked in brisk, loose strokes that appeared precise and effortless. In spite of his concentration, his face softened. Hannah tried to settle herself into waiting and watching the fire, but she couldn't resist another look toward the drawing. The fire cast a fragile light across Billy, but it was the globe of light from the candle that captured his intensity and seemed to radiate from the heat of his focus on the page, his eyes no longer shifting to look toward Hannah but engrossed in his rendering.

When he finished, he slapped the paper facedown on the table. Hannah wanted to see the drawing, but she refused to ask him for it. As if he'd forgotten the drawing altogether, he gathered a couple twigs from the kindling box, and a piece of string, and sat down again with his props. What was he fiddling with now? He pondered, and huffed, and made sketches. Was he drunk? Of course he was. He was a drinker and a fool, and she'd asked him to stay.

Billy looked up, disoriented, his face full of shadows. The lighthouse beam flashed through the curtains, reminding Hannah why she was here. How would she have managed these past weeks without John if she hadn't been able to rely on the steady demands of the light: fill the oil, light the lanterns, keep the logbook. Every time the beam flashed through her house, she thought, *I am the lightkeeper.*

Billy blew across the sheet of paper and admired his work before holding it up for Hannah. There she was, her sweeping hair windblown around her face. He'd captured her amused yet doleful eyes, her small nose and high cheekbones, the planes of her face. His drawing revealed Hannah to herself more than any mirror. He'd rendered the distance in her expression and the light in her eye that was curiosity and nostalgia.

"You don't like it?" Billy asked tentatively.

"No, that's not it at all," she said. "You draw well. It's startling to see myself."

"You do like it then?"

"Yes," Hannah said, trying to find something in the room to focus on that wasn't the drawing.

"You can have it for another belt," he said.

She grabbed the bottle, then blew out the lanterns and the candle until the only light was the flash from the lighthouse. Then she went to her room. When her door slammed shut, the clatter of the cast-iron latch hung like a shrill note in the air.

"Okay then," Billy said. "That's fine. Good night, then."

Hannah listened from her bedroom as he climbed the ladder to the loft where he slept now. He didn't even get undressed before falling into a snore. She thought of the drawing faceup on the table and took her candle back into the kitchen to look at it. She held the candle over the table. He'd observed her in a most intimate way. Why should this startle her? They spent every day working together. She'd gotten used to coming down from the lights and meeting him in the kitchen, or waiting for him to come in from the field for supper. But his drawing painted a different portrait of him than the one she'd carried in her mind. She'd thought him rough and insensitive, but here he was sketching her in the most sympathetic way. Every day they had lived together, he wasn't lost in his own thoughts; he was with her.

12

<hr />

Jan 21: Winds > 19, SW, A schooner moving along at a good clip near parallel to shore, topsails taken in and a reefed main, another farther north.

Jan 21: Winds > 25, NE, Sm sch hd E, sm brig, hd E shore

TWO DAYS AFTER TESTING THE SURFBOAT, THE northeast wind drove hard onto the shore. "We need to be at the ready," Hannah told Billy. "Get everything you'll need to get a fire going down there."

Billy hurried to the barn and packed the small cart with wood, whale oil, a life ring, and blankets, then covered it all with a canvas tarp. He'd learned to pack the cart quickly with everything they needed. Even if the storm was tapering off, they had to be prepared for survivors. Hannah watched him out the front window as he pushed the cart over the uneven yard toward the dunes. He worked with an animal force. She was drawn to him as he maneuvered the wagon against some frailty in himself, as if he was ruined and working against it. There was a wildness about him, the way he strode across the lawn, loose in his body and urgent. When Billy turned for the house, she hurried to the lighthouse passageway before he came back in.

The afternoon became a monotony of drinking coffee, carrying in wood to dry by the fire, trips up the lighthouse, and endless waiting. Billy fell asleep in his chair at the table and Hannah resigned herself to lying down in her room. Without rest they'd be useless. She lay fully clothed beneath a single quilt, but she couldn't sleep. She ran her hand along the front of her pants. How long had it been since she'd felt her own pleasure? She relaxed into the surge of feeling, moving beneath the blanket in rhythm to her own breath. She drove herself hard upon her hand, feeling for the places that heightened her pleasure. She kept an ear out for Billy. He could wake up and glance into her room, but she didn't stop until the warm flush was over. Then the loneliness overcame her. She turned her face into the pillow to bury her tears. Only then did she finally rest.

When a snap in the wind woke her, she leapt from the tangle of quilts to stand at the window. Sails like broken wings in the soft gray air. Surf battered the hull, the keel caught in the shoals. The sounds were as familiar as her own quickening breath.

There was Billy standing in the doorway to her room. Panic held his eyes open wide. She wanted to press herself against him to quell the raft of her loneliness and quiet his fear. She stepped toward him, aware of his fear. He was thinking of his own shipwreck. "You can do this, Billy. I need you to help me."

"Everything's in the cart ready to go," he said.

Hannah went into the kitchen and peered through the window. "Rain's fallen off, that's good." Her voice was calm as she pushed the front door open against the wind. The storm felt good on her face, the cold air a relief.

Once outside, Hannah pushed through the wind toward the tops of the stairs and descended in the flourish of her green scarf and trailing wool coat. Billy fastened his cart to the rope they'd used to haul him up the dunes a few months ago. He lowered the gear, let the rope out slowly, and felt the cart as it bounced over beach plum and scrub to land on the beach.

By the time he reached the beach, Hannah had already flipped the surfboat, so much lighter than the old skiff, and loaded it with the extra-long rope and life ring. The wreck tilted in the waves not more than a hundred yards from shore, the sails shredded like thin cotton sheets, the masts like winter trees stripped bare. The surf tapered off as the wind died down. They said nothing as they pushed the boat to water's edge where it bobbed in the shallows. Hannah settled herself on the middle seat while Billy held the boat steady. With the oars set, Hannah sighted the wreck, then turned to Billy. She knew with certainty that she could trust him. "You'll get that fire going and set the tarp."

"I got it. Be quick, Hannah." When she gave him a final nod, he rushed the boat through the surf and shoved off toward the wreck. The surfboat rode up on a cresting wave, tilting toward vertical. The length of Hannah's body, her feet against the stern seat for leverage, her arms down and pulling back on the oars, with the bow of the boat rising above her, appeared to him then as an angel rising up from the sea. But there was no ether to her presence, no heavenly wings to carry her, only the strength of her arms and a determination that frightened him in its pursuit of survivors.

She rowed hard against the breakers, checking over her right shoulder now and again to make sure that she was on course. The bow of the boat lifted and held itself high in the waves. Hannah felt powerful in the knowledge of her own stamina as the boat responded to the slightest shift of her oars, and she began to close in on the wreck. Billy's fire flared on the shore, and above, the white column of the lighthouse. Flotsam knocked against the hull and caught her oars. She listened for the telltale noise, water sloshing over decks or calls for help, but heard nothing, and so rowed harder, throwing her back into each pull upon the oars, hauling against the weight of the ocean to send the boat forward until she heard sails flapping. Above the wash of water over the ship's decks, a loud thumping racket caught Hannah's attention. As she approached, she heard muffled cries from the cabin.

"Hallooo! Anybody there?"

More muffled cries, louder this time. In that instant, she dismissed every warning she'd heard from John. *Never get close to a wreck, Hannah. The masts crack in the wind, and when the hull fills with water, it can suck you and everything else down with it to the bottom. I have to keep my distance if I've any hope of saving anyone.* She turned and sought out Billy's fire on the beach, the black smoke a thin trail winding up. The pounding started again, a desperate racket that drove her alongside the wreck. *No, Hannah*, John's voice warned from the back of her mind, but she couldn't stop herself. There were men onboard.

The gunwale was underwater, and the waves lifted and dropped the skiff so that it rose above the sinking ship then slammed down below it, lifted up, then slammed down again.

The breakers crashed over the decks. Hannah held on, ducked her head, and peered through the salt spray. If she tied the skiff to the rail and the ship went down, it would take the skiff with it. She stood with her legs straddling the center seat, feeling the sea in her knees, and keeping her eye on the ship's rail that rose as the skiff dropped. When the rail rose to meet the skiff, she quickly looped the rope through it and tied a slipknot with nervous hands.

Satisfied that if the ship began to sink, a quick tug on the rope would free the skiff so that she could pull it back to her, she climbed onto the submerged deck of the wreck. The frigid water filled her boots as she made her way toward the hatch cover where the pounding continued, louder now. Even pushing with all her weight didn't budge the hatch cover. It was locked from the inside. *Unlock it. Find the latch.*

"Help!" Voices hysterical and desperate came through the hatch.

Hannah turned around and searched the deck for anything she could use to bash the hatch open. The water inched up her shins. She couldn't let herself think about the cold. She had to keep moving. *Think, Hannah, think!* She found a heavy belaying pin and swung it viciously at the hatch. Each blow against hard wood reverberated painfully up her arm, but she kept at it until a sharp pain overtook her elbow and she had to rest. The boat shifted and threw her off balance, until she gripped a handrail along the cabin. Her heart battered the cage of her ribs as she beat more violently at the hatch. "Hold on, hold on, I'll be right back."

She dragged the skiff's line to a cleat on the deck and tied it against her better judgment. Slogging her way aft, she held on to the cabin rail for balance and searched for anything that would free the hatch cover. Her feet had gone from numb to unbearable pain. A hatchet caught her eye. It was lashed to a bulwark underwater. She plunged her arm down to release it from its leather holster, and made her way back to the voices. "Step back. I've got it now. Step back!"

Beneath the blows from the ax, the hatch splintered and then she went at it more brutally. The ship tilted once again, groaned, and trembled. She eyed her skiff and continued heaving her arm back and thrashing it forward. Some terrified violence drove her. As the ship pitched hard to starboard, the hatch split wide open. Water rushed over the decks and rose from inside the ship to fill the cabin. She clutched the handrail once again, and this time the water was so high she let her legs float back while she peered inside. She took a deep breath and pulled herself under using the brass handrail that led down. Her clothes ballooned as they filled with water. The blur of a girl's dress billowed and she reached out, caught the fabric in her frozen hand. The boat shifted and the girl, her ghostly blue skin and frail limbs, spun away like an apparition. Hannah was out of breath now and dragged herself up by the railing until she broke the surface. One suck of breath and she went under again. Books floated past, a woman's scarf, a wooden spoon. Where was the girl? Into the depths of the cabin, past the chart table and benches, Hannah ventured, but there was no one. The pain in her chest exploded in a rush of air and she kicked against the anchor of her clothing, pulled hard on the railing, and kicked again until she broke through the surface to suck in the air.

The surfboat was still tied alongside the wreck, pitching in the waves. Hannah struggled to pull the skiff close enough to climb aboard, but she lost her footing and fell backward. The rope fell from her fingers; the boat drifted. She dove after the rope, caught it in one hand, and pulled herself toward the skiff. With her hands on the gunwale, she worked her way to the middle of the boat. When a wave lifted her, she swung her leg over the side and dropped into the bilge, now six inches deep with water. Her mind reeled. The ship was going to plummet. Her jaw rattled, limbs quivered as she set to rowing toward shore. Rowing hard was the only way to warm up. The surf continued to batter the disintegrating hull, and the masts and crossbeams strained like the sound of terror itself. The air vibrated with warning as the ship caved in. Masts thick as tree trunks snapped like skinny branches. From only fifty feet away, the sinking ship mesmerized and horrified her. Hannah heard the suck of water as the ocean pulled the wreck to the bottom. She stared until nothing was left but a foamy wash that faded across the ocean. The world went quiet, almost silent. Water swirled and rippled where the ship had been, and broken spars and shreds of sail and random bits of debris floated to the surface and knocked against the skiff.

Hannah trembled but rowed as hard as she could, using her breath to pull through each stroke. The air chambers Everett had built in the bow held it above the waves, and the boat sailed through the water. The lighthouse beam beckoned and she followed like a child called in from the cold.

On the beach, she staggered out of the boat. Billy grabbed her beneath her shoulders as she fell forward. He lifted her upright, then slung her arm over his shoulder. She let his strength take over where hers had succumbed. Her left side rested against him as he carried her to the fire and settled her on an over-turned crate. From the bottle kept in the locker beneath the stairs, he poured a mug full of whiskey. "You gotta get warm, Hannah. I'll see to the boat."

Hannah knelt at the fire and gasped for air, just as she had when she'd come up from underwater, but she was sobbing now and pulling at her wet clothes. She stripped off her gloves, wool sweater, and boots, and leaned in close to the fire to absorb the heat. She couldn't contain the sobs that rattled her rib cage. In her delirium, she tore off her trousers and shirt, until she stood in her underthings, as if the heat could assuage her grief.

She didn't hear Billy approach amid the sound of her crying and the crackling fire, and she didn't care enough to pull herself together, couldn't even if she wanted to. "It was a child," she sobbed. "I tried…they were right there, then the wreck shifted and started to go down and I almost…but they floated away…I couldn't—"

Billy wrapped her in heavy wool blankets and positioned her in the lee of the tarp out of the wind. He sat in the sand beside her, pulling the blankets tight in front of her, swaddling her like a child. "You're slurring your words. You've got chilled to the bone, Hannah. We have to get you up to the house before you catch a fever." He shook her by the shoulders to focus her attention. "Get hold of yourself. We have to go." He gathered Hannah's clothing, packed the rest of the gear back into the cart, and kicked sand over the fire. Hannah stood near the bottom of the stairs wrapped in blankets. "Up we go," he said, helping Hannah to her feet. "Can you make it up the steps?"

"Yes, yes." She tried to stand, but she was light-headed. There had to be a better way to do the rescues. With one arm over Billy's shoulder, Hannah let him lead her up.

Jan 22: Winds > 15, NE, schooner Neptune's Daughter of Boston total loss.

Hannah didn't mention the little girl again. She slept and slept, and when the lights needed tending, Billy shook her awake and followed her to watch how she trimmed the wicks and filled the oil and lit the tiny fires. Mostly, he was afraid she'd fall down the stairs or burn herself in her half sleep. One morning, she said, "I'll show you in case something happens to me."

"Those are the first words you've spoken in days," he said. "I want no part. It's the only thing getting you out of that bed."

She stopped talking after that.

In between trips to the lights, Hannah slept the dreamless sleep of the dead, a sleep in which she did not worry about the lights or the fog that rolled in on the wake of the nor'easter, or the bodies held captive in their watery deaths. When the sun crept through her windows and lit dusty bands of air, she pulled the quilts over her head. She couldn't get the image of the little girl's billowing dress from her head. The only feeling she could imagine upon waking was an inescapable darkness. She slept, and occasionally heard pots clanging on the stove, or the gentle stream of water from the pump at the kitchen sink, but never a voice until one afternoon when Tom stood by her bed. When she stirred, he retreated to the kitchen.

"How's she doing?" Tom asked. "I brought some beef from Hallet's. Maybe it'll help her get on her feet."

"She's had a terrible fever," Billy said. "She just gets up to tend the lights and doesn't say a word. Like walking in her sleep. She ought to be turning the corner, don't you think?"

Hannah heard them talking in the kitchen now, two grown men, worried and helpless. Her body ached from lying in bed. She had to get up, stretch, move. When she pushed back the covers and sat up, a fog rolled through her head. She stood slowly, her legs wobbly as she made her way out of her familiar, curtained room.

"I'm not dead, you know," Hannah said, shuffling into the kitchen.

"Well, I came to see for myself," Tom said. He gave Billy a look meant to drive him away, and Billy removed himself to the barn.

"I know what you're going to say, Tom, so don't even bother."

"I'm going to bother."

"Well don't. I went too far, I know that. But it was a young girl. I heard her calling out, and then I finally got down the hatch. She was so close." Hannah began to cry, but hardened herself. "I don't regret it. I'd do it again."

"But the girl's drowned. You nearly killed yourself for nothing," Tom said, angry. "It was a reckless thing to do."

"If I'd gotten out there faster, I might have saved her."

"Hannah, you know you should never board a sinking ship. You shouldn't even be out there."

"I can't talk about it anymore," she said, and closed her eyes.

Tom leaned forward on his chair and pushed himself up, as if exhausted by trying to talk sense to Hannah. "You know I care for you, Hannah. I should be the one here with you, not this stranger. Let me take care of you. It's what John would want."

His love was familiar and complete and she wanted to relax into it, but she said, "I can't right now, and it's not fair to bring John into it."

"You must know I love you. I've loved you since…"

He watched her closely, but she didn't move or give away any feeling. At the door, he turned, as if to say one last thing but thinking better of it, he left her to her silence.

After Tom's visit, Billy returned and Hannah read out loud last week's marine list for notice of *Neptune's Daughter*.

MARINE LIST

Disasters, &c.

Sloop Connecticut, (of New Bedford or vicinity), Gibbs, with rough rice and cotton, fm New River, NC for Charleston, is stated in a slip from the Charleston Courier of 21st inst, to have gone ashore on Pumpkin Island. Breakers night before, about 23 o'clock. Capt and crew remained in the rigging until next morning when they were providentially taken off, saving nothing but what they stood in. About ten minutes after they were taken off, the mast, to the rigging of which they had been clinging, went by the board, carrying with it everything attached, and had not they been rescued then, all must have met with a watery grave, as the vessel was full of water, and a tremendous sea running. Vessel and cargo total loss.

Sch Convert, (of Bath) Austin, fm Wilmington NC for Boston, struck on Cohasset Rocks early this morning, was got off leaking badly, and to prevent her sinking was run on Peddocks Island. She is full of water; cargo of naval stores, and 50 hhds of molasses—latter on deck.

Sch Neptune's Daughter, of and fm Wilmington D with 4800 bu corn, for Boston, even of 25th inst, went aground off Dangerfield: cargo fully insured in Boston. Total wreck. No salvage. All lives lost inc Captain Jones Silva of Delaware, wife Hester, daughter Ella 8 yrs old.

"Here it is," she said, defeated.

Billy looked up from his drawing. "Did your husband row into the storms?"

"No, he stayed ashore to watch the lights. Sometimes after the storm, he rowed out."

"You did what your husband wouldn't do. You went aboard that ship."

"It didn't help."

"You think you'd be doing any of this if he was here? Any of this lifesaving?"

"Yes, I do."

Billy took a gulp of water and drank it down like the hair of the dog. "Were you helping him when he was here?"

"No, I wasn't."

"You were certainly willing and able, more than anyone I suppose."

Hannah stood from her chair and ran her hands down the front of her trousers as if they were a skirt she was trying to flatten. Why was she letting him upset her? He'd never even met John.

"Go ahead, think on it, Hannah. Look at it close up." Billy wiped his chin on his sleeve. His eyes were not unkind.

Hannah spun around and glared into his face. "You think you know what it means to lose your husband? Your longest relationship has been with a bottle. You've never committed yourself to anything."

He only nodded as if she were right and he understood her anger—and this, his understanding, infuriated her. She closed her eyes and tried to deny the possibility that he was right. She told herself that if John had returned, he would've let her row into the surf. He would see how good she was. But the other, deeper truth continued to rear itself up, like a buoy shoved under the waves that bounces to the surface. John had a need to protect her that would always keep her ashore.

In her confusion she fled the house and Billy's pestering question. Tom would've discouraged her from rowing into the surf, but he wouldn't have tried to stop her. She walked along the edge of the cliff and counted ships along the horizon, a series of light gray wings against the sky.

13

S HIP AHOY!" THE CALL RANG OUT FROM ALOFT. THE MORNING
mist had burned off, and only wisps of clouds streaked the
azure skies. The first mate rang the bell, and the crew of the *Alice K*
went belowdecks to gather arms. They fell into a loose formation
on the leeward rail, waiting for Jack to call orders.

"All hands on deck," he said, pulling his jacket over his thick
torso and taking the steps two at a time up to the deck. His
dark eyes were sharp, exhilarated, as he adjusted the pistol in
his holster and the cutlass that he wore slung through a sash on
his other hip.

Blue, who was always ready, always alert, had to go
below for her pistol and machete. She'd been distracted by
Mark opening his shirt to her. "Goddamnitalltohell. I never
should've let that man—" She cursed her way along the companionway into the fo'c'sle, buckled the heavy leather belt at
her waist, and went up to the deck, her machete swinging at
her hips. Onboard the *Alice K*, she didn't hide her identity, but
on a raid she wore men's clothing and tied her hair up under
her hat. She buttoned her shirt and jacket and covered her
head with an indigo scarf. In a fight, her hair eventually came
down and the overtaken crew would realize that a woman had
beaten them.

Jack was amidships. She joined him to monitor their steady progress toward the merchant runner. Blue fingered her pistol. A feeling like dread washed over her as they neared the ship and Jack started commanding the crew. She waited for the usual rush of excitement to lift her into action, but instead she watched the pirates swearing and posturing, working themselves into a fury.

By the time they sailed alongside their prey and feigned friendship, Blue stood back from the rail and scanned the faces of the crew for Mark. Not finding him, she then shifted her attention toward the ship as they approached and prepared to board. Even as they boarded and Jack issued orders to the overtaken vessel, Blue couldn't rally her rage. She slipped belowdecks to search out the captain's cabin. A sea chest was fastened to the floorboards by the captain's bunk. She used the butt of her pistol to smash the lock. The chest contained the captain's letters, jewelry, a gold watch, and a knife with a scrimshawed handle. Blue tore a blanket from the bunk and folded the valuables into the middle, rolled the blanket into a bundle, and started up for the companionway. A tall sailor with red curly hair stopped her midstep, his right fist clasped around the leather-wrapped handle of a cutlass, his body poised and ready to slice at her.

"Drop it. Now!" he said.

Blue's hand was on her pistol, hidden beneath an armload of booty, and as commanded, she dropped the sack. At the same time she leveled her weapon and fired. The sailor's eyes flew open and his body slammed back against the white-painted paneling and slid down the wall. Blue bent to grab the sack and slung it over one shoulder. She stepped over the sailor's crumpled legs and climbed onto the deck near the stern, where she could cross onto the *Alice K* without notice. She stowed her loot under the whaleboat.

With the merchant crew defeated, the pirates carried crates, barrels, and boxes of cargo to stash in the hold of the *Alice K*, and then they went back for more. Briggs oversaw the men as they used a yardarm like a crane to hoist the heavy crates, swinging the spar over the hold and lowering a line on block and tackle to fasten to the crate, then lifting it up and swinging it over the decks until it lined up over the *Alice K*'s hold where it was lowered and settled into position.

Jack stood by the defeated captain, nudging the pistol into his side at regular intervals as a reminder of what would come should the overtaken crew break ranks and revolt. "Not so bad, now, is it, Simpson?" Jack asked. "We get what we want, and you get away with your life. The ship's owner has insurance to cover your loss, mate. It works out for everyone. Don't you agree?" He picked at his teeth with his marlinespike and spat downwind before returning his attention to the steady stream of boxes and crates being hauled aboard the *Alice K* by his men.

The crew looted the carpenter's tool chest, stole as much food and silverware as they could find from the galley. Jack called for Blue and waited for her to appear at his side. "Find those two sailors we rescued, make sure they're earning their keep. If they're not, get rid of 'em."

"Right." Blue nodded, although she felt a moment of panic that she quelled by lurching into action. She found Mark and Jeb in the hold, among crates and sacks of grain and flour.

They hovered over a small sea chest, the backs of their heads bobbing as they worked at picking the lock with the tip of a cutlass. "What's this?" Blue asked, standing over them with her pistol drawn. "Move aside," she said, not meeting Mark's eyes. "I said move!" Blue stepped toward them and pulled back the hammer on her pistol. The two sailors covered their ears against the deafening blast. The shot was true. The lock fell into pieces, parts of the wooden chest splintering from the blast. She threw back the lid of the trunk and unfolded a white coverlet carefully spread over the contents. Were the gold pieces real or a figment of her ransacked imagination? The two sailors gasped, awestruck, and stood to watch as Blue filled her pockets with coins, slid them into her boots, her stockings, her undergarments, then removed the handkerchief from her head and filled it with coins, wrapped it up, and tied it inside her jacket. Her hair hung in tangled knots around her shoulders. Turning to leave the hold, she said, "Take some coins for yourselves and say nothing. Then deliver the rest of the gold to Jack as if you found it. It might save your lives."

Back on deck, she did not mention the chest of gold to Jack. A dead sailor slumped against the cabin, his shirt soaked with blood that had formed a pool around him. Blue signaled one of Jack's crew to help her drag him to the rail. His head flopped from side to side and his limbs hung heavy. They wrestled his weight over the rail. He was somebody's husband or brother or lover. Why had he risked his life over somebody else's property? Didn't these stupid men see that they weren't losing anything themselves? They lived under the thumbs of ship owners who made the big profits and paid the sailors pennies only to work them to the bone so that they could live in their large houses atop hills overlooking the sea that delivered their soft, pampered lifestyle. *Now that is pirating*, Blue thought.

The dead sailor floated for a moment across the waves. Blue watched as his body tilted and sank so that he went from a man below the water's surface to a dark cloud drifting down to nothing at all. She turned from the rail and moved slowly to keep her coins from jangling. What had possessed her to steal the gold coins? She crossed the plank to the *Alice K*. If Jack found the stolen coins, he would shoot her on the spot or make a spectacle out of killing her before the men. Every pirate signed the ship's bylaws and understood the code. With the rest of the crew, she always accepted her share of the loot without question. Now she felt like a stranger among the crew. The mere fact of her disavowal let her know that she had turned away from the pirates. Just like she'd crossed over a line joining the pirates, she'd now crossed a line in stealing from them, and she could not go back.

She watched the sea chest swing back and forth in small strokes between Mark and Jeb as they carried it onboard the *Alice K*. They must've shown Jack the gold, as Blue had instructed. So why did Jack look angry, twirling a loose end of rope between his thumb and forefinger?

She waited for him to speak.

"Those two rescued men found a chest with gold pieces in the hold below. The captain never told me about it when I asked him what he had of value onboard. He should have." Jack's eyebrows flattened to a straight line across his brow.

"What will you do?"

"I've no choice," Jack said, stepping to the rail to watch the sea chest make its way to the hold of the *Alice K.*

"I'll take care of it then," Blue said, and Jack waved her on as he turned and started back to the *Alice K.* Blue found the stranded captain at the helm where Jack had tied him—hands behind his back and fastened to a spoke in the large wheel. She cut the captain free of the wheel with her cutlass and sheathed it at her waist. "Come with me," she said, her words sharp and flat as a knife's blade.

"What for?" the captain asked. His skin was tan, but not yet weathered. He couldn't have been more than twenty-three or twenty-four years of age, Blue thought, herding him ahead of her amidships. He wore a navy blue waistcoat with brass buttons that caught the sun and cast a glitter like gold coins.

She backed him up against the mast. "Take off your jacket," she said.

"Why?"

"I don't want to get holes in it when I shoot you. Take it off!" The chilly tone of her voice sounded distant and strange. She felt that she was watching from slightly above, as if perched in the rigging close enough to overhear the cruel conversation, but not in any way an actual participant.

"But why? I complied with your captain's orders. I did what he said."

"You told him nothing about the sea chest in the hold." She watched her hand reach to unbutton the man's coat, and when he fell to his knees, she watched her own arm jerk him up by twisting his arm behind him so that he yelped with the torque on his shoulder. The man stood on his feet and let her unbutton his jacket and strip it back from his chest and shoulders. Blue felt the heat of his body and his fear as she tore the jacket down so that the sleeves hung from his hands, which were still fastened behind his back with rope that cut bloody wounds into his wrists.

The captain's head hung, and when he looked up, his gray eyes angry and sad, he said, "But I thought—" Blue stood back and considered the unfortunate captain. With her cutlass, she cut the rope at his bloody wrists and told him not to move a muscle as she removed the sleeves of his coat from his forearms. She held the garment up to examine it from all sides before sliding it on over her own sweat-soaked shirt. Blue fastened the shining buttons and tugged the coat down at the waist so that the fine blue fabric lay flat. Then she looked hard into the captain's frightened face.

"What do you think of it?"

The sweat jeweled on his forehead, his head and shoulders hunkered down as if braced for a blow.

She nudged him with the muzzle. "I asked what do you think?" she said.

"Handsome," he said.

"Lucky for you." The pirate crew was back on the *Alice K*. His own crew were wounded or hiding below. "Now listen to me, young captain. Get below, away from your men and any living thing for two nights and two days until we're long past the horizon. I'm warning you. You'll be a dead man if you cross me."

He looked at her in disbelief. "Yes, yes. I'll do it," he said, collapsing with relief.

Blue walked him to the hatchway and shoved him down the steps so that he landed in a heap. She ducked below the hatch and pulled him up, then pushed him ahead of her along the companionway. Pistol in hand, she waited for the captain to disappear down the hatch amidships. Then she fired a single shot into the seam between the deck and the hull of the ship. The shot that Jack would hear and think that she'd killed the captain. As she climbed through the hatch into the air, the ship began pitching slightly. She felt tired, more tired than she'd ever been.

The walk to the *Alice K* felt endless. She passed Johnson sorting through a box of cargo, and Briggs ordering everyone where to stow the foodstuffs, building materials, precious metals, and money. Blue ducked down the companionway and nearly fell into her hammock, into a dreamless sleep that could've lasted minutes or days or years. She fought waking up, but the carousing overhead kept pulling her from oblivion. Still, she dove for that blank slate, that black nothing of sleep until the noise finally won and her mind came alive and she knew where she was.

Blue climbed from her hammock, ducked under the wood beams. She took the narrow steps and stuck her head into the night air, a warm breeze from the southeast. Loneliness swept through her. The baby's final wheeze had left her hollow as a gun barrel. Everything after that had been emptiness.

The sounds of the *Alice K* rose more distinct to Blue's ears. The wooden seams creaked, and the rigging settled and groaned and snapped against the mast.

Blue walked along the rail, around the cannons bolted into

the sides of the ship. She stopped at the whaleboat fastened atop the deck. The white hull glowed under the night sky like the belly of a whale, exposed and dangerous. She peered beneath the overturned boat and scanned the ground for Mark's feet. She didn't know what she wanted with the sailor, even as she ducked under the boat and slid into the protective dark. "It's Blue," she said.

"I know," Mark said.

"You're always here." Blue shuffled her body toward his voice until she was leaning against the hull next to him.

"There's something I have to show you." He took Blue's hand. "It's not what you think."

He slid her hand over his breast, and she let her fingers graze his soft skin. She forgot for a moment what she was feeling for, a scar maybe or some other disfigurement, but what she felt was a wide, cloth strap. He guided her hand beneath the strap, then loosened it and slid her hand farther, until she felt a breast pressed flat, but rounder and fuller than her own. Blue yanked her hand back.

"My name is Mary. Mary Burke of South Boston."

Blue tried to remember the last time she'd had contact with a woman. It had been the midwife who delivered her baby.

"So why are you dressed like this? Why are you at sea?"

"I've been at sea nine years or thereabouts. My mother died when I was fourteen, and my aunt raised me until I was sixteen. She sent me to work in the kitchen of a rich lady's house on Beacon Hill." Her story seemed to tumble out with the relief of having finally been asked. "I worked there just five days before running off with her purse. I ran downhill, straight to the water, and wandered the docks. There was a steady stream of men and ships coming and going. Women walked the docks for money. I saw then what I'd done. I'd left the only way I had to survive. I sat on the dock and cried, thinking I'd have to lie down for money. I watched a brig set sail out of the harbor until the sails dissolved into the sky and I thought, wherever that ship's going, I want to go. So I cut my hair and spent that lady's money on sailing clothes and found myself work as a cabin boy. It wasn't hard to pass. Worked my way up to the crew and finally served as boatswain. It's been nine years."

"You've passed as a man all those years?"

"Some might've guessed I was a woman, but I did my job and passed. Nothing was said about it."

"If Jack finds out, you're dead. The men'll have their way with you. You'd be fair game as far as they're concerned."

"Jack's not going to find out, is he?"

Blue held still as Mary leaned her face in close and let her cheek brush Blue's cheek. Mary's lips brushed her cheek and lips, and Blue waited for her to lean toward her before she kissed her on the mouth with a ferocity that was sorrow. Her desire frightened her, as she shoved Mary down on the deck, passed her lips over Mary's neck. She tugged at the cloth strap with Mary's help until her breasts came loose. Mary guided her hand beneath the waist of her trousers, which she'd sprung open with one quick motion of her hand. The smell of her skin and her sex was purely female, sweet and acrid and complicated, familiar as her own but different.

She held Mary in the palm of her hand and answered every push of Mary's hips, until nothing existed but Mary's stifled cries.

When Mary tried to nudge Blue onto her back, Blue resisted. "No, like this," she said, straddling Mary's hips. Mary released Blue's trousers as deftly as she'd released her own. It was the first time Mary wasn't talking, but Blue heard murmuring as if from the seams of the boat. Blue took her pleasure, knees pressed into the deck, palms against the hull, until she shuddered and forgot everything but the rush of sex pushing up now through the core of her body and washing her mind clean.

Her own snoring woke her in the dark beneath the boat. Four bells rang out—the night watch changing. Johnson was on deck to receive the telescope and lantern from the sailor who'd been in charge before him. She rolled onto her back and fastened her trousers, then looked up at the ribs of the whaleboat arching over them. Mary slept with her head on a canvas bag, her mouth hanging open, oblivious as Blue drifted into the dark.

Blue's bunk hung at an angle that forced her body to roll. The morning sun blared through a small porthole, forcing her eyes to squint as she reached for the water flask. There was a tapping against the glass, steady as a rat clawing in the walls. Tap. Tap. Tap.

There it was again, with a voice this time. "Blue, you in there? Blue, it's me. I must see you," Mary said, her voice both demanding and plaintive.

Blue opened the hatch and peered through for any sign of Jack before swinging it wide enough for Mary to climb down into the cabin.

Mary leaned her weight into Blue and kissed her neck.

Blue pushed her away and sat on the sea chest, head in her hands. "I have to get off this ship."

Mary stood before her, eyes wide.

"This has nothing to do with you."

Mary took a step back from Blue. "I'm staying," she said, as if she realized it just then. She placed her hand against Blue's cheek, and with a determined silence, she left the fo'c'sle.

Blue stood before the looking glass. Her face looked older to her, creased around the mouth and dark with sun, eyes distant and wild. When was the last time she'd seen herself? With her left hand, she took a clump of blond hair and pulled it taut, then scissored her rigging knife back and forth until the hair came loose and only a short tuft of blond remained. Blue worked her way around her skull with the knife until she'd cut off all of her hair. Then she wet her hand and tried to flatten the goose down, but it wouldn't lie down.

Her long hair had been her banner. Even though she wore it up during raids, it always came unfurled, a flag for her own country, the nation of female pirates. There were other women like her, women with no means to live on their own. Women who did what they had to do in order to survive. The men she'd captured had been aghast to be taken over by a woman. It was an affront to have their crew slaughtered by the hands that should be holding a baby. To cower down by the bulwark in fear of a woman was an embarrassment that prevented most men from reporting her. And who would have believed them? Forever they would carry the curse of that woman with the blond mane. She gathered her locks from the floor and dropped them into a tin box and closed the box tight, and then she lay down again, the tin box clutched to her chest.

Jack stood with Nate at the helm. He had a matchstick in his mouth that he chewed between his back teeth, and he pointed one rough finger at the compass, then out toward the bow of the boat. When he spied Blue, he leaned in to give Nate a series of orders, and then slapped him on the back and spun on his heel to face the stern.

He joined Blue where she stood looking into the ship's wake, then up to the sky at wispy clouds elongated over the horizon. Jack didn't say anything about her hair even as he took it in. "You drunk?"

"Not yet."

He nodded and spat over the side. He walked away, his coat loose and flapping, brass buttons clattering in the wind. Blue listened to the musical sound of his retreat. Then her gaze drifted up to the rigging and the crow's nest atop the mast. She swung herself onto the ratlines and climbed up, the rough-hewn rope scraping her palms, her legs swinging with the sway of the rope ladder. Near the top of the mast, she pulled herself to the crow's nest and stepped onto the small platform with nothing but the metal rail at her waist to keep her safe. As far as she could see, waves foamed and rolled in white arcs. Not a ship in sight or any land, only the boat and wind and water and sky. She couldn't stay aboard the *Alice K*. Not after stealing the gold, which she stashed in the false bottom of her sea chest. Not after letting the young captain go. She had to get off this ship.

The only way to escape was when Jack and the crew went ashore with Therese and her women. They would be drunk and distracted; they'd expect her to stay on the ship as she had in the past. The wind swept the thoughts from her mind until she couldn't think beyond the pressure of air and the rocking motion of the ship and the sturdy rail at her waist that held her close as a lover.

14

IN THE EARLY MORNING, WRAPPED TIGHT IN A JACKET buttoned over her white flannel nightgown, Hannah bent her torso into the wind and walked to the lip of the dune where she stood amid withered scrub brush and vines. A tangled knot of air writhed and tumbled between her and the ocean. Eight-foot swells the color of cracked glass crashed onto the beach in a milky froth, spraying the air with mist. Hannah's breath quickened, and her pulse throbbed with the violence of it. She squatted down out of the wind and poked at the frozen earth with the broken end of a stick, and she found herself digging viciously, digging and digging until she became aware of herself and stopped. In the surfboat, she felt her own power lifted and enhanced. She wanted to put the boat to work, but she needed to be able to rely on Billy staying away from the bottle.

On her way back into the house, she looked toward Tom's yard, but he wasn't there. She felt lonely for him then. Was she foolish not to marry him, though he hadn't said anything about marriage? Hadn't she thought about him often since that day on the beach? Hadn't she watched the graceful way he moved across a room? Hadn't she noticed his hands, strong from working wood, and imagined them on her body? She wanted someone she could rely on.

Inside, Billy had made a pot of coffee and looked to be pouring his first cup. The hair on one side of his head pressed straight up with sleep.

She dropped her jacket on a chair, pulled her cardigan close, and stifled a shiver that ran through her entire being.

"You've got to lay off the drinking," Hannah said, with more anger than she intended.

He squinted against the pain in his head. His surly expression, watery eyes, and puffy face all made her want to slap him. He reminded her of her father. But she waited until the feeling settled down. "There's only so much you can do around here if you're drinking. These are people's lives we're looking after. How can I count on you if you're drunk or suffering the day after?"

He was silent, his lips a tight crease.

"I'm talking about you being someone I can trust. You have to take responsibility for your post." Hannah turned away from him. "Otherwise you can leave."

His face filled with surprise, then despair, his eyes boring into her, then away. Hannah was afraid. She didn't know what he was capable of. She went to the kitchen counter and eyed the rolling pin. If he came at her, she could swing the pin right at his head. She was strong enough to hurt him. She'd seen a man's rage. She'd seen how her father taking a drink here and there could turn into pitchers of milk thrown against the wall. Seen how a man could turn his anger into a machine that worked without stopping, hammering against anything that got in its way.

She turned from the counter and took in his stricken face. Billy saw that he'd frightened her, and his rage looked to have turned in on himself. His shame drove him to a far chair where he sat opening and closing his fists as if to exorcise some fiendish impulse. Then he sat with his head in his hands, as if everything bad about him had collected in the orb of his skull and he couldn't bear the weight of it.

"I don't want you to have to leave," Hannah said.

"I said I'd quit last night. It's not like I never thought of quitting," he said. "Nothing good ever came of it." He ran his charcoaled fingers back and forth across the tops of his trousers to rub the stains out but they persisted. He looked up, waited for Hannah to say something, but she didn't speak. "Onboard, we drank to break the monotony. Then it was because I couldn't stand the life and I needed to take the edge off. I drank and drank until after a while it didn't do anything for me. I could drink all I wanted and I still felt the same as I did before I drank a sip," he said.

Still, she wasn't in the mood to feel sorry for him. "You have to lay off."

"It won't feel good to quit."

Hannah sat down in a chair opposite him. She wanted to understand why he drank. Her father said he drank to ease the pain in his back, but she knew it was something deeper; his drinking had started long before he hurt himself. When had Billy started drinking? "You said you sailed in the Caribbean. What were you doing there?"

He slouched down into his chair as if he could disappear into it.

"You're always going to be a stranger here if you don't let me know you."

He looked out the window toward nothing, his jaw clenched tight. Then he fixed his gray eyes on her. "There's things I don't know how to say. If I could tell you—" He shook his head and rose from the chair, slump-shouldered and frowning. He went outside to the barn, no jacket or hat, nothing to protect him.

Tom appeared that afternoon carrying a package under one arm, his green eyes flashing happiness when Hannah opened the door. He was handsome in his seaman's jacket, his ruddy cheeks flushed with cold.

He placed the package on the table and dropped his coat onto a chair. "Where's Billy?"

"He went out to the barn hours ago."

"I've brought you something," Tom said, and he sat at the table. "Come, sit."

Hannah sat in the chair at the head of the table and received the gift Tom slid in front of her. It was wrapped in newspaper from Barnstable.

"You don't have to buy me presents. That's ridiculous," she said.

"Just open it, will you?"

"Okay, okay," she said, running one finger under the seam between layers, then carefully folding back the paper. Inside, was a maple box, finished to a high shine, with brass hinges on one side.

"It's beautiful," she said.

"Open it up," Tom said, a look of mischief on his face.

The compass inside tilted to remain parallel to the earth so that even when you carried it in the boat that rose and fell in the surf, the compass would remain readable and true to course.

"That should help you in the storms and fog."

"It's the most thoughtful gift. Did you make it?"

"Just the box, the compass I found. I also made a cubby for it in the bilge of the surfboat so that you can read it from your position at the oars."

"When on earth—"

"You're not always down there. I found the time."

Hannah was moved not only that he would give her a gift, but also that the gift acknowledged she wouldn't stop the rescues. She leaned over to kiss him on the cheek, but he turned his lips toward her. She let her lips hover near his, taking in his salty scent before she kissed him on the mouth. His kiss moved through her body, strange and familiar. When he pulled away from her, he held her by the shoulders and looked into her face. "It should be me here with you," he said.

The next morning, the wind drove itself hard upon the house; it jangled the blue glass bottles on the sills and thrashed the shutters. Hannah felt a hot rush of excitement at the prospect of a storm. She had been rowing the surfboat for weeks now and developed a familiarity and ease with the boat as her arms and legs built muscle.

"Jesus, Mary, and Joseph!" Billy shouted in the loft, rousing himself from bed. "What in the hell was that?"

"We got a nor'easter coming in. Not for a while, but it's coming," Hannah said. "I'm going up to check the lights, you batten down the hatches."

"Yes, ma'am," he said.

As she passed through the kitchen, she heard him swearing and struggling in the dark to find the ladder leading down from the loft. "Don't land on your rump in my kitchen," she said.

"No, ma'am," he said, caught up by the tone in her voice.

Hannah hurried through the passageway toward the spiral stairs leading up to the lights. She climbed quickly. The howl of wind trembled in the sturdy column of the lighthouse. On the landing, all but one lantern burned, and the effect dazzled the lenses with a fierce light. Hannah squinted and turned her head to the side as she struck a match. The windows shivered in their frames as she cupped her hand around the flame, feeling the heat of the fire that would magnify and gather to cast a beam far across the water. This was the first thing she could do to save a man. Keep the lights going through the storm. Once the nor'easter hit, it wouldn't let up until it had blown itself out.

With all the lanterns aflame, Hannah checked the level of the whale oil and used a long-handled scissor to trim the wicks. What an exhilarating feeling, knowing that she could help a floundering ship navigate these waters. She wiped the windows with clean rags and vinegar, reaching every corner, clearing the soot and dust. One last glance at the lights, then she went down.

Billy stood sopping wet in the kitchen, a pool of water collecting at his feet. "I've wrapped us in pretty tight," he said.

"Got the shutters closed, the barn door locked, and the storm doors fastened and bolted. Stoked the fire."

"Good," Hannah said, rubbing her hands together and stepping in front of the fire that Billy had nurtured into flames.

"Now what?" he asked.

"We wait, and we watch." Hannah sat by the fire while Billy paced, then leaned back against the kitchen counter and picked at his nails. "You can wipe up that puddle. Then come over here. I want to hear about what happened when your ship went aground."

Billy used a rag from the kitchen to clean the floor then sat in a chair near Hannah. "You want me to tell you about it?"

Hannah nodded.

"The captain was holding our course and watching this lighthouse. I could see the flash of light when it was only a pinprick out the porthole of my berth. Then it got bigger and bigger and closer and closer, and word was that if we stayed close to shore, but not too close, we'd be safe. I nearly fell asleep because the boat wasn't pitching so much as when we were out in deep water. I was in that part of sleep where you're dreaming, but you're still awake, when I heard a crash, like the world getting ripped open. Water rushed into the bilge and the whole ship started shaking.

"Everything happened fast, no time to do anything. All hands ran to the upper decks. The ship tilted hard to port and you could feel the weight of water pulling her over. Something takes hold of you in a storm like that. On deck, the crew was frantic to loosen the sails because the wind was driving us hard onto the shoals. The captain was shouting orders to loosen sail, but no one would climb up the rigging. We were too heeled over and the masts were creaking, about to break. I worked my way along the gunwale, holding on against the surf, until I got to the lifeboats. One of the mates, Tomas, helped me lower the first boat, but it capsized and sank. He looked so young right then. I thought he might cry. I led him to the second lifeboat, and we held firm while more of the crew and passengers piled in and the first mate, James, manned the oars. The ship listed in the breakers as we rowed away. A sailor called Brennan, he was the one you found on the beach, leapt over the side hoping to swim for shore. He swam toward the lifeboat but went under pretty quick. We all turned away then, from him, the wreck, everything that was death. Next thing I remember I was getting yanked out of the water into your boat."

"If I'd gotten there earlier maybe some of your shipmates would've made it," Hannah said.

"No one can survive a storm like that. Not even you with that fancy boat of yours," Billy said. He got up abruptly and climbed the ladder to the loft. "I've got something to show you," he said, and he climbed back down the ladder, a roll of paper under his arm. He spread his drawings out across the dining table while Hannah moved the candlesticks and butter crock. "There's a way to make a rig, like you wanted. I'm thinking you set an anchor in the sand to make a lifeline secure on shore. Maybe get me and your friend Tom to bury you a post six feet deep with only the top exposed to show the fastening ring. You'll have to row out to the ship with the other end of the lifeline so the crew can fasten the line to the mast. Once I get the signal from the ship, I run this life seat out to them."

The next drawing was of a ship's life ring with a seat sewn in the center. It hung within a tripod of ropes gathered above at a block and tackle system. "The life seat runs along the lifeline, and I pull it to and from the ship with a hawser line from shore."

"That's all well and good, but what kind of a seat is going to withstand a storm wind?"

"I'm thinking it's sewn from heavy canvas sailcloth, stitched with waxed marlin strong enough to hold the heaviest man, like what they use for sails."

Hannah was silent, scanning the drawings. He'd thought things through pretty well. She followed each line in his sketches, surprised at the detail and intelligence of the system Billy had worked out. His drawings were crisp and clear, full of ideas they could really work with. "Seems possible," she said finally.

"Wait here," Billy said, and followed the passageway that ran from the house to the barn. Hannah sat in front of the stove listening to the rain. The wind had picked up and gusted against the northeast corner of the house. She traced the lines in her palm and thought about the last sinking hours aboard that ship, but she'd never been close enough to death to understand those last moments.

Billy came back carrying a huge lifesaving ring. It was one that John had collected from a wreck and stored in the barn. Billy hefted the life ring onto the table. He'd already stitched a seat out of sailcloth in the center, with two holes for legs so that a man could sit in it with his arms over the side of the ring. The edges of canvas were double-stitched to keep from fraying. If the rope running to shore collapsed and the ring hit the water, it would float and with the attached safety line, the sailor could be pulled to shore. The ring was designed to hang from a block and tackle that ran along a rope to the ship, just as he'd drawn it. "You send the ring out to the ship. Then you pull them to shore with this extra line here. It looks strange, but it might work, depending on the wind and how it's secured to the ship. Of course, you have to reach the ship before it's sunk too far." Billy held the rig up so that Hannah could examine it from every angle.

"Able-bodied sailors won't have any trouble climbing into the thing," Hannah said.

"If the wind is too heavy, no one will be able to maneuver it," Billy said. "If the ship is falling apart, or the masts snap, this would be far too dangerous. Anyone with serious injuries won't be able to use it. But it's better than nothing, which is what you have now. And better than you alone in the surfboat. If you want, and weather permits, you can even tow the old skiff behind you out to the wreck and carry in survivors that way as well. But there are risks."

"Anything we can do to improve a man's chances will be good news, don't you think?"

"I built a test rig in the barn. If you want to see it—"

"I can't believe you've been hiding this."

"I haven't been hiding it. I've been working on it."

"So show me."

She followed him along the passageway into the barn, which he'd transformed into a testing area. He'd rigged a rope from a cleat on the wall stud up to a ceiling beam at the loft about forty feet off the ground so that the rope triangulated the barn.

A system of block and tackle hung from the rope, and Billy hooked the life ring to it. Wind rattled the roof shingles and seeped through the barn boards; rain pattered the walls.

"Show me how it works," Hannah said, her face flushed with excitement.

"I've only tried pulling the life ring up and down from the loft with this hawser line. I've experimented with bags of grain in the seat, and I worked out a few kinks in the block and tackle."

He showed Hannah the hawser line that drew the ring closer, and the lines that would run out to a stranded vessel, reviewing the details as if to double-check his work. While he pointed out the features of the rig, Hannah followed along lengths of rope and over pulleys to the lifesaving ring. He spoke with an authority she hadn't seen in him before, a confidence that lured her in.

"So who's going to be the first to try it?"

"It's not ready. I haven't fully tested it yet."

"What are your concerns?"

"I don't know if the seat will hold, if the lines will run with the weight of a person pulling down on them, or if the hawser line is strong enough to pull the life ring in. What if someone climbed into this thing, and then I couldn't pull them in?"

"You could cut the line and they'd float to shore. That's the way you designed it, right?"

"I need a little more time," Billy said, fiddling with the rope in his hands. The wind blew through cracks in the barn boards and swung the ropes overhead. Hannah unrolled her wool turtleneck up to her chin.

"Well, it's going to work, isn't it?" Hannah asked.

"Yes, soon."

Hannah watched to see what he'd do next, but he only coiled the ropes to run free.

"Maybe we should try it out," Hannah said, "and see how it works."

"I'll put a big sack of grain in the seat and run it up to the loft. That'll give you a pretty good idea of what we're dealing with here."

"A sack of grain doesn't mean anything to me. You need a person, someone with arms and legs that move, someone with real fear."

"Where are we going to get a half-drowned, terrified sailor?"

"I'll try it myself." Hannah's resolve steadied her as she stepped toward the life ring. "I'll get into the seat, and you can lift me just high enough so that my feet lift off the floor, to see if it holds."

Billy nudged the life ring with his elbow where it hung from the block and tackle, then followed the rope up into the beams, making sure that the rigging was strung right and the ropes would hold. "I need to give it another couple of days, try it out with a few more bags of grain, make sure it can stand the weight."

Hannah grabbed the hawser line and drew the life ring down to her so that the cork was near her waist.

Billy took hold of the life ring, but she yanked it back and held on to the block and tackle for balance as she climbed into the seat and pulled the ring up snug. "It'll be okay," she said. "Now pull me up a little at a time, just enough to get me off the ground."

"God, you are stubborn." Billy worked the rope that dragged the block and tackle toward the loft. Hannah stood on her toes and then her toes left the floor and she was in the air, the block and tackle taking her weight. He let her dangle like that, kicking her feet and jostling her weight to be sure the rig would hold.

"It barely creaks, Billy. I knew it was solid, but I didn't know it was this solid. Now lower me down from here. I've got an idea."

Once she was out of the contraption, she climbed the ladder to the loft. "I'll be a sailor on a sinking ship, and I've fastened the lifeline to my mast. Now you're going to send the buoy out to me, okay?"

"Aye, aye, sir," Billy said.

Hannah tugged a thin rope that ran along the thicker lifeline and drew the life ring toward her. "That's it," Billy said. "Keep going until you pull the rig aboard."

Hannah sat on the edge of the loft and put her feet through the seat. The wind thrashed the side of the barn now and rain came through seams of wood. Hannah shivered as she spoke. "No drowning man is going to have the luxury of sitting down," she said, and pulled her feet loose and stood up again. She'd have to climb into the rig where it hung over the open air, just as a stricken sailor would have to climb above the surf and step off a tilting deck into a swinging piece of cork that was the life ring. Hannah clutched the block and tackle and stuck her legs down through the canvas seat, lowered herself down until it took her weight and the only thing between her and the floor was Billy's apparatus.

Why did she trust him? How could she explain that she'd

learned something about him through his drawings and his careful construction of the rig? What would John say if he saw her swinging from the beams in the barn, suspended aloft by a web of ropes constructed by a hard-drinking sailor?

Billy caught her eye and held her gaze until her fear passed. "You're sitting pretty good. I'm going to let you down slow," Billy said. The wind scattered the hay across the floor.

Hannah didn't look down, only at Billy. All the while the air below felt like a threat, but she refused to be frightened. She let Billy's eyes hold her and keep her from looking anywhere but straight ahead along the length of rope that led to him. When her feet brushed the floor, she nearly toppled over. Billy caught her under the arms, and Hannah stood amid his working smells: the salty odor of his sweat, and coffee on his breath, and the smell that must have been just him, just Billy.

"Let's try it again." She wanted to feel him on the other end of the rope, and the thrill of the open air beneath her as she waited to land beside him.

15

HER LAST NIGHT ON THE *ALICE K,* THE SHIP WAS AT
anchor in Jamaica. While the crew caroused with
Therese's women, and Jack negotiated the sale of their stolen
goods, Blue stole a roll of bandages from the medicine box.
She knew she could only take some of her stolen gold, or the
weight would drown her when she went overboard. The
safest shore was a hundred yards away across a rippling surface
of water. With the coins in a pillowcase, she wrapped them
around her waist, then held the bundle in place with the
bandage wrapped like a cumbersome belt. There was nothing
in her sea chest she could bring: not her gun or machete, nor
Daniel's coat, nor the drawings she'd made of the ship and
the pirates themselves. She let the heavy lid drop and left the
fo'c'sle for the upper deck. Spots of lantern light glowed along
the shore. If she swam east, away from the village, anyone who
might return to the ship from shore wouldn't cross her path.

A rope ladder hung down the railing where the pirates
climbed down earlier into the women's canoes. Blue climbed
down, the ship's hull a dark wall rising. She bounced on the
ladder to test the weight of the gold before she lowered herself
into the lagoon. With one hand grabbing the ladder, she tried
to tread water. Arms working, legs kicking, she let go. She

swam hard then toward the eastern shore. She'd known what to expect with Jack and the crew, and now she'd thrown her life to the wind. The gold was the only thing between her and destitution. The gold would protect her. This gave her strength as she swam against the weight of it. Every once in a while she looked up to measure her distance from shore, then she plunged again into her steady stroke.

When she reached the beach, she crawled on her stomach across the sand, the weight of the gold like a stone attached at her waist. A low barrier of bushes lifted into trees where she could walk bent over. Then the woods thickened, and she walked upright in search of shelter. A fallen tree draped with bougainvillea created a kind of tent filled with the fecund odors of rich soil, banana leaves, and flowering trees. She unwrapped the bandage at her waist and the pillowcase full of gold dropped to the ground. With a thick stick, she dug a hole and buried the gold, then covered the ground with dried palm and foliage. The sound of the pirates in the near distance felt both familiar and frightening; the strangeness of the world around her startled her in its intimacy. She slept on top of the gold, vigilant and half dreaming. Branches jabbed her in the ribs, and the damp soil soaked into her clothes until she woke shivering. What was that sound? There it was again: the clatter of the anchor chain being hauled aboard the *Alice K.*

The sight of the sails taking shape against the orange sky as the ship steered away from the lagoon filled her with relief and sadness. Then as the *Alice K* sailed around the outcrop of cliffs to the west, fear got the best of her and she cursed her stupidity. She'd never be safe again. Even on her own with the gold wrapped again at her waist, she would always be the pirate, Blue.

She found the path hidden under foliage and worked her way back toward the lagoon. Her body stank; her clothes, covered in dirt, stuck to her skin. On the edge of the tiny village, she squatted behind a row of azalea and watched the women cleaning up after the pirates, sweeping huts, washing clothes in wooden tubs. She stepped from behind the bushes and let the trail carry her around the lagoon. Ishema saw her first and dropped her broom on the ground. She wrapped her thick fingers around Blue's arm and dragged her forward. "You're disgusting. You stink, but you are not dead yet."

Therese stood on her porch, the arc of her body soothing in its calm posture. Her eyes, curious and intent, asked the question without her saying a word.

"I had to leave," Blue said, and she fell to the ground.

Therese waved to one of the women, and she brought Blue a cup of water.

"Go on. Drink it," Ishema said.

Therese led them into her hut where the shades were drawn, the walls covered with floral tapestries. "You shouldn't have come here. You're dangerous to us now. You'll get us killed."

"Sit," Ishema said, pointing to the bed.

Therese opened a sea chest in the corner of the room and dropped a pile of men's clothes on the floor in front of Blue. "We can't hide you. You have to leave here," she said. "Change."

Blue took off her shirt and unwound the bandage around her

waist. The pillowcase of gold coins fell to the floor in a dull thud. A handful of gold coins spilled onto the floor.

"What's this?" Therese asked.

"It's all I have," Blue told her. Naked before Therese, she felt exposed beyond the fact of her skin.

"He'll kill you if he finds you," Therese told her.

Blue let Ishema help her wash, not bothering to cover herself. "You've changed," Ishema said, lifting Blue's arm to wash her armpit. Blue stood compliant as a child. "You've grown hard, barely any hips at all. You'll pass easy in these clothes." Ishema wrapped a blanket around Blue and pushed her into a chair. She took care of Blue like she had when Blue lost the baby. Blue wanted her to stop and not to stop. She wanted to get off the island and feel safe again, but she felt safe in the care of these women, who knew how to take care of themselves and didn't need anyone to tell them how to live.

With Therese's unflinching gaze upon her, Blue dropped the blanket and pulled on a pair of brown twill trousers and fastened them at the waist.

Ishema unwound a skein of cotton webbing.

"You hold it tight right here," she said, and pressed the end beneath Blue's armpit. Blue obeyed while she wrapped the bandage around her back several times to flatten her already small breasts so that the expanse of her chest and sternum, ribs and abdomen appeared as male as her trousers. She stuck her fingers beneath the cotton and tried to loosen it to make it more comfortable, but Ishema had wrapped her in tight.

"Stop fiddling. You have to get used to it," Ishema said.

Blue pulled a white undershirt over her head and tucked

it into the waist of her pants. She ran her hands over her flat breasts, feeling the folds of the bandage. She wore a linen shirt buttoned up the front, leather suspenders and a brown frock coat that didn't match the trousers but was close enough. With each piece of clothing, she felt some part of herself fall away. She'd worn men's clothes aboard the *Alice K*, but even with her rough manners and swinging stride, she'd never thought of herself as anything but a woman. This man taking shape before her eyes had never occurred to her.

Ishema trimmed her short hair over her ears and in the back with a straight line of bangs in the front.

"Now shake my hand," Ishema said.

Blue took Ishema's hand in her own and made a handshake.

"Firmer," Ishema told her, "like a man."

Blue grasped her hand with a tight hold and gave a stiff shake.

"That's it. Now walk across this room, with purpose. Think of men you've seen on deck."

Blue followed orders. She walked, sat with her legs apart, spat on the floor, and gulped her water like a sailor, her hand around the glass as if she was about to throw it across the room.

"You're a natural," Therese said. "Ishema will take you to the harbor, find you passage north."

Blue studied herself in the glass, dazed by her new identity. Her short hair accentuated the hard lines of her face, carved from weight loss and work. The tailored cut of the frock coat along her sides showed the sinewy strength of a man bristling with restless energy.

"Carry yourself well," Therese said. "Be a man."

Ishema gave her a canvas bag for her gold, with some bread,

chicken, and papaya. "Take this," she said. "Don't be stupid. Trust no one."

Blue followed Ishema along the dirt road into town and listened to her instructions. "Find your man's voice, a lower voice. Watch how they move, how they talk. You'll fit in." Ishema looked around at the fruit stalls as she spoke. She bought pineapple from a vendor near the dock and then left Blue on a bench with the fruit and her bag of gold coins. "You stay here. I'll be back."

Blue watched a group of men talking in front of the outfitter shop. One smoked a pipe with his hand cupped around the bowl and his eyes on the business of the harbor. Another blew his nose into his hand and wiped it on his pants, while he watched a round-bottomed woman walk away from the dock. He took no trouble to hide his interest. The man next to him stuck an elbow in his ribs, and they all snickered; to Blue, they were no different than the pirates.

When Ishema returned, she held a packet of papers out to Blue. "You go on that one, north, away from here. You don't look back to this place. You forget about us."

The only way to thank Ishema was to follow her instructions. Blue walked toward the ship, the *Cynthia Rose.* At the sight of a crewman checking passenger tickets, she hesitated. She had no gun, no machete, nothing to protect herself. The crewman was young, like Johnson, but rosy-cheeked and doughy with an extra puff of chin and a jacket that strained its buttons over his belly. Blue assumed an attitude of impatience; she took on something of her threatening glare. The young man looked over her ticket quickly and stepped aside to let her onto the ship.

Blue stood by aft cabin and searched the docks for Ishema, but she was gone.

The *Cynthia Rose* left that afternoon. Ishema had registered Blue as William Pike of Portland, Maine, an importer and exporter of coffee, spices, and healing remedies from the islands, trading primarily out of Portland and New Bedford. Her small starboard cabin held a bunk, a small washbasin, a sea chest with a lock, and a single cabinet. She dumped the gold into the sea chest, locked it, and put the key in the bottom of her boot. The whitewashed woodwork was speckled with mildew, the oiled floorboards worn smooth from passengers who'd come before. She let herself drop onto the bunk, and she slept as if she'd been taken out of time.

When Blue woke foggy and parched, she rolled onto her feet and felt the sweltering heat in her cabin. She put on her frock coat and went up on deck for air. The island of Jamaica was no longer visible, nor any land at all. At a water bucket near the aft cabin, she took a drink. The captain, John Otis, stood by the wheel. He was nearly six feet tall with a square head and pockmarked cheeks livid red. He wore a light blue captain's uniform with red piping, silver buttons that reflected the sun in kaleidoscopic patterns.

Blue tried to avoid him by ducking behind a bulwark, but when he finished giving orders to the first mate, he made a point to introduce himself. What if her voice gave her away, or some reluctance in her demeanor? With him standing in front of her, it was too late to worry. She gave him a firm handshake and answered his questions about her business in as few words as she could conceive. He was interested in her experiences on the island and spoke to her with a respect that she hadn't experienced from a man before. *If he knew I was a woman, he wouldn't say a word to me, but in men's clothes I've got an opinion worth hearing.* She found a nerve in her man's voice, deeper and lower, and took great pleasure in lying to him about her buying trip and her eagerness to return to her family. Her wonderful wife, Rosemary, mother to their four children, would be waiting with dinner laid out, the children fed and gone to bed. Rosemary was lovely, in both manner and attractiveness. "And she knows how to spend my money," Blue said. Part of her longed for Rosemary right then, for the smell of roast chicken and a table set by the fire, the rustlings of children in their beds and a quiet house. A safe life that would elude her until the day she died.

"You're a lucky man," the captain said. "My wife died of fever some years ago. I've learned that a seaman's life is no life for a lady."

"That's true, Captain, and women are bad luck on ships, after all. But you must miss her."

"I have women," he said.

At rest in the berth Therese had purchased, Blue tried to consider Therese's generosity as a sign of something good about herself, but the woman's kindness did nothing to penetrate her desolation. She couldn't shake herself loose from the knowledge of her life aboard the *Alice K.* The farther she traveled from Jamaica, the more she felt the horror of all that she'd seen and done, as if the safety of distance allowed her to look more closely.

She stayed in her cabin most days. Even dressed in a man's

attire, she was still herself. She'd constructed William Pike with
such little effort and time, she worried she'd be found out.
The swagger came easily and felt natural enough. Had trying
to survive onboard the *Alice K*, living among those men, made
her one of them? The comfortable men's clothing was a relief,
no stays or corsets. Not that she'd adhered to that over the
past years. Nonetheless, strutting about in trousers and a frock
coat suited her. William Pike had been waiting for her to step
into those very trousers, button this linen shirt and pull on his
collar. She discovered in William Pike a hidden part of herself,
and only by practice and circumstance had he risen to see the
light of day.

One evening, she was invited to join Captain Otis in his quarters for a drink. They sat in cushioned chairs and drank brandy
from crystal glasses. Blue imitated the way the captain sniffed
his liquor before he sipped, unlike the pirates who gulped from
a tin cup. Blue realized that she'd have to remember at least a
hint of the refinement of manners from her early life if she was
to fit into regular society.

The captain's quarters had the curved shape of the ship's
stern and were painted a deep green, slightly faded, which gave
the room a rough feel. A row of daguerreotypes, likely family
members, decorated one wall. Lantern light cast the room in an
amber glow. The captain leaned back in his chair, swirling the
liquor in his glass and staring at Blue. She sat, legs spread, feet
square on the floor, and eased back into her chair.

Captain Otis looked her over, from her surly expression to her well-polished boots. "I've been told you've built trade relationships among the Jamaicans. That's part of your success, I suppose."

"Treating them fairly, like equals, has earned their trust."

"That's difficult for many businessmen."

"True, they want something for nothing." The lies came easily. William Pike spoke with authority.

"Do you do business with the same people on each of your trips?"

"I typically purchase the same goods, so yes."

"It's hard to imagine them as businessmen."

"And women."

"Really?"

Blue glanced toward the navigation table where brass instruments lay scattered across a chart. She ran her hand along her jaw, as if bored by his conversation, and scratched an imaginary beard. Her skin was weathered and too tanned for him to notice that she didn't have a beard.

When she took her leave, John Otis shook her hand, and wished her well on her voyage. "You'll be home soon enough," he said. "Your wife needn't worry. You're safe aboard the *Cynthia Rose*."

The captain believed in William Pike. Blue stood at the stern rail. She wished her past could drift away in the foamy wake left in the ship's path. William Pike turned from the rail and strode toward the cabin, his boots steady against the deck.

"Evening, Mr. Pike," a crewmen called after him, but he ignored the voice. He was William Pike, and everyone knew it. Now, he knew it, too.

16

THE NEXT MORNING, WHEN BILLY BEGAN TO RUSTLE around in the loft, Hannah called up to him, "Looks like a good one today. You might want to get yourself up and moving before you waste the whole day."

"Methinks me needs a bath," he said.

"About time," Hannah said.

"You're still angry, aren't you?" Billy asked, climbing down the ladder and landing with a heavy thud in the middle of the room.

"Why should I be? You can't make me angry, Billy, I hardly know you."

"You know me as good as anyone and you're mad 'cause you know I'm right. You wouldn't be doing your rescues if your husband was here."

Hannah stood and faced him with her shoulders squared. "John and I were partners in all things. But you could never know that. If he saw me handle that boat in the surf, he'd want me out there." She lied, because it was none of his business and she couldn't stand the smug expression on his face. "We'd be partners in the truest sense of the word, sharing all the responsibilities of this place."

"And he'd help with the house chores, the sewing and

laundry?" He wasn't malicious, only curious and perhaps trying to make a point she didn't want to admit.

Hannah could no more picture John sewing than she could picture herself killing a chicken, but she lied, "Sewing's no different than repairing sails on a ship, and John's done plenty of that. But men are men, after all," she conceded, "and there's only so much they can tolerate from a woman. It's almost like it hurt his pride for me to do real work. He felt it was his duty to protect me from that, and there was something about my ability to do his work that could make him feel weak, as if he was supposed to be stronger than me, and if he wasn't, well then we at least have to keep up appearances."

Billy nodded as he poured water from the bucket into the washbasin to clean his face. Unlike John, Billy didn't rush through his chores. He took his time to enjoy the feel of the water under his fingers. No slamming and rushing around like John. It interested her how men could be so different. She'd only lived with her father and John, and they were more alike in their habits. Billy was different with his baggy shirt hanging from his shoulders and his skinny ankles poking out the bottom of his trousers.

At that moment, Hannah felt the urge to reach out and touch his shoulder, as if to say, all is okay between us, but instead, she said, "I'll be out in the barn for a while. If you want to bathe, you know where the tub is."

In the barn, Hannah ducked beneath the lifeline Billy had rigged from the loft to the far corner where the wall met the floor. She had to credit his ingenuity. Standing over John's workbench, she looked at the confusion of hammers, screwdrivers, and planes. She poked through the disarray until she found a heavy hammer with a comfortable wooden grip, shaped by John's thick, square hand, and a fistful of long nails and two strips of wood for repairing any cracks in the existing fence. Fully armed, Hannah stepped outside into the chilling air. The open blisters on her hands still burned from her foray into the storm. She needed gloves if she was going to work on the fences, and so she dropped her gear into the wheelbarrow on her way back into the house.

Hannah swung through the door and saw Billy standing near the kitchen sink, his white linen shirt tucked into his pant waist and hanging down like a skirt so that his naked torso was revealed as he bathed over the basin. Hannah wanted to see what he did when he thought he was alone, but her eyes focused on the steam rising from the washbasin. A washcloth was draped neatly over the metal rim, and he picked it up, ran it along his arm slowly as if letting the warmth seep into his bones. The kitchen windows cast squares of light that fell onto the floor just before Billy's feet, which were bare and white as paper, the bones protruding beneath the skin like branches. His trousers reached his anklebone, which stuck out like a knot in a tree. He was rooted to this earth and solid. She wanted to reach out and touch him, but she remained still, as her eyes moved up his legs, to his thin torso, tapered to his waist. She stepped back to take in the length of him, as if there was some way to understand his curve of waist. Then he turned slowly toward her to reveal his upper body, the firm set of his shoulders, and his flat stomach, and there, right there, two small breasts.

Hannah searched his face, searched as if to find him beneath this woman, but he *was* this woman.

Billy met her gaze. Staring into the level depths of his eyes, the gray-blue clouds of them, Hannah tried to understand what she was seeing before her. She wanted to speak but found no words.

She stepped closer, as if to see more clearly. "Who are you?"

Billy didn't answer, but he didn't look away. His eyes held Hannah like two gentle hands.

"You've been living in my house pretending to be a man," Hannah stammered. She thought of the bandages wrapped around his chest, the muscles in his arms, and his sailor's swagger. She tried to match the man she knew as Billy with this woman standing before her. Billy with breasts, but more than that, the slight curve of hips, the sad, tender look in his eyes that gave him an allure she wanted to deny. He'd never told her anything about his past. It terrified her that she could be so naive as to let someone like him into her house.

She turned away and went to the kitchen counter where she could look out the windows over the ocean. She'd always thought she would stand here with John, that her life would be spent with him watching over the coast. Now this man had intruded on her safety with his strangeness.

"Hannah," he said.

The woman who was Billy stepped toward her, but she avoided him. "Quiet! Just be quiet! What kind of person are you? I trusted you. You *let* me trust you." She nearly spat the words and then turned from him. Her anger got away from her like a skiff let loose in a hurricane, and it shamed her. But who was she to be ashamed with this stranger in her house? When she spoke, her voice was softer and revealed her hurt in a way that pierced Billy. "Why? I want to know why."

Billy stepped toward her, but she turned her back to him.

"I want you to leave," Hannah said. "Get out."

"Where do you want me to go?"

She turned to face him now. "Just get away from me! Get out of my house!"

He didn't gather his sketchbook or clothes from the loft, no food or extra socks. When the door closed behind him, Hannah fell into a chair at the dining table. The sky hung low over the yard, heavy with oncoming rain. She wouldn't cry. Not after his lies. She found her gloves and stepped outside, the cold like a hard slap across her face. How could she have been so wrong? Her foolishness drove her outside to sit on the edge of the porch, her head in her hands, and her gloves soaked with tears.

17

~~~~~~~~~~

HANNAH TRIED TO CONVINCE HERSELF THAT IF SHE could fix the fence, she could hold back her anger. How could she not have seen that those small hands were a woman's? Two hours since she'd seen Billy naked, and with each swing of the hammer toward the post, Hannah ticked through the deceptions. The bandage around Billy's chest was not treatment for broken ribs, but a disguise to flatten small breasts. *Breasts!* She spit like a man and worked like a man, but Billy was a *she*. Her muscles roped beneath her skin, as if her blood was thicker or pumped harder.

The most Hannah was able to learn about Billy she learned working alongside her, watching her throw herself into a task until she exhausted her energy, or the way she worked and reworked her drawings for the rig. Yet, behind Billy's swagger something softer lingered. Hannah recognized it in the careful way she watched out for her during the rescues, and in the portrait she'd drawn with Hannah's hair wild around her face, her sorrow palpable on the page. It had startled her in its intimacy. *No man could know me like that.* Still, she had not recognized Billy as a woman. How could she know? She recalled the way Billy stumbled around the room when she first woke on the hearth, as if land was an unsteady thing. Then later how she'd swaggered along the beach like she owned it, like she'd earned it and deserved it. But there had been a quality to Billy's listening, a kind of presence that had startled her in its affinity.

Hannah's anger took charge of the hammer, driving iron nails into the post where the fence had splintered. Nothing would hold it together now, but still she pounded until the wood collapsed. There were so many times Billy could've told her the truth. When she'd first woken in her living room. Hannah had saved her life after all. Didn't she deserve the courtesy of knowing who this person really was? Or when Billy decided to stay on, what about then? Billy was a liar and a sneak. Hannah couldn't trust her or anything she said. Hannah sat on the ground and swung the hammer into the frozen earth again and again, bombarding the dirt with her rage and a sadness she didn't want to claim.

Hannah leaned against the fence post, the hammer dangling from one hand, the weight of it an anchor against an endless sky that could have swept her up with the sheer force of everything she didn't know.

Billy stayed away for four days, then one morning she appeared in the doorway like an apparition. Hannah was sorting through clothing she'd tossed onto the chair by the front door. Inside the windowpanes, crystals of ice froze the glass. She didn't want to look at Billy, yet an ocean swell of feeling rose within her.

"You might as well come in," she said.

Hannah led them into the kitchen where Billy took a seat at the table and waited for Hannah to speak. She moved crumbs back and forth with the edge of a spoon. The dishrag in Hannah's hand surprised her each time she folded it. Over and again, she folded it. If she had any sense at all, she wouldn't have let Billy in. She would demand that she leave. But she couldn't speak. She needed Billy if she wanted to keep the lighthouse and the rescues going. The past four days had been long and burdensome, with barn chores and repairs piling up on top of her lighthouse duties. Yet, she'd let herself get attached to someone who was untrustworthy, a liar.

"I don't know anything about you," Hannah said finally, pushing the hair from her eyes, oceanic now with emotion. "You have to explain this to me. You can't pretend to be one thing and turn out to be another." She wound the dishrag around her hands, then threw it down in the center of the table. "You've been living in my house."

"It was the only way—"

"No, it wasn't. That's no excuse for not telling me. You lied to me!" Hannah paced back and forth by the table.

"You have to let me explain," Billy said. She stood from the table and shoved her chair in. "I signed on to the *Cynthia Rose* as William Pike for my own safety."

"I saved your life! I deserve the truth. You could've told me at any time." She tried to keep her voice down. She spun from Billy to face the fireplace. Arms across her chest, she stared into the ashes.

"I'm telling you now, Hannah." When Billy stepped toward her, she moved away, as if she was being chased.

"What kind of a person does this? Do you think you're a man? Is that what you want?"

Billy stood before her like a wall, refusing to give in to her rage. "No, that's not what I want. I had to do this, Hannah. Now it's just easier."

"Easier for who? For you? What did you suppose I would think?"

Billy leaned back against the wall and watched Hannah drop herself into the chair by the table. The wind outside shivered in the windows. It was time to get a fire going.

"I need to trust you, but you've hidden yourself all this time. You've made me and everyone else believe you were William Pike."

"It's still me, Hannah."

"But you're not who I thought you were. You're a stranger to me now. What am I supposed to think?" She wanted Tom to walk in the door with his familiar ease and set things right. He'd know what to do. But she didn't want to admit her failure. Was the Billy who'd drawn her likeness a fake? Did he pretend his intimacy and care for her?

Hannah couldn't take her eyes from the place where Billy flattened her small breasts with a cotton wrap. She couldn't forget the thin torso curved down into the hard lines of a female waist. A woman's body with a man's demeanor that was in part natural and in part practiced until it got down into her and became her. The woman was barely detectable beneath the sailor's swagger. What had seemed a man's silent reserve was in fact a woman's desire not to be known.

"I don't understand why you continue with this disguise. Is it your preference?"

"I became William Pike for my own safety. Now it just feels

more like myself. If I could live as a woman dressed like this, without having to be a wife or a servant or a whore, I would, but the world isn't like that, Hannah."

"You weren't afraid of being found out?"

"At first I was, but once I passed with the men on the ship, I got comfortable. I'm not the first, you know. There're other women who do what they have to do to get by. I met a woman who dressed as a man to sign on to a whaler."

"I can't imagine that."

"Well, it's true."

"Still, you've lied to me. You've met people, Tom, Everett, the others." Hannah shook her hands by her head as if to clarify her thoughts. "It would've been easier if you'd arrived as a woman to avoid the gossip of my taking in a strange man. So what do we do now?"

"I'll continue to live as William Pike, your workman. This is who I am now, Hannah. I can't go back."

"What's your real name?"

"It's Blue."

"I'll call you Billy."

No matter what Hannah was doing—washing the dishes, fetching eggs from the coop, climbing the lighthouse stairs—she wondered how Billy had trained herself into that swagger, those rough manners and muscled arms. What was Billy and what was the disguise? Standing on the front porch, she watched Billy carry the toolbox toward the far fence, holding it out to one side with her elbow flexed, using the strength of her arm like a man. Hannah had come to rely on Billy's strength, on her hard work and companionship.

She wanted to trust her again, this stranger moving through her house with the same smells and bad habits. Nothing in her demeanor had changed. Not the way she cleaned her fingernails with her knife when she thought Hannah couldn't see her, nor the way she poked at the fire with a piece of kindling.

One night, as they sat in front of the fire, Hannah stared hard at Billy, about to say something, but she stopped herself.

"Just say it," Billy said.

"Why? I just don't understand why."

"I'm still the same person, Hannah."

Her gaze lost in the orange and yellow glow of the fire, Hannah tried to understand who Billy was as a woman, who she was as the man Billy, and who she was now, this tangled combination of both. She didn't know if it mattered. She was still the Billy who'd created the lifesaving rig, the Billy she'd pulled from the water. Billy had helped her recover after the little girl drowned. She worked hard around the lighthouse and looked out for Hannah during the storms. Had she really done anything wrong? Yes, she'd lied. Still, Billy was this person sitting beside her, the same person who'd been sitting beside her for months now.

"We need to work on the lifesaving rig," Billy said. "How long before we can test it on the water?"

"How do you propose we do that?" She held Billy's gaze.

"You'll anchor the old skiff offshore, then come in and run the line out to it. Even though there's no mast, we can test the system for running the rig back and forth over the water."

"If that works, we'll have to take our chances and use it on a rescue. There's no further way to test it," Hannah said. She stared into the fire, calm now and filled with thoughts of the lifesaving rig stretched over the water, running men from ship to shore while Billy maneuvered the ropes.

The next morning, Hannah stormed the kitchen, her skirt flapping around long johns, jacket flailing around her body as if trying to get hold. Water ran down the drainpipes from the gutters, and rain pelted Billy as she rubbed at her eyes to wake herself up. "You can't go out in this. We have to wait until it blows over."

"It's not going to blow over. Hurry up."

Hannah waited by the door, checking the length of wick on the lantern. Billy stepped into a pair of damp trousers and scurried down the ladder from the loft. She stuffed a hunk of cheese into her pocket and drank from the remains of Hannah's coffee. With one arm through the life ring, she carried it over her shoulder like a different kind of woman might carry a purse.

Outside, the violence of the rain silenced them. Hannah signaled Billy with a nod of her head, *this way*, or a flick of her hand, *over there*. Billy followed Hannah down the swaying staircase, matching each footstep one to the other so that she didn't slip on the small treads and fall to the beach below. The wind against the stairs terrified Billy. Rain ran down her jacket, chilling her through the oilskin. Hannah glided down the stairs as if there was no cold, no rain. She sailed on the wind, her skirt ballooning beneath her jacket.

On the beach, wet sand sucked at Billy's feet, and the weight of the life ring on her shoulder made walking strenuous. They patrolled to the north, heads down against the wind and rain. Billy scanned the waves for unfamiliar flecks of color, anything that should not be there, then her eyes drifted down to the beach where Hannah had pulled her from the wreck of the *Cynthia Rose*. Why was she following Hannah through the rain?

"We're not going to find anything," Billy said.

"You don't know that."

A black wooden doll floated in on the wash. It stared out with startled white eyes, a yellow gash of a mouth, and red brush strokes of hair. Billy had seen dolls like this one. Ishema had put one on the shelf by her bed. The Jamaican children carried these dolls like totems. Women sold them in the streets and on the docks to travelers.

"What's that?" Hannah asked, stepping toward her, her breath hot, cheeks flushed with exercise. "Some kind of doll?"

Billy nodded.

"We ought to go out and take a look around, don't you think?" Hannah waded in to pluck the doll from the surf. She scanned the surfboat where Billy had organized the ropes and the life ring. "C'mon, what are you waiting for?"

They pushed the surfboat into the breakers, and Billy rowed them out past the surf to deep water. The sky smoldered. Billy matched the rhythm of the oars with the rise and fall of the boat. When the bow rose too high, she lifted herself up to avoid the shock of slamming down.

"Keep your eye out," Hannah said.

A cluster of seagulls rose from the distance and dove near the boat, squawking like hungry children. There was the faintest snap of tattered sails. She held the oars still for a moment. The sounds of the wreck of the *Cynthia Rose* swam through her, the men crying out as they leapt into the water, and her holding on to the creaking mast so that she didn't get swept into the cold. Then she'd found herself in the water all the same.

Hannah slapped her on the leg. "Look alive. You want to do rescues, you have to stay alert."

"There's something over there!" Billy pointed to the small brig with its decks tilted at a steep incline and the bottom rail underwater. Several men stood on the high rail waving, one of them holding a small child, a Negro girl in a pale blue shift who clung to the man like an animal. Surf battered the windward side of the boat. A wall of water splashed the rail and soaked the men who hunched against the cold. Sails fluttered overhead, shredded and regretful. As they rowed closer, the hull took on greater proportions, its size exaggerated by the strange angle it formed against the sea, like an iceberg with most of its bulk underwater.

"Bring us alongside, but not close enough for them to climb aboard. They'll swamp us," Hannah shouted, making sure the lifeline was available to run free and clear.

"Hallo! Over here! We're saved!" one of the men shouted in desperation and relief.

Hannah surveyed the group of people, noting their size and weight and shape, their physical condition. The mast tilted over waves that sloshed the ship's remains as the men braced their feet against the bulwark for balance. Billy scanned the crew for reasons of her own, her head down but her eyes furtive, always alert.

Hannah yelled through her cupped hands. "Listen, all you there! We've only room for four or five at a time," Hannah said. "We'll come back for the last of you."

"Drag us behind the boat," a thin, shivering man hollered. "I'll gladly be dragged through the water than left to sink on this barge."

"You can't. You'll freeze," Hannah said.

The man raised his arms up and shouted louder now, using his entire body to propel his voice across the water. "I'll take my chances. I'll not lose my life to this ship. I'd rather drown a different way if I'm to drown at all."

"Who's the captain here?" Hannah called. Billy held the oars steady, and understanding that there was some order to Hannah's line of reasoning, she let Hannah lead the rescue.

"He's drowned."

"All right then. You'll listen to me and obey my command, or you'll be left behind. We'll take one aboard at a time as long as we stay afloat. The rest of you we'll drag on a line with the life ring. You first, sir, you with the child. Sit right in front there."

The man clambered down off the rail, leaving the girl to drop herself into the bow of the boat where she scrambled and tucked her small body into the curve of the stem. The man took the seat Hannah indicated and watched as the second man climbed down and sat beside him. "We're floating good," Hannah said, "you two next." She waved her arms to hurry them across. The short, bearded man nearly leapt into the air and landed in the stern seat, followed by another seemingly identical sailor. The last man Hannah chose was a young sailor who looked malnourished and blue around the lips. "You, come on. You two who are last, wait there while I set the lines," and she fastened the life line off the transom so the life ring floated not more than thirty feet aft of them.

Billy noted that she'd chosen the two sturdiest men to ride in the water, figuring they had the best chances of surviving. "I want the bigger of you to lie across the top of the ring, and then the next one to lie across him. That way you won't be directly in the water." Hannah held the life ring where the first sailor could lay himself across, and once the two were situated awkwardly upon their makeshift raft, she set them adrift behind the surfboat.

"Are you sure you're the only survivors? Have you checked belowdecks?"

The survivors nodded. As the wreck tilted in the waves, the ship's bell clanged.

"They've perished, the lot of them," a young fellow said, his voice so despondent that Hannah took him at his word. She sat on the seat beside Billy. "It'll take both of us pulling on the oars," she said, and Billy nodded and they set themselves to rowing. With the weight of the men, the boat sat lower in the water, and they had to work harder to make headway. They each worked an oar, matching their motion one to the other, shoulders pressing into each other, breathing synchronized. The closer they drew to shore, the more the riptide dragged the boat north of the lighthouse. The men remained quiet, shifting and grunting, whispering and pointing.

"Will we make it?" one of the men cried out.

"We gotta keep rowing through it."

Hannah and Billy didn't speak but moved in unison, bodies pressed hard against each other on the small seat, inhaling as they pushed the oars forward, exhaling as they pulled back. The men and the child sat quietly, turning to spy the lighthouse then casting their glances down to empty, puckered hands. Their breath cast clouds that drifted over their heads. There was no talking now, just the sound of the oars in the water and the heavy breathing of Hannah and Billy as they rowed. From their perch amidships, they watched the two sailors in the water on the life ring; they waved every so often to signal their well-being.

Billy knew they cleared the riptide when the thunder of waves on the beach reached her, and they rowed south again. Near the lighthouse, the men looked to Hannah to give word before they climbed out of the boat and hurried ashore. They hovered in a tight group by the base of the stairs as if no amount of land would ever be enough. Hannah and Billy pulled in the lifeline and the last two men stumbled onto the beach shivering with cold. The young girl stood in the center of the men, her thin arms at her sides, while Hannah and Billy coiled the lines and hauled the surfboat back to the dunes. The men watched and waited, uncertain of what they were waiting for beyond some signal that they should move from their huddled position. With no words, Hannah led them up the stairs and they followed one at a time, each waiting for the next and pulling themselves up on the railing when the strength of their legs couldn't match the task. Billy lifted the small girl onto her back and carried her. "You're okay," she said, but the girl said nothing.

The men skulked into the house like a pack of animals. The tall-est among them had been the one to ride in the bottom of the life ring against the water. His lips were blue, his jaw hammering with cold as he removed his jacket and stood by the fire. The rest followed suit, looking into each other's faces for confirma-tion of their survival. How lucky they were to be in this good woman's house. In spite of their bruises and scrapes and the gash over one man's eye, they couldn't believe their luck. They were almost afraid to speak for fear of breaking their lucky streak, or so it appeared to Billy as she stoked the fire and pointed to a set of hooks where the men could hang their coats to dry.

The little girl sat on the floor against the hearth, her long limbs like crooked branches knobbed at the knees and elbows, eyes pegged on one of the sailors, fat enough to bust his jacket, his red, puffy face frothing with cold and rage.

"What are you staring at, girl?" he said, loosening the buttons at the collar.

She leaned one shoulder forward as if to protect herself, her brown eyes cast down. She looked so slight and stricken.

The doll jabbed Billy from where it was stuffed in the waist of her pants, and she held it out, but the girl only stared at it. "Is this yours?" Billy said. The girl reached for the doll and clutched it in her fist.

"Me go on drop now," she said quietly. "Mi neva been so col."

Hannah watched Billy navigate the room with ease, com-fortable among the sailors as she handed out blankets and stuck the bellows into the fire. When Billy stood up, the candlelight cast the hollows of her cheeks in shadow and reflected in her gray eyes. Hannah was drawn to her then, to her gentle voice and lithe body moving gently among the sailors, as if any abrupt motion would only traumatize them further. Billy understood the men's distress firsthand. At the stove, she poured hot tea into cups and instructed the girl to set them on the table, but the girl shook her head no. Tears trailed down her salt-crusted cheeks.

The man who'd carried the girl from the wreck rubbed the sphere of his belly and belched into the room. "Where's the privy at? Eh?"

"Round back," Hannah said.

The men hung about the fire, exhausted and spent, sitting on the floor with knees drawn up, bare feet blue from the cold. Those with boots pulled them off to dry on the hot bricks. One of the older sailors banged on a younger crew member's chest as he coughed, then moved on to wrap a cut hand in a makeshift bandage until Hannah came with her medicine box and settled herself among them. Those who complained she tended to first. A bandage, a splint, alcohol poured across a wound to prevent infection. It was not the time to hold back on adding a shot of whiskey to the coffee, and she left the bottle on the counter for any one of them to take a shot. Right there on the counter. Light through the bottle cast an amber shadow that Billy could taste, but she ignored it as she poured drams to warm the sailors.

Hannah passed blankets around to the men and brought the bag of hand-me-down clothes. The men sorted through the clothes for something dry to wear. Their noises stirred the room, the quiet and thankful murmuring after a rescue, all these strangers amazed at their survival, obvious in their cohesion as a crew. With the exception of miscreant sailor, they were comfortable in the proximity of each other's bodies as they huddled together and tried to find an easy position on the floor.

Billy had moved to the kitchen and was adding potatoes and carrots to a large pot of chicken soup, stretching the meal for two into one large meal for six men, a child, and themselves, until Tom showed up with a chicken, two loaves of bread, butter, and bourbon in a large basket. Hannah welcomed him with his supplies and his flashing green eyes, and Billy put him to work cutting the chicken into small pieces.

The men broke bits of bread and dunked it into the broth. They ate noisily. They didn't seem to notice anything different about Billy. She was a man among men, and they accepted her. Hannah watched Billy as she spoke to one of the sailors about the wreck, leaning into the man with an intimacy only men shared. "Many's lost," the man said. "Can't even count 'em all yet."

"You're here. That's all that matters," Tom said.

"I never been so afraid. Like a little girl. I woulda cried for my mother if I thought there was a chance in hell she'd come to save me."

"There's no shame in it," Billy said. "You were waiting to die. Fear like that, it's natural."

"I'll never get over it."

"Have some soup," Tom said. "Get yourself warmed up."

The girl clutched the doll in one hand. She held her lips together and shook her head, refusing food. "See him dea? Look pon dat man how im pack up im mout when im a nyam." The girl indicated the fat man who had been holding on to her at the wreck, telling Billy that he packed his mouth full when he was eating.

"You think I don't understand that darkie voodoo horse-shit?" the man said, soup spilling from his mouth down his rotund belly.

Tom stood from the table and hovered over the man.

"You will not talk like that in this house," Hannah said, her voice like a hammer thrown down. "What is your name?" she asked the girl.

"Mesha," the girl said.

"You come sit here next to me. No one will bother you here. Not while they are in my house."

Tom sat, his fists clenched. Billy did not take her eyes from the man, and when he met her gaze, she saw his wickedness exposed like the bottom of a board pulled from the dirt, rotten with wormholes and nothing good left to build on. This man was ruin itself. He watched her leave the table, eyeing her face, her hands. She felt his eyes on her back as she placed her bowl in the sink. He'd saved the girl, probably because he owned her. Less feeling for her than for that silver buckle on his belt, which he was about to lose. She'd see to that.

18

BILLY WOKE WITH A START, KICKED IN THE HEAD BY bad dreams and a flash of anger hot enough to remind her where she'd been in this world. The lighthouse beam swooped over the room. She was here in Dangerfield now, but the shipwrecked men's snores and coughing, their mutterings in sleep brought Billy belowdecks on the *Alice K*. She strode into the living room as if across a ship's deck and kicked the fat man awake. In his sleep and confusion he swatted her away. She kicked him harder and he scrambled to his feet. "What the—?"

"Get up, follow me," Billy said, stabbing words that held the command of her rage. She shoved him toward the passageway that led to the barn and closed the door behind them so that no one would hear. "You're a coward. I should kill you."

The man's eyes, watery and red, stared out at her, not comprehending what he'd done to upset her. "But you just rescued me. What do you want to kill me for?"

"You took that Jamaican girl from her family. You took her from where she belonged."

"For good money," he said.

Billy caught her breath and reconsidered her line of reasoning. "What did she cost you? Tell me!" When the man hesitated,

Billy punched him in the stomach so that he fell onto his knees, doubled over. "You were going to use her for yourself."

Billy kicked him, throwing him back on the floor. Blood ran from his nose. "I could kill you! Go on. Get up, you worthless dog. Get out of here! You're a pig." She spat the words at him like bullets.

"Where will I go? I've no money. I've lost everything 'cept what I got in the house," he said, wiping the snot and blood from his nose with his filthy hand.

"Get up, get out. Now! Follow the road and I'll spare your life."

He stared into her blue eyes with a familiarity she wanted to smack off his face. Who did he think he was looking at her like that?

"I know who you are, that lady pirate! There's a bounty on your head. They'll hang you when I come back for you, me and the men you've robbed! You think you can escape what you've done? You think you save a few poor sods and you're free? You'll never be free. You'll always be looking over your shoulder, wondering when or where that one knowing face has come to claim you. Then it will be over and I hope I'm there to see the day, you sanctimonious, no-good—"

The man's eyes bulged. He spat and drooled venom until Billy picked him up by his still-damp shirt collar and shoved him to the barn door. She slid it open enough for him to step through and then pushed him into a heap on the cold ground. "Get up, or I'll kill you!" Her hands trembled with the lightning force of her rage, and it took all of her strength not to unleash herself, wrap her hands around his throat, and squeeze the breath out of him.

"You think I'm the first you'll find along these shores who'll know you? You're on a major shipping lane."

"Shut up," Billy said. Maybe he was right, but she'd deal with others as she dealt with him. She could be ruthless if she had to.

The man leaned against the barn to leverage his hideous weight into a standing position and started walking in his stocking feet toward the road. Every few steps he swung his head around to see if Billy was still watching, and after a while he stopped turning and just walked.

Billy turned back toward the house and saw Hannah standing on the front porch, a blanket wrapped around her shoulder. She went back into the barn, and Hannah returned to the house, where men huddled around the fire and shifted about, hungry and adrift. Billy's violence both frightened her and put her at ease. That Billy was capable of such spitting rage on behalf of the girl. Hannah had watched her kick that man, punch him, and shove him around. Billy could've killed the man if she'd chosen to, like Tom on the beach, who'd been ready to kill to save her. She hadn't been able to hear what Billy said to the man, but he left at her command.

There were things Billy would never tell her, things she didn't need to know. Wherever Billy had been before she'd arrived at the lighthouse, whatever she'd done, she meant to undo it, that was clear.

Hannah moved among the sailors, some of whom coughed or spoke softly to one another, recounting the wreck. Their words rose like mist into the room. *Splintered like a toy boat. Nothing left to hold on to. Did you see him go under? There was men in the hold. I know it.*

One of the men pulled out a chair for her. "Here you go, missus. You set yourself down." He shivered even now in the heat of the kitchen. His hair had dried into a blond frizz, bushy eyebrows to match, and a sharp chin with barely any stubble. "Ellis here was our galley cook, and he's pretty decent, though I've never seen him at it on flat land. My name's Jody Evans."

"One of your men is missing," Hannah said, the image of him walking shoeless down the drive fresh in her mind.

"Hope that coot took a long walk off a short pier's what I hope," a man called Izzy said. He was short and squat with wild black hair and a beard to match. First thing he'd done when he came inside was take off his jacket to reveal a blouse with the sleeves ripped off and arms tattooed to the shoulders, proud as a lion. He could've been trouble anywhere else, but in the wake of a wreck and the humility of being rescued, and by a woman no less, he was tame.

"He didn't seem the type to be caring for the girl."

"If he was caring for that girl, she'd be better off drowned," Izzy said.

"Girl looked desperate the minute she came onboard," Ellis said. "She was afraid for her life. You could see it clear as day."

"I used to see her and her little brother down by the docks near Montego Bay," Jody said. "They scavenged fruit and vegetables that fell off the carts. Sometimes they dove from the pilings for coins."

"The little buggers get rich doing that. I swear."

"I doubt it."

"Still."

Their voices drifted over the room like one voice. "Her father sold soup right where our ship docked. Scrappy little guy, good for nothing. Most his teeth gone but that gold one in front."

"Where will she go now that her keeper has gone?"

"Just another cast-off nigger child."

"We'll take her with us. I'll get her sorted out, ma'am. Name is Joe." He reached a large hand across to her and shook her hand firmly but not hard enough to hurt her. "She has family, as you've heard. I came to know her aboard the *Alexandria*. I hope to ship out of Boston on a southbound ship promptly. I'll see to her transit to Montego Bay."

"You're very kind," she said, searching beyond his sincerity for any signs of ill will, but the man was warm, genuine.

"She's a good girl. She worked in the kitchen and swept the berths for the crew. She fed the small goat and the chickens they kept onboard for food, and she played with them and loved them with the reserve of a child who knows that the chickens are grown for eating."

"We owe you and your man our lives," Joe said.

Hannah was relieved. They believed that Billy was a man, as she had believed. She hadn't been so naive after all. And if they hadn't believed it, what then? Rumors and scandal that could jeopardize her position at the lighthouse.

Joe sat down across from her, his arms folded like tree branches, thick and difficult to maneuver. The bones of his face were built like a wall, and his forehead rose to a sea of dark hair.

"Quite seriously, ma'am, we owe you our lives. We would've perished out there if you hadn't come along. We want to repay you somehow, with work or money or whatever it is you want."

But she was tired and there were too many people hover-ing around her fire. She only wanted them out of her house. "That's very kind," she said. "I only want your health, and your safe journey home."

Feb 16: Winds > 30 NE, rain

Feb 17: Ship aground, Alexandria, 7 survivors, NE 10

Feb 18: Alexandria sunk, no sign left of wreck, crew to Boston, wind SW 12, two brig, one schooner

The sailors packed themselves into the wagon like chickens in a crate. Mesha sat amid their heat and comfort, an oversize wool coat fastened at her waist with her former owner's leather belt, the silver buckle glinting at her midriff. The coat sleeves frayed at the wrists, and she pulled at the loose threads with her teeth. Joe stood by the wagon and adjusted his cap in a line over his eyebrows. He shook Hannah's hand and climbed onto the seat beside Billy. He watched Hannah recede into the distance until he couldn't see her anymore. They traveled the rutted road toward the harbor. The girl whispered with one of the men and then cried halfway to the harbor, and after that it was quiet except for the wheels clamoring over rocks in the road and men coughing and spitting over the side of the wagon.

After a while, the sounds of the harbor rattled on the wind. The men moved around in the back of the wagon to get a view of the water.

"I'm de only girl," Mesha said. "Girl. Boy. Girl. Boy." She

pointed to one of the men, then herself, then another of the men, then herself, on and on, until Izzy hushed her with an arm around her shoulders. "Whe we goin? Will dey be chilren? Why me de only one?"

The sight of masts rose above the trees, then around the next corner, sails curved like wings. "The packet's docked along the back here," Billy said, guiding the horse through wagons and skiffs up on cradles and men milling about with duffel bags or standing around smoking their clay pipes.

When Billy brought the wagon to a halt, the stronger men climbed out and walked along the dock eyeing the packet. Billy introduced Joe to the packet captain, Henry Mechum, whom she had gotten to know during her visits to the harbor. As the men climbed aboard, Mesha cried furiously. She stood on the dock and held fast to a piling. "No. No. No."

The men gathered around her, cooed and cajoled her. "It's okay, miss, you've seen the worst of it."

"There's nothing wrong with being afraid," Joe said. "We all are, but we're going to get on that boat together and sail to Boston, and when we step foot on those streets we'll all feel much better because we'll know there was no reason for us to be afraid."

"I don't want to go. No." The girl cast a pleading look toward Billy, who could only turn away. She'd gotten rid of the man who'd taken Mesha from her family. There was nothing else she could do for this girl. That was what she told herself as she walked off, passing a cluster of sailors standing in front of the grocery.

"G'morning," one of them said.

Billy tipped her hat without showing her face, and the rest grunted in her direction. A flock of boys huddled over a game of marbles with the focused intent of men at the helm. Boy. Girl. Boy. Billy did not look back at the packet or listen for the girl. At the fishmonger she bought a big piece of cod, some shrimp, a strip of haddock, and a bunch of scallops. Her next stop was the bakery for bread, and then over to Millie Bragg, who worked on the cod flakes with an authority that frightened most men.

"How you doing today, Millie?"

"Same as every other day."

Billy held out a folded wad of money that Millie stuffed into her bodice between two tremendous breasts. Their soft flesh bulged against her corset and dress so that the fabric looked about ready to burst and set loose its fearsome cargo. Millie's face was full and square, her features stacked one on top of the other like rocks.

"My oldest's fourteen now and wants to go out on a whaler. Near died when he told me that. After his father, I don't think I could live with another gone to sea." She flipped the gutted cod and flung salt across the white meat and worked her way down the flake, her skirt hem shortened to keep the fabric from the mud and fish guts.

"It's hard to keep a man ashore in this town."

"Well, he's just going to have to learn something else."

"No doubt he will," Billy said, and received the bottle that Millie had strapped under her skirt, tucking it into her jacket. "I'll be seeing you."

"No doubt," she said, not looking up from the flake.

Billy sat atop the wagon, the bottle a comfort against her chest. She wanted to erase the sound of Mesha's voice from her mind. The girl was everything about Jamaica and all that came after. She reached for the bottle and took a hard swig. The rum ran down her chin and she wiped it on the back of her hand and took another drink. With the horse in motion, her mind wandered and she took the long way back to the lighthouse, around the Mill Pond and up Old County Road.

Tom landed on the porch after the men left. He congratulated her on a successful rescue and made tea for her while she sat in front of the fire. "I'm glad you had Billy to help you," he said.

"Yes," Hannah said.

"But he can't stay forever, Hannah."

Hannah drank her tea and stared into the fire. She didn't want to think about Billy leaving.

Tom placed his hand over Hannah's where it rested on the arm of her chair.

"I want us to be married, Hannah," he said. "I'll help you with the rescues if that makes a difference. My furniture business is doing well, and I've saved money. We can live here at the lighthouse, and I'll keep my house for our retirement. We can have a good life together." He got on one knee then, his face lit up by the fire, the ring he held flashing in the light.

"Hannah Snow, will you marry me?" he said. "I'll do everything in my power to make you happy."

Hannah placed her tea on the table. "Stand up," she said.

Tom remained before her on one knee. "I love you, but I can't wait any longer. I must know. Please, Hannah, be sensible."

She placed her hands on his cheeks and kissed his forehead.

"I know you love me," Tom said.

"Oh, I do, I do."

"So marry me."

"I can't."

Tom stood then, and slid the ring into his pocket. "Don't tell me it's Billy. Please don't tell me that."

"I won't marry again, Tom, regardless of the circumstances."

"Don't you see how wonderful it could be?"

"Yes, but I was married to John for many years, and I don't want another husband."

They went back and forth until Tom was utterly frustrated.

"I need to take a wife," he said. "My career, my age…if it can't be you."

"Is that a threat?"

"No." Tom hesitated. He looked down into the leather creases of his boots and brushed his palms along the thighs of his linen trousers. "I've been courting someone in Barnstable. I knew you wouldn't have me, Hannah, but I had to ask you one last time. You understand?"

Hannah stiffened. "I'm not going to ask you who. Not yet."

He sat beside her and they held hands in front of the fire for a long time before Tom took his leave.

19

THE LETTER ARRIVED THAT AFTERNOON, DELIVERED by Sam Potts on special order from Mrs. Nora Paine. "I'll need you to sign here, ma'am," the man said.

Dear Hannah,

I'm sorry to write with this news. Your husband's body has been found. Evan Pierce and his father were hunting near Dennis Pond and found John, covered in leaves beneath a lean-to of branches, where the men hide while waiting for deer. They were quite shaken and saddened to bring this news to our family, and they helped your father take John to the undertaker. We'll bury him in the family plot on Summer Street, if that's what you want. Please send word as soon as you can, and let us know when you'll arrive.

I hesitate telling you in a letter but want to spare you the misery of not knowing. John was badly beaten and showed signs of having put up a struggle: bruises on his fists, blood beneath his fingernails. A bullet wound in his stomach ended his fight. With the wagon gone, we can only assume that he was robbed on his way home, perhaps mistaken for a merchant who carried money. Of course, there's no way to know.

I'm saddened for you, dearest Hannah, and my only consolation is that you will have some peace knowing that he is properly buried among loving family.

All my love, and condolences,
Your loving mother

Hannah dropped the letter on the floor and stared out the front window toward the road, where her husband should've appeared atop his wagon all those months ago. The windowpane shivered in the wood frame. She placed her hand against the cold glass to steady it. When had she given up waiting for John? Her life had changed almost imperceptibly at first. Then day by day, week by week, she'd moved on without him.

A dull ache clenched like a fist in her chest. She went to the kitchen window and stared at a line of three ships pointing south, sails ghostlike against an ashen sky. At John's desk she opened the logbook to record the wind direction and speed she'd taken earlier. Notes made, she flipped back through the book until she reached John's careful script, so different from her own loose marks. She ran her fingers over the square letters, down rows of numbers and names of ships, to his last marks in the logbook. The emptiness she felt upon turning the page to her own notations overwhelmed her, and she sobbed. The finality was what she'd wanted, but now she wished she didn't have to know. Not knowing had allowed her to go on with always the possibility of his return.

In the bedroom, she absently gathered her clothing into a suitcase. What do you wear to your husband's funeral? Whatever she didn't have, her mother would provide for her. She went to the kitchen to wash the dishes, but each plate felt unfamiliar in her hands. Each bowl seemed to take hours to wash. She didn't notice that she was shaking, until a cup slid from her hands. Hannah left the rest of the dishes in the sink and rushed along the lighthouse passageway as if she would find John at the other end. She climbed the stairs to the lighthouse landing. This was the only place where she felt him with her. Not in Barnstable or in a cemetery or anywhere else. This had been their home, and this was where she'd said good-bye to him months ago. Saying good-bye to him again felt like an unnecessary grief. She wanted to feel the relief his body was meant to bring, but she only felt newly scathed by loss, and an emptiness around her as wide as the ocean's graveyard.

Billy reached the lighthouse by early afternoon and half the bottle was gone. The girl's voice still hung in her ears. Billy unbridled Nellie and leaned against the horse for balance as she led her to a stall. She spilled oats across the floor as she filled the bucket, then she let the horse eat a carrot from her hand. "Atta girl," Billy said, patting the horse's rump as she left the stall, waiting to hear the latch click before walking away.

She slid the box of fish from the back of the wagon and

carried it into the house. The smell recalled the early days of pregnancy when she couldn't stand any strong odors.

Billy lifted a heavy pot onto the stove and let the flames burn full blast. When she heard Hannah's boots scrape the passageway, she wiped her hands distractedly on the dishrag and bent down to hide the bottle in the cabinet beneath the sink, behind the potatoes and onions where the bottle settled itself in the corner. She closed the cabinet and stood as Hannah turned into the room.

"What's wrong?" Hannah asked.

"Nothing. Why?"

"You look scared."

Billy shook her head. Hannah's nostrils flared and her eyes widened as she smelled the liquor. "If you're going to drink, at least have the dignity not to lie." Hannah stood with her arms across her chest and stepped back from Billy. Everything about her, from the smell of liquor on her breath to her sullen expression, disgusted Hannah. She hated her then for wearing John's shirt, hated her for living and breathing in the kitchen where her husband should be. She wanted to slap her, to shake her awake. Her mother pretended not to notice her father's regular trips to the woodpile, but Hannah couldn't stand it, not for another minute.

"I want you out," she said without raising her voice. "I can't stand your lying and drinking. You told me you were done with that."

Billy walked past the chairs scattered around the dining table and felt Hannah's eyes on her. "It's just that girl, Mesha…just this once, that's all."

"I don't want to hear it. It doesn't matter to me why you're drunk. I can't trust you, and I want you out of my house." The anger Hannah felt upon saying these words startled her. How could Billy do this when Hannah had to go to her husband's funeral? Even though Billy didn't know about John yet, Hannah felt especially hurt.

"What's wrong with you?" Billy held Hannah's furious gaze and tried not to look away.

"You can leave in the morning," Hannah said.

"I can leave right now."

"Don't be foolish," Hannah said.

"So now I'm foolish? After everything I've done around here you're going to kick me out?"

"You can stay in the barn tonight. Be gone in the morning."

Billy knocked over a chair on her way out of the house. Hannah didn't bother to pick it up.

Hannah prevailed upon Tom to take care of the lighthouse while she went to Barnstable. Her family held a private, grave-side service. John's parents couldn't afford to make the journey, and so sent their sympathies along with money for a wreath. Hannah stood beneath the bare oak trees, their branches etched against a silver-gray sky as if in charcoal, and tried to connect the casket perched by the grave with the man who'd been her husband. Her father had identified John's body and discouraged her from viewing him to say good-bye. After so many months in the woods, he was no longer her husband. The wind rushed over the Paine family and stirred up the odors of moist earth, rotting leaves, and fresh-cut wood from the new casket. The minister read from his Bible, and they stood with heads bowed, but Hannah didn't hear his words. When the minister stopped talking, she was grateful for the quiet. Her father dropped a handful of dirt into the grave, but it wasn't until Hannah released dirt from her own hand onto the casket that she fully realized the extent of her loss. She started to fall onto the ground, but her father caught her by the elbow. He wrapped his arms around her until she let go a sob that shook her body.

Her parents' friends stopped by, delivering beef stews, whole chickens, vegetable casseroles, and pies. They wanted to talk with Hannah about John, what a fine man he was, how they'd searched and come up empty, and now this, by chance. They wanted to talk about what could've happened to him, like the townspeople gathered onshore after shipwreck, endlessly trying to figure out how the ship could've gone aground. Hannah tried to avoid these people with their good intentions and occasional tears. She said, "Thank you," and took her leave and nobody questioned her or thought she was rude.

Every day was like every other day—one after the next. She cried and ate the food her mother prepared from the offerings of friends. Her parents were always close. They moved around her tentatively, as if testing for injury, and she let them. Why not let them take care of her? She felt sick, worse than sick. She wanted to turn herself inside out and empty out her grief once and for all, but it lingered and broke free at unpredictable moments. One night, her mother reached across the table and placed her hand over Hannah's, and Hannah broke down. One night, she woke to the sound of her own sobbing.

The next morning, her father asked her to help with the lobster traps. They bundled up in the cold and wore gloves with the fingertips cut off so that they could mend the nets. Hannah retied the torn nets with twine and replaced broken wood slats as easily as she'd done it as a girl. She moved from one trap to the next, lost in the network of twine.

Her father worked slower, his fingers arthritic and stiff. When he went for his liquor bottle by the woodpile, Hannah ignored him.

"It's my back," he said. "I can't bend over like that for long." He sat and drank for a while without working.

The broken traps made Hannah think of the flotsam John used to gather after a storm. He often called her out to the barn to view his collection: a broken oar, a block and tackle severed in a storm, or a frayed length of rope. Garbage, she thought, but she watched his meaningful gaze and said, "You'll figure it out. You always do."

He used the block and tackle to rig the system for hauling sailors and gear up from the beach. And now Billy used a scavenged lifesaving ring for the ship-to-shore rescue device. There was a use for everything, just as John had told her. She could hear his voice as clearly as if he were speaking over her shoulder, but she kept herself from turning around. Her fingers in the net held her focus. There was no way back to a place where John existed.

The sun bore down on them through the cold. Hannah unbuttoned her coat and stretched out her fingers, relieved when her father began talking about boats bought and sold and who was bringing in the biggest catch, anything to distract her from her own thoughts.

"I don't suppose Tom told you his news, not with everything that's going on."

Hannah looked up from her work, her fingers tying a knot into the net.

"He's been courting Cassandra Wainwright."

Hannah couldn't breathe for a moment. Even though he'd warned her, she couldn't stifle her surprise. "Cassandra Wainwright? Isn't she kind of prim?"

"Seems an unlikely match, but I've heard they're seeing quite a bit of each other," her father said.

"But he just—"

"What?"

"Nothing," Hannah said, stunned.

Hannah couldn't think of what to say. She felt betrayed, even though she'd turned him down. She'd known Cassandra growing up. She was everything that Hannah was not: wealthy, conventional, and well-mannered.

"She'll be visiting Dangerfield soon. I've heard she's quite curious."

"Well, I better rescue Tom from the lighthouse. He's got business to attend to, I'm sure," Hannah said. How was she going to manage the lighthouse without Billy, and with Tom focused on a new woman? She pulled a knot of twine tight and cut the end with a rigging knife. After weeks in Barnstable, and her father's traps mended and stacked, it was time to go home.

The ride took all day, and Hannah was exhausted as she put the horse up in his stall. She wanted a bath and to go straight to bed, but she didn't have the energy to get the tub or heat the water. Her body ached from the ride, and from crying. The passageway from the barn was dark, and she dropped her bag on the floor as if she was releasing a burden heavier than her suitcase. In the living room, she threw her coat onto a chair and sat before the fire. The heat eased her muscles and she closed her eyes. Tom must be up tending the lights. When she heard him come around the corner, she turned, but it wasn't Tom standing in the half-light.

Billy stepped into the room as if waiting for Hannah to kick her out again, but Hannah was relieved. After her trip to Barnstable, and Tom's upcoming marriage, she wanted something to stay the same.

"May I come in?" Billy asked.

"You might as well," Hannah said.

Billy sat in the chair beside Hannah and stared into the fire, silent, as if preparing what to say. "I want to prove to you that I can do this," she said. "You need the help."

"I can't rely on you when you're drinking."

Billy turned to face Hannah, and with the utmost earnestness, she said, "I promise you, Hannah, that I will not take a drink so long as I live under your roof."

"You've promised that before, haven't you?"

"It's different now. I've got a stake in things here."

Against her better judgment, Hannah wanted to believe that

Billy could work on the lifesaving rig and help her succeed with the rescues. She didn't want to give up when they were so close. "We'll see how it goes," Hannah said.

20

CASSANDRA WAINWRIGHT ARRIVED IN DANGERFIELD with all the pomp of royalty. Her sister Freda chaperoned the excursion, and they traveled in a black cabriolet with red piping and two yellow streamers trailing in the wind. The driver wore a black suit with a white blouse buttoned to the neck and held his hands before him in a formal posture, guiding the horses by flicking the reins lightly on their backs. Billy was in the southwest corner of the yard when she heard the wheels straining over holes in the road. The driver pulled back on the reins to slow the horses and keep from jostling his passengers and their cargo. Five trunks stacked in successively smaller sizes bounced on the back of the buggy, pressing against the leather straps and creating a precarious rumble. There had been some dissension among the girl's family about her making the trip without a chaperone. Cassandra, a fiery if sheltered twenty-three-year-old, had refused her mother's company, and after days of quarreling had settled on Freda, a spinster of twenty-nine years old, but a good companion for the long ride. She'd pay respectable attention to the goings-on between the couple but wouldn't stick her nose in where it didn't belong.

Billy stood from where she was bent over a long trunk of oak. Once it was planted six feet down into the ground, this would act as a mast to test the lifesaving rig. Standing over the pole where it lay on the ground, Billy tried to envision the ropes running up to a crossbar where Hannah would wait like a shipwrecked sailor. She laid two pieces of wood on the ground to form the crossbar, and then set supports coming in at an angle. She bent over the mast pounding nails.

Tom walked up and startled her from the swing of her hammer. He wore his best wool trousers and a fine cotton shirt beneath a black frock jacket. In his gray work overalls and fishing boots, he'd blended into the landscape. Now his life edged beyond the peripheries of their yards and past the town lying between the lighthouse and the harbor.

"I thought you were entertaining your lady friend," Billy said. "How's she like the place?"

"Good enough," he said, his lithe frame swaying in his clothes as if the sea rolled beneath him, but it was only nerves and the desire to move. "I painted some of the rooms, bought new linens, curtains, things like that. Hannah's mother helped choose fabrics. Of course it must seem pretty rough to Cassie, still."

"It's a comfortable house," Billy said.

"She's used to more company." Tom eyed the mast, hands shoved deep in his pockets now. He hadn't worn an overcoat and his jaw clenched against chattering. "Hannah home? I want to ask her if we can come by for a visit."

"Yep."

"You'll let me know if you need a hand getting this thing in the ground?"

"There's something else I need." She told him her idea for

installing a ship's bell at the top of the stairs, with a rope handle running down to the beach that Hannah could use to signal that she was okay, or if she needed help.

"That's the best idea I've heard in a while," Tom said. "You have a bell?"

"Yep."

Billy washed her face and neck in the kitchen sink. She rubbed the dirt from her hands and dried herself before removing her sweat-soaked shirt and unwrapping the bandages that held her breasts flat. Once released, she stretched her back and the feeling returned to her breasts. Without the bandage her breath came easier, her ribs rose and fell in normal rhythms. Her reflection in the mirror surprised her, her pale breasts released from their wrap, the imprints of the cloth a lattice of smooth marks.

Since the wreck she'd gained weight so that she was no longer all muscle and bone, and her breasts began to look like a woman's again. Small, tiny even, but still a woman's. Only when she was naked did she feel completely like a woman, no confusion of gender in her small breasts or what lay between her legs. When she dressed and stepped into the world, her disguise not only compensated the privations of her sex, but also protected her most private self. She'd fought hard on the *Intrepid* for the privilege of working the sails and navigating the ship. She'd battled the men on the *Alice K* for her survival until she proved herself one of them. William Pike had taken shape inside her as a means of survival. Now the swagger she'd learned with the pirate crew, and the men's clothes she'd donned in Jamaica, felt as much a part of her as the color of her hair or the blue veins that rose on the back of her hands. This strange tilting between sexes left her feeling like neither one nor the other, but a combination of both that she couldn't fully decipher, but it was her, the real her, William Pike.

She tossed the dirty water out the window and stood for a moment with the cool air on her skin, rubbing the feeling into her breasts, feeling them there so strange and forgotten.

When Hannah broke the spell of her privacy, Billy turned from the window. They watched each other, spry as cats. The air in the room weighed on them in spite of the cold breeze until finally Hannah stepped forward to break their silence.

"What is it like?" she asked. "Is it uncomfortable?"

Billy picked up the bandage and rubbed it between her fingers to show Hannah.

"It's another kind of corset," Hannah said. She took the strap but didn't take her eyes from Billy's taut stomach, her nearly flat breasts.

Billy turned to get her shirt. She folded the towel onto the counter by the sink and put the soap in the dish. Every one of her movements vibrated through Hannah, and she tried to not watch, but she was transfixed. Billy turned from the counter and shrugged her shirt on. She placed her hand on Hannah's arm, as if to say *I know.*

"I need to feed the chickens," Hannah said, and abruptly left the room. She didn't know what she was feeling, this strange mixture of dread and desire. How could she have feelings like this for Billy? In the yard, she turned and stared blankly toward the barn. Oh yes, she needed to feed the chickens.

It was rare to get visitors from Barnstable. Hannah stood in front of the mirror and admired her fine skirt, rose-colored plaid on a background of sand, a burgundy velvet bodice with covered buttons. She ran her fingers over the ivory stitching as if to assure herself that every last thread was in place. Her dark hair spun easily into a bun, and the white nape of her neck shone pale against the rich colors and textures of her clothing. The last time she'd worn this dress was in Barnstable when she first met John, but it wasn't the loss of John she felt. It was the loss of the possibility of a marriage to Tom. He'd given up on her finally and left her to contend with her feelings for Billy. She'd turned him down, but how could he choose Cassandra Wainwright of all people?

Cassandra had grown up in Barnstable not a mile from Hannah, but they had never met. Hannah was four years older and the difference in age kept them apart. Cassandra's father, Charles Wainwright III, owned a fishing business with concerns as far-reaching as Boston and New Bedford, not to mention the fleet he ran out of Barnstable harbor. Hannah knew many of the men and boys who worked in the fleet, but none of the Wainwrights themselves bothered with the stink of fishing.

As Hannah pulled at the tight bodice of her dress, she realized that Cassandra would be a new neighbor, possibly a friend. Anyone who interested Tom had to be worth knowing. She would have news of Barnstable, and maybe of Hannah's family and friends. Since John's disappearance, her feeling of connection to her past had all but washed away. John had met her family and spent time with her in Barnstable, so that coming to Dangerfield had felt an extension of her world more than a departure. With John gone, the tie was frayed. She wanted to reach back and grasp her past firmly in both hands, but she didn't want to give up anything of her life in Dangerfield.

Hannah chose a cameo necklace, the ivory silhouette of her maternal grandmother atop a faded ebony oval. She fastened the gold chain about her neck so that the pendant rested in the center of her chest, and she pressed her hand to it as if to calm her heart. Cassandra would know the story of John's disappearance, that he was dead. Hannah didn't want sympathy. She didn't want to discuss John or wear a widow's black attire. She was getting along just fine. That's what Cassandra could tell people when she returned to Barnstable. *Hannah Snow is getting along just fine.*

She rubbed salve into her hands, wishing her skin wasn't rough from work, the creases in her palms not stained with oil. What about Billy? What if Cassandra went back to Barnstable and told people that Hannah was living with a strange man in her house? Or what if Billy couldn't pass as a man now that she'd filled out a little around the hips? She couldn't help feeling that she was hiding a secret more frightening than the fact of a strange man living in her house.

Would the women sense the familiarity she had with Billy? What would they think? Why wasn't she afraid of Billy's naked body in her kitchen? She was more intrigued than frightened, and this troubled her. She shuddered at the thought of being found out. Billy sat in the front room with one foot propped on a chair as she spliced a piece of rope around the lifesaving ring, which looked huge in the middle of the floor. The swish of Hannah's skirts preceded her, and Billy could not take her eyes from the lift of her breasts captured in the bodice, the shimmer of burgundy velvet, the soft sheen of fabric over baleen hoops. Hannah's lips appeared fuller, the depths of her eyes brighter.

"They're going to be here soon. You can't do that in the house," she said, gathering discarded clothing from the furniture and piling it in her bedroom. "I've been giving it some thought." Hannah adjusted the cameo back and forth on her chest, though it sat perfectly centered. "Cassandra and her sister are expecting a widow in mourning."

"You're not even wearing black. You're dressed to impress someone you don't really know."

"I do know them. They're Barnstable women, and they won't understand how we live. They'll gossip."

"What are you saying? You want me to leave?"

"It's just for a little while, so I don't have to lie or make up explanations. You have to be Billy, my hired man. Keep your place when they're here and don't be too familiar."

Billy left the life ring half finished on the floor. She grabbed her coat, slammed the front door, and stepped into the cold like she meant to do it harm.

Cassandra and Freda arrived at Hannah's in the cabriolet with Tom sitting up high with the driver. He swung himself down off the seat before the buggy came to a full stop, the flaps of his jacket in flight behind him, birdlike. He held the buggy door wide and raised a hand for Freda as she balanced on the narrow step, pulling along the cage of her skirts as she stepped to the ground in her white-buttoned boots.

Hannah walked straight to Freda and offered her hand in friendship. "I'm Hannah Snow, the lighthouse keeper and Tom's friend. How kind of you to visit."

"I'm Freda, Cassie's eldest sister and chaperone."

"Nice to make your acquaintance," Hannah said. Freda was a big woman with a square, handsome face that gave her a brutish look, perhaps because of the scowl that seemed a permanent aspect of her countenance. She had thick arms and a large waist but moved rather lightly, and her melodious voice was as unexpected and lithe as her gait. Everything physical about Freda existed in direct contrast to the delighted sparkle in her olive green eyes. What at first appeared a scowl turned out to be nothing more than worry and a bookish sort of shyness that she tried to shield behind wire-rimmed spectacles.

Cassandra stepped out of the buggy as if onto a stage and waved as she took Tom's hand. Her pale blue dress and pale skin gave her the sheltered look of a child. She was pretty in an impractical way.

"This is Cassie. Cassie, this is Hannah, the lighthouse keeper here at Dangerfield."

Hannah stepped forward to take Cassie's arm. "You must come in and see the lighthouse," she said. "Tom has told me so much about you."

"I brought you a little gift," Cassie said. "A package of tea from China. Daddy got it on one of his voyages."

"How lovely. I'm going to save it for a particularly cold night."

Inside, the women settled themselves around the table, and Hannah set the pot on the stove. She poured boiling water into the white china pitcher with tiny yellow flowers on it, a gift from her mother.

"How many years have you been living at the lighthouse?" Cassie asked. Tom sat beside her, gazing at her as if seeing her for the first time, then glancing to Hannah to see if she noticed, but Hannah couldn't look at him.

"Over six years now. My husband John had been here for several years, and once we married, I joined him. He built sections of the house that you see here with lumber salvaged from shipwrecks." Hannah nodded toward the far wall. "That crossbeam that holds the roof up came from a ship's deck, and the cornice here also washed up on the beach. My husband made good use of what he found."

"Like Tom's lovely tables," Freda said, sipping her tea.

"Tom's turned practicality into an art form. We can't claim to be anywhere near as creative or clever as that," Hannah said.

Tom went to the fire, uncomfortable now that the attention had turned to him.

"If you ride out to the harbor, you'll see there are fishnets used for chicken coops," Hannah said, "and oars for fence posts and salvaged block and tackle hanging from over the barns to lift and lower bales of hay."

"Yes, Tom took us on a ride in that direction earlier today.

Quite interesting," Freda said. She spoke as if the world was an object placed before her for intellectual consideration.

"Sailors are resourceful. They have what they have and they put it to good use. Fishnet on a chicken coop makes perfect sense to them," Cassie said, delighted, and without taking a breath, she continued. "I'm so sorry to hear about your husband. How are you getting on?"

"I'm grateful for my duties here. Keeping our home and keeping the lights going is what John would've wanted."

"You're very brave, very brave indeed," Cassie said. "I don't know anyone who would hold up so well under the circumstances." She broke off a piece of orange cranberry bread from her plate and popped it into her mouth. Something in the tone of her voice triggered a nagging feeling that Hannah should appear to be more undone by her grief. Any woman who truly cared about her husband would simply not be able to go on.

"I have difficult days, of course," Hannah said. "But the demands of the lights keep me focused on my responsibilities as a lightkeeper's wife." Hannah knew they would not understand how she could step into John's role as lighthouse keeper, or how she could live with a strange man she'd rescued from the sea.

"Yes, I'm sure," Cassie said. Tom nodded, brushing crumbs from his jacket. He stroked his sideburns where they grew long near his jaw. Hannah noticed his new riding jacket, the pressed cotton shirt, the slicked-back hair, all of it reaching for something just above him, whether it was money or status, she couldn't tell. Maybe it was to impress her or maybe it was the love of this woman he sought with his finery.

She understood his attraction to Cassie. Even her casual dress had been sewn from a polished fabric, an exotic floral design of green and gold cut to accentuate her tiny figure and show her delicate wrists. Her hands pale and soft, the fingernails smooth and clear as tiny pieces of glass, reminded Hannah of a child's hands not yet put to work. And her face captivated with a freedom of expression and delight that animated her brown eyes. She was likable, she deferred to her audience while maintaining her own opinion, she could take a joke, she could listen. When she gazed at Tom, her eyes widened, and she nodded in agreement with most of what he said, not out of a dim-witted womanly duty but with a real like-mindedness that made Hannah envious and lonely.

"Where's Billy? I thought he'd be here," Tom said.

Hannah smiled. "Tom loves to include the help. It's one of the things I like about him. He doesn't see himself above anybody."

"Billy's more than just the help," Tom said. "He's—"

"He's gone down to the harbor for supplies," Hannah said, giving Tom a look meant to keep him from saying anything further.

"Yes, well. I suppose Cassie will meet him another time," Tom said.

"Has Tom told you of his success? He's become quite the sensation in Barnstable with a reputation as a fine furniture maker. He's considered an artist. Father thinks he can make a name for himself in New York City. Go ahead, Tom, tell her."

"Well, yes, ah, Cassie's father, Charles, he's a fine man, very helpful, a mentor to me really. The furniture has done so well that the limited supply has driven the prices up very high. Because I can only produce so much furniture by myself, Charles suggested a manufacturing model. I could build the furniture with a crew of men, and we could produce more pieces. In fact, we could have many pieces of furniture in the works at any one time. The key, he said, and this is fascinating, really, is that we need to find the exact point where the supply of furniture does not exceed the demand so that the prices stay high and people still feel that they are buying something unique and special." Tom became especially animated, pacing back and forth as he spoke and looking into Hannah's eyes to make sure that she was following his logic. "That's what they're paying for, the story, the handmade quality, the attention to detail. If too many pieces of furniture were to make it to market, they would not command the same prices. If the prices go down, or if too many people acquire the furniture, buyers lose interest. The key is to find the balance."

"Sounds like you will be making the trip back and forth to Barnstable quite often," Hannah said. "To gather wood and build and whatnot."

"We hope to keep two homes," Cassie said.

"We'll have to see how our business plans shape up," Tom said. "It could very well work."

"Yes," Cassie said, turning to Hannah. "So how about a tour of the lights for a couple of town ladies?"

Hannah rose and escorted the women to look out the kitchen windows and into the bedroom, where she explained the historic features of the keeper's cottage, the arrangement of the windows at awkward intervals along the wall to allow a wide view of the coast.

"How quaint," Freda said, stepping carefully over uneven floorboards. "You sacrifice so much in order to carry out your duties."

"I don't see it as a sacrifice, though, Freda. I enjoy this view the way you might enjoy a wonderful library filled with your favorite books."

"Don't you get lonely, Hannah?" Cassie asked. "Don't you miss the parties and the friends you grew up with? Do you remember Evan Pierce? He's a lawyer now. He works for my father now and again."

Hannah did feel her loneliness then, listening to Cassie talk. She was ready for them all to leave, ready for Billy's return.

Hannah led her guests along the passageway to the lighthouse, and they looked up into the column at the curving stairs. Cassie looked straight up the middle at the black steps forming concentric circles that got smaller and smaller toward the top. "My, that's a long climb."

Freda watched from the side, as if the mere suggestion of heights was enough to make her nauseous. "How do you get up those stairs in your skirts?"

"Well," Hannah said, "it's difficult. With John gone, I realized that men wear trousers for good reason. This may sound ridiculous, but as I stepped into my husband's role as lighthouse keeper, I found it convenient to step into his trousers as well."

Cassie slapped Freda on the arm. "Hah! Did you hear that? Hannah Snow, you are outrageous. Men's trousers indeed. Wait till I tell—"

"Oh no. Please, if my mother hears of it, she'll never leave me alone. Please don't speak of it, Cassie."

"All right, if you insist. It will be our secret. But it's going to be hard to resist. You're quite the outlaw, Mrs. Snow."

Hannah laughed, leading them back to the house. "No, not really. I'm just practical." In the living room, she pulled the curtain back and peered up the road for Billy, but there was no sign of her. What would she think of this curious girl that Tom was going to marry? She felt tired now, and bored with these women. Where was Billy? She'd been gone for hours. Her visitors talked, but their voices sounded far away. Billy had been so angry. Had she forgotten that Hannah was keeping her on for the winter even after her lies and her foolish drinking? Couldn't she see that Hannah needed her help? Didn't that mean anything?

When Hannah turned her attention back to her guests, Cassie had settled into a chair, her dress rustling around her. Tom stood to one side of her. Freda wiped her seat cushion fastidiously with her handkerchief before sitting down with her spine straight, her hands folded on her skirt. They were waiting politely for her.

"Hannah, Cassie was just saying how she remembers you from Barnstable," Tom said.

"You don't remember me because you were one of the older girls and I was just a little one, but I remember you out on the boat with your father. You didn't care about anything but fishing. You went everywhere with your father. My mother used to say you were that man's shadow and if you wanted to grow into any kind of lady you were going to have to stay home. That's how she was. But all the girls admired you. We wanted to spend time with our fathers. All we did as little girls was play house, play with dolls, and run from boys. Oh, and take piano class. It was all so dull."

Hannah smiled and looked at Freda, certain that Freda had never admired her. Tom couldn't keep still. Hannah watched him poke the fire, stack kindling, and gaze around at the women as if they would tell him what to do next.

Twilight lasted forever that evening, a silver light stretching along the horizon, bladelike. Billy kicked through some rubbish behind the grocery store. Millie didn't have anything for her, and she shouldn't be buying anything from Millie anyways, but her mind was in ruins. Not the cold wind, not her heart beating hard enough to crack her ribs, not the scraping in her gut, nothing eased the underwater feeling she moved through like a swimmer with rocks roped to her boots. She realized her desire for Hannah in the utter ache that permeated her body. Hannah had kicked her out, like some kind of expendable hired help. She slogged up the alley and back around to the front of the grocery store.

All these people in town with their friendly faces, all these people who waved hello and knew each other, had known each other for years, had lost husbands and sons and brothers together, survived winters and fished together. Their warmth and camaraderie exaggerated her own loneliness. She headed toward the docks, where there had to be some sailors on shore leave with a pint to spare. She needed a drink. The clouds broke apart now, streaked with light from the disappearing sun. Finally, dark swept over the street like a blanket.

On the dock a fiddler played and men sang around lanterns that splashed light across the dark water. Billy leaned against a post and listened. The plaintive fiddle, joined now by a mandolin, eased her sadness and for a moment she was not a stranger. How could Millie be out of liquor? She regretted leaving the light-house in a rage. A drink would ease her back. But Hannah might kick her out for good if she got drunk. It was probably exactly what Hannah was expecting. She would sniff the air around Billy. No. Not this time. She wouldn't smell of it this time. How could she return to the lighthouse? Where else could she go? She pushed herself forward and toward the road. She felt weak on her way up the hill that led out of the village. When a wagon pulled alongside, she hopped onto the back and sat with her legs dangling. The driver coughed and spat over the side, coughed and spat again. His breath rasped loudly in the still air. She slid off the wagon when they reached the main road, and she watched as the driver headed north toward Provincetown, his figure fading into the dark. There was the lighthouse beam flashing through the trees. Her heart lifted. If only she could harden herself against longing, but she was tired, desperation had ground her down, and there was the light, calling her back.

Hannah changed back into her work clothes, relieved to be free of the constrictions of her bodice and polite company. As much as it interested her to hear news of Barnstable, the familiar family names she'd known growing up—Cobb, Hutchinson, Worthington, Collins—she tired of the talk. Her responsibilities kept her from the whorl of emotions eddying within her. If she could climb the lighthouse stairs, those names would echo and quickly recede, as if Cassie had never come and spoken them in her house. What did people think about her living at the lighthouse now that John was gone? She'd been too self-conscious to ask Cassie outright. Still, she wondered as she stood at the sink. Was that Billy coming up the porch? Hannah tipped her head to listen for footsteps, but it was only the wind pushing a wood chair across the boards.

Hannah went out to the barn, lantern swinging from one hand. The pale light swirled about the expansive dark in the barn. Only emptiness, a rock in her stomach. The ropes Billy had used the first time they tested the lifesaving rig hung coiled on the back wall. Hannah remembered how she had trusted Billy to guide her down to safety, and how she trusted Billy now to help her with the rescues. She should've let Billy stay, but she was afraid of what the women would think. She was a coward, and she regretted her decision. Nellie rustled in her stall, the heavy clomp of her hooves reassuring. "Are you out here?"

She turned in a circle, shining the light along the walls and then walking into the corners where the shadows thickened. She searched each stall and climbed up to the loft. What if Billy was gone for good? There was nothing keeping her here. She could take this opportunity to move on to whatever awaited her on her route north. If Billy didn't come back, it would be Hannah's fault.

"You can't stay out here forever," Hannah said, her voice tiny in all that dark.

In full stride from the road, Billy rattled the floorboards on the porch. She entered the room like a northeast wind. On the table, the remnants of tea, a half loaf of cranberry bread and empty teacups, reminded Billy why she'd been asked to leave, and the disorder of her longing and her fear ruined her. *Hope was a fool's dream.*

Hannah met her at the door. "I'm sorry," Hannah said.

Billy held up her hands to stop Hannah's words. "It doesn't matter." The gaunt look, the squint in her eye that wouldn't look at Hannah directly.

"I want you here. It was a mistake to ask you to leave. Do you hear me?"

"I'm too tired to listen to this, Hannah."

But Hannah stepped through the gravelly sound of Billy's voice. The way Billy's body moved like a blade, her forehead knotted and strained, didn't frighten Hannah. She took Billy's face in her two hands and spoke, even as Billy's eyes looked into the corner of the room. "I need you here. It was a mistake. I'm sorry."

Billy couldn't resist the feel of Hannah's hands, nor her insistent need to pull Billy back. "But you asked me to leave. I'm not good enough for your friends."

"That's not it. I was afraid." The pleading, half-desperate look in Hannah's eyes confused her. She shook herself loose, stepped back.

"You're not afraid of anything, Hannah."

"That's not true. I was afraid what they would think of us if they sensed our friendship. What they would say back in Barnstable. Then I was afraid you were gone, and that was worse."

Billy didn't respond. Hannah grabbed her by the upper arms and shook her. "Can you forgive me? Will you stay?"

With the relief of Hannah's plea, all the grief she'd carried down to the harbor fell from her like a heavy coat. "I was never going to leave," she said.

21

Mr. and Mrs. Charles Wainwright III
of Barnstable, Massachusetts
Request your presence at the marriage of their daughter
Cassandra Rose
to
Mr. Thomas Edward Atkins
of Dangerfield, Massachusetts
Saturday, March 30, 1844
St. Mary's Church 2 pm
Reception to follow at Wind Rush Estate
Main Street, Barnstable

WEDDING! BARNSTABLE! ABSOLUTELY NOT. HANNAH struggled with the wick in the lantern. The lever that controlled its height wouldn't budge. She wiggled it back and forth, and shook the lantern. How could she go to Barnstable when John had gone missing there? When she imagined seeing people from her past who still lived in the houses they grew up in and worked on their fathers' fishing boats or married the women their mothers picked for them, she wanted to loosen her collar and gasp for air. She went to John's desk and stood over the logbook, turned a few pages and ran her finger down his rows of entries. His careful marks made her feel as though he were in the room. For a moment she longed for the way her life was when he was in it. What would he think of her now?

She imagined the wedding, the whispering behind her back amid the earnest condolences. *Hannah, how are you getting along?* She was getting along just fine because she was here in Dangerfield tending the lights and not in Barnstable where her dead husband had last been seen. And how could Tom not have warned her? He was so focused on his need for a wife that he forgot about her feelings. All it had taken was for her to turn him down, and he'd given in to Cassandra. No, she could not think of that now. She didn't need to witness Tom getting married. She slid the invitation into the back of the logbook where she hoped to forget it.

A fluttering rattle on the northeast corner of the house drove Hannah up and into her boots. She pulled her woolen shawl on tight over her nightgown as she strode toward the stone hollow of the lighthouse. Hand clasped on the cold iron rail, she ascended the spiraling stairs. She cleaned the magnifying lenses before she lit each lantern, then worked her way around the lights the way John had shown her. Once he'd taken care of the lights, he kept his vigil by the fire and waited out the storm. He only ventured down to the beach to look for survivors at the tail end of the storm. His risks were calculated. He protected himself to ensure that the lights remained a beacon that sailors could trust. That was the difference between them. Hannah couldn't bear knowing that there could be men in the surf fighting for their lives. She had to get in the boat. She had to help.

As Hannah rounded the corner into the kitchen, Billy was sitting by the fire with the poker, which she nudged into the charred and broken logs. Her desire for Hannah distracted her now from her daily chores, from watching out for her fingers when she pounded the hammer, from standing back from the ax as she swung into a wide piece of spruce. Her desire could ruin her. She could lose her position here, hurt herself, or succumb to drinking, and so she tried to disown it. This worked so long as she focused on building the lifesaving apparatus, installing the bell system that could alert her if Hannah needed help on the beach. It worked until Hannah came in from a storm, her eyes alive with excitement, her body bristling with energy. Until Hannah leaned forward in the candlelight, her high cheekbones and the planes of her face cast in shadow. It worked until right now, when Hannah entered the room with her hair down over her shoulders, her nightgown knotted at her thigh.

"I didn't mean to wake you," Hannah said, reaching over Billy to light the candle. Her nightgown brushed against Billy, her skin so close to Billy's shirt Billy nearly vibrated with fear.

The slow patter of rain started all at once, and wind rushed beneath the door. They both tipped their heads to listen and gauge the storm by the force of rain against the house. "I wanted to remind you about those loose shingles by my bedroom."

"Soon as it clears, I'll fix it."

"I know you're busy with the lifesaving rig. That's more important, of course."

If the lifesaving rig didn't work, they'd be limited in their rescues. Part of Hannah understood that while she could take the risk and row into a storm, she couldn't always save the sailors, and she wanted to save all of them. She felt desperate to get the rig up and working. She took a damp pair of trousers from the back of a chair and slid them on beneath her nightgown. Then she faced the fire and pulled her nightgown off over her head. Billy turned away while Hannah layered herself in woolens.

She wanted to remind Hannah of the danger, but the wind was less than a gale and Hannah had been out in worse. There would be no stopping her. That's why Billy had installed the bell as a signaling system. The old ship's bell she'd discovered in the barn rang with a sound that carried on the wind for a distance. She'd nailed it to a post at the top of the stairs and ran a heavy rope through eye hooks from the bell down to the beach. Every half hour Hannah was to ring the bell twice for an all clear. If there was a wreck or she needed help, she was to ring the bell continuously and Billy would respond. She'd gotten Hannah to agree that she would not go out in the boat alone.

"You'll use the signals and wait?" Billy said.

"Yes." Hannah slid an arm into her jacket and glancing at the tide chart to see when there would be low tide, when a ship was more likely to run aground. As Hannah stepped into the weather, a suck of air pulled the door shut behind her.

Billy kept her vigil by the window so that she would be sure to hear the bell. She busied herself splicing lines for the lifesaving rig, drawing pictures of how she imagined the rig would work once the mast was in the ground. She had a piece of paper with the time written for every half hour—8:00, 8:30, 9:00—so that she could mark each time Hannah rang the bell. The first half hour dragged and Billy sat by the window. The rain tapped the glass, and the glass fogged, and she waited. Hannah hadn't dragged the boat into the water, had she? No, Billy reassured herself. She put her rope work aside and stood to stretch and stoke the fire. Standing in the heat of the fire, she rearranged the pictures on the mantel.

The daguerreotype of John caught her attention. She'd seen it every day, but only now began to take it in. Hannah's husband leaned slightly to the left toward his wife, his frock coat and collar trim and neat. His trousers hung loose and slightly too long, his boots shabby beneath the cuffs. He wore his hair slicked back and long sideburns that made the line of his jaw more pronounced. He held his left hand to his lapel in the traditional manner meant to appear stately. A dimple in his chin looked like a crooked scar, off center and tilted to one side. But most striking were his eyes, which seemed to call out with mournful acknowledgment, as if they had seen all the world had to offer and knew better than to trust it.

The bell rang clear through the wind and rain, two steady clanging signals. Hannah was still on the beach. Everything was okay. Billy marked the half hour in her log and went back to her rope work.

For hours Hannah patrolled, first walking north a half mile toward the post she'd planted to let her know if she'd gone far enough. Then south to the place where the dunes rolled back and the sand turned rusty orange. The storm tide ran north along the beach as fast as a person could walk. In the movement of her body she felt reassured. The ocean reminded her who she was. The overwhelming force of it put her right in her place. She pulled her collar up, tucked her scarf tight around her neck, and headed north again with wind in her face. She was nearly at the stairs when the wind rushed hard from the northeast. The staircase whined. The canvas tarp over the surfboat snapped in the wind.

Silver light, like something exposed.

The outline of a ship two hundred feet out. One great white sail caught in the flashing light. The hull a shadow leaning toward the safety of the lighthouse.

Hannah yanked on the bell rope. Over and over, she rang the signal for a shipwreck. Would Billy hear her in the wind? The vessel was close enough to shore to use the lifesaving rig. She dug behind the stairs for the gear, pushing aside the toolbox and a sack of life jackets, until she had the ropes, life ring, and sand anchor lined up on the beach. Again, she rang the bell. *Where was Billy?* She wasn't going to take any risks this time. The schooner was over fifty feet long and tilted so that the decks rose like a hill, the lower rail almost underwater. A lifeboat from the sinking ship floated belly up in the waves, but there was no sign of anyone in the water. Only shades of sandy green where the bottom lay close to the surface.

Hannah dragged the ropes onto a canvas tarp, which she took and tried to drag to the surfboat. She was sweating in her clothes in spite of the cold. The ropes were too heavy for one person to lift, but still she pulled the tarp against the wind.

When Billy called out, Hannah felt buoyed by the sound. She wiped her sandy gloves on the back of her trousers. "Hurry the hell up!" she yelled through the clamor of wind and sea.

Spars croaked and strained. Salt spray flew over the surfboat and sloshed in the bilge as Hannah maneuvered the surfboat alongside the schooner's aft rail. The masts leaned over, ready to snap with the weight of water filling the sails. The ship's crew had been caught with no time to take down the canvases. Men clung to the bulwark. The bow of the schooner lifted and sank the stern. The keel dug itself deeper into the sandy bottom, and the great strain shivered through the hull, a hollow moan, and then the rush of water into the lower cabin.

"Who's in command?" Hannah shouted through the wind, careful to maintain a safe distance between the surfboat and the wreck. A sailor with a gray walrus mustache waded through the flooded deck and looked at her, taken aback.

"I'm the captain!" He wore his black collar up against the wind, his legs solid and braced against the sea.

"I've got a rig to get your men to shore."

Hannah threw the heaving stick, which was a small block of wood attached to the free end of rope by a smaller length of twine. He caught the stick and hauled the rope aboard until he reached the paddle end upon which Billy had painted the instructions.

Make the tail of the pulley fast to lower mast. If mast gone, then to best place you can find. See that rope in pulley runs free, and show signal to shore.

"Hurry," she said. The captain looked worried, but Hannah

pointed at the coiled ropes. A breaker lifted the surfboat, and dropped, then lifted again so that the surfboat slammed into the schooner's rail. With one of the oars, Hannah pushed away from the ship and rowed clear while the men scrambled back. The captain looked toward the lighthouse, standing in water up to his thighs, and waved a man down from the rail. He shoved the instructions into the man's hands and pushed him toward the mast.

"How many on board?"

"Thirteen," the captain said.

"Give me eight. Seas are coming up. I can't come back out, but we'll get you ashore with the lifesaving rig." Hannah rowed alongside the schooner. Before the captain had time to give any orders, one of the sailors leapt across into the surfboat in his panic, tipping the boat hard to one side with the force of his weight landing in the bow. He hit his head on the seat and groaned before righting himself, hands to his head and squinting against the pain.

The rest of the crew followed orders, standing back from the rail until they were told to cross. Those instructed to stay behind held the surfboat alongside or watched the lifesaving lines to keep them clear.

The next sailor dropped his legs into the boat, then let the rest of his weight down slowly and folded himself onto the seat beside the first. Their tattered jackets, wet boots, pants that stuck to their legs left them exposed to the cold. "For chrissake, hurry up," Hannah said, helping the next man across while the surfboat rocked against the schooner.

With the last man onboard, Hannah cast off. The weight of

the men helped balance the boat in the waves. She put one of the sailors to work unloading the rope one coil at a time so that it drifted slack behind them, but not so slack that they lost sight of it underwater. "Just make sure the lines don't get tangled. Don't take your eyes off it," Hannah said.

"What the hell is this?" the tattooed man asked.

"Shut your mouth." The young sailor's voice punctured the air like a spike. His pale skin and dark eyes had no look of hardness or weather about them. He wore his hair cut close, and when he worried his frayed jacket cuff, his hands moved tenderly as a whisper while all around was a chaos of wind and storm currents carrying the surfboat north. Hannah compensated for the north-running tide by rowing slightly south.

She was focused on her rowing, pulling back and aiming for Billy. *It'll get your shipmates ashore. We just have to move fast.*

Near the beach, Hannah pulled the oars in and jumped into surf to her knees. She ordered the men to help haul the surfboat clear of the water. They moved sluggishly, weighed down by wet clothing, cold, and fatigue. If she could keep them moving, they'd warm up. "There's a pile of wood and dry matches by the stairs," she told them. "Get a fire going. Hurry up."

Billy had set the crossbar: two ten-foot boards bolted together and crossed near the top to form an "X". She hauled the rope, heavy now as it stretched through the water, and hooked it to the sand anchor she'd constructed from two six-foot boards crossed and bolted at their centers. After she made sure the lines ran clear through the block and tackle, she hauled the free end to pull them taut, and the crossbar lifted and sustained the bridge of rope from shore to the stranded schooner.

Hannah eyed the system of pulleys as Billy worked the rope to run the life ring toward the ship. She remembered how light she'd felt riding in the life seat above the ground and the solid feeling of the rig. But how would it feel to a man coming ashore over frothy seas with wind straining the rig and an unstable vessel? The canvas seat in the life ring had to hold the heavier weight of a man, the captain had to fasten the ropes properly, and the sailors had to be able to climb into the rig without fouling the lines or tearing the coarse stitches. *It's going to work. Don't worry. It'll work.* Hannah forced her mind to focus on the rig reaching across the water.

Once the life ring reached the wreck, Billy waited, attuned for the slightest vibration, but it was a man's weight sagging the line that let her know it was time to haul the rig to shore. She stood back to get leverage and work the ropes. The tattooed sailor stood behind her to haul on the lines, his body leaning forward with Billy and pulling back with all of his strength. Faster and faster they pulled. The sailors gathered around, watching the ropes strain the pulleys. "Keep going," Billy said, out of breath, her arms rubbery and burning. "He's almost here."

The sailor approached the beach, arms draped over the ring. He was alert, watchful. "Hurry up, bring him in," one of his shipmates said. The rig carried him as far as the crossbar and he dangled there like a child in a swing.

Billy figured it had taken about twenty minutes to get the rig out to the ship and back ashore with the sailor. They had four more men to bring in, including the captain. That was over an hour to go, and the waves were getting huge. Hannah couldn't go out in the skiff now, not in these seas. They had to rely on the rig. "Get him out," Hannah said.

"And make fast work of it," Billy said. The crew swept into motion like a dark cloud, one indistinguishable from the next, with their wet clothes clinging to their bodies, their shoulders hunched and sticking together as if for warmth, but it was fear kept them close like that.

Billy lowered the life ring, and the crew yelled orders back and forth to each other as they helped the sailor from the seat. The man was at least six feet tall once he struggled to his feet, with rosy skin and a helmet of black hair. Billy recognized him at once, and when Briggs caught his breath and walked up the beach, she kept her eyes on her work. As soon as Hannah cleared the lines, Billy sent the life ring out again. The wind gathered from the northeast, and the rig creaked where it ran through the pulleys. The life seat swayed on the lines. Billy felt the vessel shift and jostle the rig. The lines lurched and then settled down again, and the men who were not tending the rescued sailor hovered around the rig.

"Is it okay?" one of the men asked, his black eyes reflecting the fire. The wreck shifted as the tide went out, which placed more weight on the keel. At some point the hull would crack, the schooner would go down and take the rig with it. They had to get the men to shore fast. Billy watched the life seat until it reached the schooner. When she felt a man on the other end, the tattooed man joined her on the ropes.

Hannah forced her way between them and stood behind Billy, then Briggs fell in line behind her. The four of them hove the weight in unison, bringing the rope in several feet at a time. The pulleys creaked and groaned with the weight of the sailor swaying the rig.

"Keep going," Hannah said. "Don't stop."

But the weight on the line felt heavier than before. When the buoy came into view, three men were clinging for their lives, one seated in the buoy as intended, one draped across him, and another dragged through the water on a rope. On shore, they fell from the life ring and told how the hull had cracked and the schooner was taking on water as the sea poured into the bilge. "There's only the captain," one of the men said. "He ordered us all off the boat."

Billy worked in a frenzy to clear the lines and get the life ring to the captain. She waited to feel a weight on the line, but the rope snapped, and she fell backward into the sand. The crossbar tipped forward, and the pulleys whirred as the ship tilted hard toward the beach. The crew ran into the surf and pulled the lines hand over fist, yelling at each other to get out of the way, and pull harder, and hurry up, hoping to find the captain, but all that came in was a frayed end of rope.

"Jesus Christ, do something," one of the men yelled.

Hannah ordered the young sailor to help her push the boat into the water. When he tried to climb aboard with her, she shoved him away.

Billy ran into the water. She lunged to get hold of the surf-boat, then grabbed Hannah by the elbow. Billy pulled Hannah out of the surfboat so hard they both fell back into the water. "It's too rough," Billy said, gasping. "You're not going out."

Hannah struggled to get free of her. "Let go of me. I won't leave him out there."

Billy shoved Hannah away from the boat and struggled up from the waves. Hannah reached for her. Her eyes squinted through the mist and blast of the sea while Billy swung one leg over the side of the boat and climbed aboard. Hannah tried to reach her against the suck of the water, but she staggered back and fell into the waves.

Billy pushed the boat from the beach with one oar, then sat on the center seat and rowed hard.

Hannah watched the surfboat rise and bow in the air over each rolling wave until it disappeared into the mist of the storm. White foam crashed on the beach at Hannah's feet. She ran to her supply bag by the base of the stairs for the spyglass. With an eye to the glass, she brought the wreck into focus, but in the rolling surf she could only make out a blur of Billy as she rose and fell near the wreck. There was no sign of the captain.

She watched through the glass, struggling for some indication of what was happening, but she lost sight of Billy and the surfboat. A bare edge of the schooner was visible above the waves, a hairline on the horizon. The waves grew taller and rolled harder onto the beach. She dropped the spyglass in the sand and ran to the little skiff.

"Come on, help me get the skiff in the water," Hannah said to the sailors.

"You can't go out, ma'am, not in that."

"I can and I will and you will help me or your captain will drown. Do you want that on your conscience?"

"No, ma'am," one of the sailors said, looking away from her like a scolded dog.

The men made light work of lifting the skiff into the water. It looked small amid the waves and Hannah knew she shouldn't take it out, but where was Billy? With two hard pulls against the waves Hannah was in deep water. The boat rose nearly vertical then dropped hard into a trough, and then lifted up again. Hannah pressed her feet against the back seat for balance and leaned her body into the rise of the boat. She could do this, she told herself, even as the skiff shivered and creaked beneath her. Never had she rowed into such a wind.

When one of the seams began to leak, she ignored it and turned to get her bearings on the wreck while a thin stream of water trickled up through the boards. She still couldn't see Billy. When a giant wave swept the boat up high in the air, Hannah's stomach dropped. She hovered over the sea, so high she could see white crested waves rolling toward shore in every direction. She clenched the oars so that she wouldn't lose them. Time stopped and held her in its hands, and she turned to search for Billy, but there was only the tilting mass of the wreck, and she was afraid. Her boat was small and the beach far away. She wanted Billy.

Then the wave began to move and her mind came back to her task. Feet against the stern seat, she set the oars. The boat dropped vertically, as if down a shaft, and slammed onto the surface of water. The bones in Hannah's buttocks yelped, her neck screamed as the boat began to take on water through a split seam. She bent forward to eye the damage. The plank on the bottom of the boat was going to go. She had to reach

the surfboat if she was going to make it. She set her oars and
rowed toward the wreck. She was close. She had to keep
rowing, and when the wreck came into view, she pulled
against the pain in her body, pulled until her body was numb
and pain was a white light that surged through her limbs.
Water leaked into the boat through the split seam, and the
boat grew heavy.

She heard the wreck, heard the way the waves crashed against
the hull then splashed into the air in the sound of defeat.
Hannah rowed against the increasing weight in the skiff, telling
herself it was no different than carrying a boatload of men. She
didn't consider the danger. She couldn't, or she wouldn't be
able to find Billy.

When she saw the surfboat, Billy wasn't in it. Hannah's
stomach clutched, as if she'd been lifted from a wave and then
dropped. The captain sat hunched over in the stern seat with a
life jacket on, one hand on either side of the rail for balance as
the boat tossed in the waves. Hannah rowed up close to him
and pulled in her oars. She reached back for the bow line and
tossed it to the captain so that he could fasten it to the stern of
the surfboat and she could float behind.

"Where's Billy?"

"He came aboard to help me. He's there behind the mast."

Hannah leaned across the boat until she spotted Billy.

"What's taking so long?"

"He wanted to see how the rope held and if we fastened it
correctly, something about the instructions on that little board
you sent out. He said something about trying to understand
what happened with the lifesaving rig."

"Billy!" Hannah yelled as loud as she could. She cupped her hands to her mouth and called into the wind. "Billy!"

When Billy heard Hannah's voice, she climbed along the rail toward the two boats tossing wildly in the waves. Hannah's feet were covered with water now, and she reached down for the baler. She scooped out water as fast as she could to empty the bilge, but the water came in fast. When a tall wave crashed over its side, a wall of water landed in the skiff, the seam split wide open, and the plank on the bottom of the boat tore from the stern seat to the bow in a sound like thunder. No baler would help her now. Another plank gave way, and the sea rushed into the boat, which went under stern first. The bow lifted then sank until only the rope rail showed beneath the surface of water. Hannah was pulled down in the rush of water as she swam toward the surfboat, toward Billy.

Waves carried her away from safety, and she watched the surfboat's white hull, full and promising, grow smaller as she drifted away on the tide.

Billy screamed from the schooner. "Hannah, swim!" She yelled at the captain, "Get the life ring."

Billy leapt from the schooner into the surfboat and untied it from the wreck, then she untied the sinking skiff and rowed toward Hannah. Hannah felt the weight of her clothes, and she struggled to remove her jacket, then her sweater, kicking her feet to keep herself afloat, but for all her strength, she wasn't a good enough swimmer.

Billy rowed parallel to the waves to avoid the rise and fall. She saw Hannah's coat, drifting just beneath the surface. Billy ordered the captain to get the life ring at the ready. Hannah had floated out of sight, and Billy rowed frantically in the direction of the tide, searching over the waves and yelling at the captain to crawl to the bow of the boat and scan the water.

"There, she's there!" He leaned forward as if his entire body could indicate the direction.

Hannah struggled against the sea, her arms already so exhausted from rowing the boat, she could barely move them. A deep ache began to settle into her. She was tired, more tired than she had ever been, and she let herself drift beneath the waves for moments at a time, until the surface was the light of another world that she could watch as if from a dream. When the pressure in her chest compelled her, she kicked herself up into the air and the relief of breathing, until she exhausted herself once again and let herself sink, deeper this time into the ease of not swimming.

"Where is she?" Billy yelled at the captain.

"She was right there."

When Hannah's head bobbed up, Billy called to her. "Hannah, Hannah!"

But Hannah didn't hear her over the sound of the wind, and she let herself sink below the surface. It wasn't so bad, she told herself. She could see the surface right there. She didn't let herself go too deep, just enough to rest. She closed her eyes to the darkness of the water and felt that she could sleep if not for the pull in her chest, the pull that exploded and made her kick to the surface for air.

"Hannah, grab the life ring!"

The captain threw the ring with remarkable precision to

Hannah's flailing arms, but she sank out of sight before she could grab it. He pulled the life ring in again and held it at the ready.

Billy maneuvered the boat as close as she could get to where she'd seen Hannah. She didn't want to get too close. What if Hannah came up, and the boat blocked her effort to get into the air? What if she knocked her head on the bottom of the boat and lost consciousness? Billy's mind raced with all of the things that could go wrong. They had to get her out of the water. The cold water alone could kill her.

This time when Hannah came up, it was only for a second, as if she only had time for a single, quick breath before she went under again. Billy kicked off her shoes, removed her jacket, and took the life ring from the captain. She jumped into the water and swam. The waves lifted her up while she struggled against them, but the current carried her toward Hannah.

She treaded water around the spot where Hannah had risen, and when Hannah came up, she kicked toward her. "Wait!" But Hannah was gone. Billy, against her better judgment and everything she knew to be true, let go of the life ring and dove below the surface of the water. She kicked down into the blur of the ocean, her eyes open and searching until she saw a sinking shape. She kicked against the pull of her trousers, kicked until she reached Hannah, drifting with her eyes closed. Billy grabbed her from behind. She reached beneath Hannah's arms and around her chest to get a firm hold before kicking toward the surface.

When they broke into the air, Billy waved with one arm for the captain, who had manned the surfboat and floated a hundred yards from where they'd come up. With Billy holding her up, Hannah rested. She stopped kicking and closed her eyes, let her feet float back and her body lean against Billy.

"Don't leave me, Hannah. Stay with me."

The captain approached in the surfboat and tossed the life ring to them. Billy hooked her free arm into the ring, and the captain braced his leg against the rail to haul them in. He leaned over and grabbed Hannah under the arms while Billy tried to help from the water as he pulled her aboard. Billy pulled herself up over the stern with the captain's help. She sat in the middle seat but was too tired to take up the oars. They drifted in the tide, the sea a storm of waves tossing them around. Waves rolled in from as far out as they could see. There was no telling where they came from, or why, they just rolled on and on, battering the shore with their endless weight.

Hannah refused to be carried up the beach. Instead, she leaned against Billy as they staggered toward the fire. Billy ordered the men to bring the boat in, and they lined up four along each side, making easy work of carrying it up the beach. "Coil these ropes," Billy said, holding Hannah against her. "Let's get this gear stowed as well." The men worked in sluggish silence. Billy was in charge now. Hannah slumped against her. The men made room for Hannah and Billy around the fire. "We saved the captain," Hannah whispered, and they gathered around to shelter her from the wind.

22

Once they were inside, Hannah dragged herself to the dining table and slumped into a chair. That's when she saw the paper Billy had used to track her progress along the beach, the careful checkmarks made at half-hour intervals, every time Hannah rang the bell. She ran her fingers over the scratches and imagined Billy sitting here waiting for the sound of the bell and then making each mark.

"You need to get into dry clothes," Billy said, and held a hand toward Hannah to help her up from the chair.

While she and Billy changed into dry clothes, the crew warmed themselves around the fire and ate soup with biscuits. The house was humid, the heat of the fire mixed with their bodies, the wet from the storm, and the men's clothes. Their silence weighed on the room, and with the thick air became its own kind of fog. They didn't want to wait for the next day's boat to Boston; they wanted to get as far away from Dangerfield as they could. Briggs sat beside Billy at the table.

"We'll want to be leaving as soon as we can," he told her. "No need to stay here."

"You need some rest," Billy said.

"We can rest on our way back to Boston. The men need to keep moving."

"If that's what you want. There's an afternoon boat."

The men cleaned up after themselves, and took one last stand by the fire, two at a time, warming their backsides before thanking Hannah for her bravery and kindness. She was disinclined to accept their gratitude, but did so as graciously as she could.

April 8: Starling aground, wind SW 15, first use of lifesaving apparatus success until ship gone down. All sailors brought to shore alive.

Once the men had left, Hannah pulled on her nightdress and felt unusually hot, her body still humming with the rescue. It could take days to come down off a rescue, days to process the strange mix of energy and exhaustion. She flung the window open and stood before it with the wind on her face, blowing her hair back. Hannah knew now what it must be like to drown, the slow giving in to rest, the quiet underwater sleep. But then she realized the last gasps and lungs filled with water were something she could never know.

Billy had kept her safe. Hannah didn't blame herself for falling into the water. She was trying to save Billy, whom she now knew didn't need saving. Not anymore.

During the rescue she'd watched Billy move with authority. What struck her most about the rescue was Billy's complete competence, her ability not only to manage the lifesaving rig, but also to direct the men in such a way as to keep them safe and make use of the ones who weren't too depleted to help.

Billy was part of her daily life. She'd entered into every hour of Hannah's awareness. Every spare moment Hannah wondered what Billy was doing, and if she would do it with her.

Hannah knew why Billy looked away from her when she changed her clothes in front of the fire. When Hannah had seen Billy half dressed, she'd stared open-eyed like an animal in the torch beam, transfixed by the woman's body beneath her very male physicality. And Billy had let her look, had wanted her to look. It was the complexity of Billy's sexuality that drew her in: a woman's heart listening to every word and understanding; the way Billy sat with her legs apart, elbows on the table while she blew across a cup of coffee; her fierce determination pushing a wheelbarrow full of mulch and fidgeting with her chest strap. She thought of how hard Billy had worked on the lifesaving rig. And the drawing she'd made of Hannah, as if she'd been able to see Hannah in her most intimate self from the very beginning. She could question herself and give herself time to figure out whether she could manage her desire, but every time she put down her pen, or picked up a plate, there Billy was, looking back at her, as if to say, *This is our life.*

Huddled together in the wagon, the men discussed their plans, who would sign on to another ship; who would visit family; who would never go to sea again. Their voices were light, drifting on a southwest breeze that carried a heavy scent of brine.

Briggs sat next to Billy on the wagon seat.

"You don't need to tell anyone you saw me," Billy whispered.

"There's a bounty for your capture and return to Jamaica.

They'll hang you, just like they hang men. Who's to say I won't be back?"

Billy stopped the wagon and shoved Briggs back by the shoulders. "You'll not tell a soul or I'll kill you right now. I saved your life, and I'm not afraid to take it back."

"I know, I know," Briggs said. "You saved my life. I was just saying—"

"You think you'd survive carrying me back there? What would they do with you once I told them who you were?"

Briggs stared into the creased leather of his soaking wet shoes where they rested on the boards. He slid his hands up and down his thighs as if preparing himself to say something, but he said nothing.

As the wagon continued along the road, Billy said, "When did you leave the crew?"

"Not long after you. I signed onto the *Starling* to get north. I'm going to Boston to get on a fishing boat, try to make some honest money, not get myself killed." Briggs spat over the side of the wagon.

The sounds of harbor wafted over the trees, and as they made the turn, the packet boat bobbed at the dock. "That's your boat," Billy said.

"Well, I hope I never see you again," Briggs said. "One wreck is enough for me. You better keep an eye on your lady friend, or she'll be the next one you drag out of the sea."

Billy delivered the men to the boat and left them talking to the men on the docks, their hands gesturing, telling their tale of the wreck. By now word had spread, and the locals wanted to hear everything, as if reliving the wreck would inure them to devastation of their own. Billy walked among them but left the reporting to the men who'd survived. They were the ones with the story to tell. As she walked toward the horse and wagon, she eyed a ship navigating out of the harbor, sails still furled. The stillness of the ship while the men waited for open water reminded her of the *Alice K.* How long since she'd thought of that? On the *Alice K*, she'd been one of the crew and understood firsthand the quiet before the action. If she had to, she could set sail again, head north, away from her past. Start over again someplace else.

She climbed atop the wagon and shook the reins until the horse lifted his head, as if sniffing the breeze before heading toward the road. Only last night, she'd been in Hannah's bed. What hot torment that had been. She'd hardly slept, moving only to accommodate Hannah's slightest motion. She'd watched the lighthouse beam swing across the room, and she held onto the familiar pulse as if it could save her from the heat of the woman beside her. Then the storm.

It frightened her to think of the danger Hannah would row into without someone there to stop her. She didn't want to leave Hannah alone, even for a minute. What if she went on the beach to survey the wreckage and something on the water drew her attention? *Is that a waving hand?* Hannah would be in the rowboat without taking time to think. How many times had Hannah done just that? She'd rowed out to save that girl from drowning, and nearly drowned herself in the process. She'd rescued Mesha and the crew on the boat from Jamaica. And she'd rescued Billy from the wreck of the *Cynthia Rose.* Weather didn't bother her. She seemed to thrive in it, as if it echoed some inner tempest. She was more alive in a storm than in the calm of an afternoon's work around the lighthouse, baking bread and feeding the chickens, washing the windows so the light shown far to sea.

Billy couldn't go on pretending that she wasn't in love with Hannah. She couldn't act as if she didn't want to take Hannah's hand and pull her close against her.

The sight of Hannah walking through the kitchen in her nightdress, the shadow of her curved figure, taunted Billy from across the room. The way Hannah looked at her sometimes made her want to leave, so intense was the depth of her gaze. To dispel that charge, she'd have to touch Hannah, but they didn't touch. That's why every time Hannah looked at Billy with love in her eyes, or something like it, Billy had to look away.

As Billy crossed the main street onto the road that took her to the lighthouse, she stretched her back and slowed the horse. The road was empty after the storm, puddles filled the muddy ruts, but the horse pulled the wagon with ease. Billy let herself be jostled over bumps in the road. She didn't want to reach the lighthouse. She couldn't go on like this. If Hannah couldn't be with her, she couldn't stay. The only person she'd ever thought to make a life with had been Daniel, and now Hannah. She couldn't play at being the workman, or best friend, when what she wanted was a lover and someone to share her life with. The thought of it terrified her, but it was true. When Hannah had slipped below the waves, Billy had panicked, as if the possibility of a life with Hannah, or any life at all, was drifting out of reach.

But all the rescues in the world wouldn't make up for her crimes. If Hannah ever discovered the truth of her identity, she'd make Billy leave. But then, Billy thought, Hannah must know at least some part of who she was. She'd seen her beat the man who'd taken Mesha, and she hadn't been afraid. Hannah wanted her at the lighthouse. She wanted Billy by her side. Of all the men in town who could handle the job, she chose Billy. The lighthouse came into view. Billy felt herself coming home.

She'd tell Hannah the truth.

When Billy returned from getting the men to the harbor, Hannah was in bed. She'd been up earlier for water and heard Billy go up to check the lights, but exhaustion was like an undertow that dragged her back beneath the quilts.

The door slammed and Billy appeared in the doorway, like a man awaiting orders.

They stared at each other, the weight of the day between them: the success of the lifesaving rig, the men saved, the disaster of the sunken skiff and Hannah in the water. Billy didn't say anything about Hannah going out alone, and Hannah didn't say anything about Billy trying to keep her ashore. They didn't talk about the confusion of their desires. All of it hung in the air between them.

"I got the men on the packet to Boston," she said. "The lights are set."

Hannah sat up, the comforter at her waist, her nightdress loose. Billy leaned in the door frame and scanned her fingernails for dirt, anything to distract herself from the sweep of skin below Hannah's neck and the suggestion of her breasts.

"You did a good job today. I rely on you, Billy. I trust you," Hannah said.

"I wanted to make sure—"

"Come sit with me," Hannah interrupted, and patted the bedside where she rested.

Billy obeyed, a clamoring inside her like bells ringing. Her steps creaked across the floorboards, and her boots felt heavy on her feet. Hannah's eyes had no more of the distance in them that she'd rendered in that first drawing, but her curiosity was alive and pulling Billy to sit on the edge of the bed. How long ago since she'd made that drawing? Even then she'd felt an intimacy that came from watching Hannah while she worked and Billy lay motionless on the hearth. She'd watched Hannah when Hannah thought she was alone. She'd seen the grief in her eyes when she thought about her husband and listened quietly when she heard Hannah crying in her bedroom; she'd seen Hannah throw a jar of peaches at the wall because she couldn't open the lid; she'd seen her work a boat like no man she'd ever known.

"You can take off your coat," Hannah said.

Billy let the coat slide from her arms onto a chair. She closed the window to a crack, then she sat on the bed. This close to Hannah, her heart drummed in her ears. She wanted to lean forward and kiss her, but she waited. Hannah slid her hand over Billy's and said something, but Billy only heard the rush of ocean in her ears. A gull called along the edge of the dune, then faded into the distance. Hannah's breath brought her back to the look in Hannah's eyes that was love and something more and Billy didn't look away.

Hannah unbuttoned Billy's shirt and pulled it gently back from her arms. She ran her fingers along the side of Billy's arm where the muscle ached from hauling the sailors to shore. It was the weight of Billy that Hannah wanted, pressing her into the bed. She unwrapped the tight fabric around Billy's chest one loop at a time, pressed her hand against the pattern the fabric had etched into Billy's skin. When Billy kissed her on the mouth, she fell back against the pillow. With her nightdress off, Hannah was pale and strong. Her beauty affected such tenderness in Billy that her breath caught in her throat. Hannah let go and all at once became fragile and exposed. Billy kissed her neck and her mouth, and she felt Hannah along her chest and arms until she was everywhere around her.

The windows rattled in their frames, a sound that grew louder as the northeast wind came up. "Listen," Hannah said.

READING GROUP GUIDE

1. *The Lightkeeper's Wife* introduces Hannah Snow, who rows into a storm to save a shipwrecked sailor. How does Hannah's determination carry through the rest of the novel, and how does it save or undo her?

2. William Pike remembers Annie in his dreams. At what point do you figure out that Annie/Blue is in fact William Pike? How believable is his/her transformation from a wife to a pirate to a man? At what points do you notice the changes, both inner and outer?

3. When John goes missing and is finally believed dead, Hannah experiences an ocean swell of grief. How does she handle it? What are the ways in which her emotions are clear, and what are the ways in which they are misplaced?

4. Hannah and Tom have an attraction between them and a past that we learn about in a flashback. Why won't Hannah accept his marriage proposal when she clearly cares for him? Why doesn't she want to marry again?

5. What do you think of Hannah's decision to take over the care of the lighthouse and pursue her rescues? What motivates her daring on the sea? Is she reckless, brave, compassionate, strong? What are her strengths and weaknesses in regard to her performing the rescues?

6. What does Annie learn from her experiences in Jamaica when her infant child dies? How does her experience there change her relationship with her husband? How does meeting Therese's society of strong women impact the rest of Annie's story?

7. Billy is haunted by his life aboard the *Alice K.* How does his life at the lighthouse help him come to terms with his past actions? Can he ever escape his past or make up for the things he's done? What are some of the ways in which his past catches up with him?

8. When is the first time we get a glimpse of the attraction between Hannah and Billy? What initially attracts them to each other, and how does their interest evolve throughout the story?

9. Billy drinks to escape his demons. Hannah's father drinks to cope with pain and not being able to work. What is the role of alcohol in the story? How does drinking impact the lives of the characters?

10. *The Lightkeeper's Wife* is initially told in flashbacks. Why do you think the author unfolded the story this way? What did she want to accomplish by withholding the fact that Billy is in fact Annie/Blue?

11. What elements of the characters' lives do you think are universal? What aspects of the characters do you identify with? Are there characters you see as "good" or "bad"? What is the role of evil in the story?

12. The characters often fail: Annie at protecting her husband's ship, Hannah at saving a little girl at sea. Men are murdered. Sailors are rescued, while some are lost. What does this tell you about life and the lives of the characters? What do the characters learn through their failures?

13. The novel takes place in Dangerfield, Barnstable, the Caribbean Sea, and Jamaica. How palpable is the sense of place? What is the role of place in the narrative? How does place impact the lives of the characters?

14. Gender and sexuality are large themes in the novel. How would you describe Billy's gender throughout the course of *The Lightkeeper's Wife*? What about Hannah? How does Billy's relationship to sex evolve throughout the narrative? How does Hannah come to accept and love Billy for who he is? Does reading the novel change how you think about gender or sexuality?

15. The story ends with Hannah and Billy coming together both in how they do the rescues and in how they form an intimate connection. How does their relationship in carrying out the rescues impact their love relationship?

A CONVERSATION WITH THE AUTHOR

Where did you get the idea for Hannah, the female light-keeper, and Blue, the lady pirate?

Hannah came to life when I saw a print of Grace Darling, a lightkeeper's daughter in the UK who became famous for rowing into a storm to rescue a drowning sailor. The print was at the Highland House museum in Truro, Massachusetts, where they had a book about female lightkeepers. When fathers or husbands died, a daughter or wife would often take over the care of a lighthouse to maintain an income. While the male lightkeepers were known for staying ashore to watch the lights, the women became known for rowing into the sea to rescue drowning sailors, perhaps out of a sense of empathy. This fascinated me. In my research of women's maritime history, I came across female pirates; how could that not grab my interest?

What was your process like for writing this novel?

Long and slow. I conducted two years of research while writing the first few drafts. I researched everything: women's maritime history, female pirates, clothing from the 1800s, famous shipwrecks, photos of Truro from the 1800s. I started with a first draft that I wrote through without listening to my internal critics. I threw everything in there, every bit of research and character and scene that came into my mind. Then I whittled it down and fleshed it out and worked it like clay. I searched for the nerve of the narrative and built from there, using that one twitch to guide me. In the case of *The Lightkeeper's Wife*, I struck a nerve every time I started to write about the relationship between Hannah and Billy, and more specifically, as it related to their gender and sexuality. I also had readers who provided feedback and helped me work the material over the years.

What is the interplay between fact and fiction in the story?

I use history as a catalyst for the story, but I don't stick to the facts. I embellish and embolden as the story unfolds. For example, Dangerfield is a fictional town based on Truro, Massachusetts, which was at one time called Dangerfield. I wanted the freedom to invent and not be tied to the specific history or place. The same is true of the pirate culture, which was in fact more prevalent in the 1700s than in the 1800s. But fiction is fiction, and I had fun with it.

What interested you in exploring gender roles in *The Lightkeeper's Wife*?

In my research about women's maritime history, I came across women who lived as men at sea. I was intrigued not only with what it would take for a woman to pass as a man, but also with how much of being a man a female character could identify with and finally take on for herself, as we see with Billy. And when Hannah puts on John's pants, she steps into aspects of gender outside the norm for her time period. Yet, while she carries out daring rescues and feats of strength, she remains a feminine figure, and Billy, even stripped of his disguise, remains more male. How can two women be so different? What is gender all about? This is some of what I wanted to explore in the novel.

How do you write sex scenes without becoming pornographic?

Sex scenes are always tricky. Like any scene, they should let us know more about the characters and further the story. Part of the work is not to get bogged down in cliché and to choose the right physical details—that is, physical details that are specific to a character and what their particular sexual experience means to the story. For example, when Hannah unwraps the strap from Billy's chest, it's sexy, but it also shows Hannah embracing Billy's complicated gender and desiring Billy as she moves from her disguise to her naked and true self.

You've written three previous books, two of interviews with other authors and one on how to interview authors and creative people. How did writing these books influence your fiction?

In writing *Conversations with American Women Writers* and *The Very Telling*, I was able to speak with authors whose work I most admired. In preparing for the interviews, I read all of the authors' works, both in their main genre and outside of it. I read other interviews with them and anything written about them, so that I became immersed in the writing life of each author. This deep study answered questions I had in my own work and generated even more questions about writing in general. I was able to sit down with each author and ask whatever questions came to mind. It was a wonderful opportunity to study and learn, as well as to publish and build relationships with other writers. So, to answer your question, how did writing those books impact my fiction—it furthered my education and helped me in the continual process of discovering my craft.

What would you say to writers working on a first book?

Read, read, read, and sit in your chair at your desk and write. Commit to a certain amount of time each day and stay in your chair. I read a great piece of advice in a Ron Carlson book: if you hit a roadblock in your writing, sit with it for twenty minutes. Don't get up to get a cup of coffee or check the mail. Don't go on the Internet. Just sit with it. Every time I've tried this, I've been able to write through my snag. Sitting is half the work of writing. So, just sit there.

ACKNOWLEDGMENTS

I want to thank the Jentel Artist Residency Program for time and support in writing *The Lightkeeper's Wife*, as well as Vermont Studio Center.

Thank you to my parents, Susan O'Leary and Charles E. Johnson, who got me in a boat as soon as I could walk, and the rest of my family who offered their support over the years, including Edward J. O'Leary III, my first lighthouse keeper. Thanks to my editor, Shana Drehs, and the good people at Sourcebooks; the Posse; and Allison Hill, Joy Johannessen, Bret Anthony Johnston, Alice Mattison, Jenny Stephens, and Randi Triant for their readings. And to Miriam Kahn for keeping my eye on the heart of the matter and staying in the boat with me through every storm. This book would not have been possible without the guidance, creative support, and friendship of Laurie Liss. Thank you to Susan Kurtzman, the other half of my writing life, who held the lantern at the door every day. She is my first reader, editor, and creative consort. She encouraged me to get the book done through every obstacle and contributed in so many ways, offering love and support and tireless edits.

ABOUT THE AUTHOR

Photo credit: Elyssa Cohen

Sarah Anne Johnson is the author of *The Very Telling*, *The Art of the Author Interview*, and *Conversations with American Women Writers*, all published by the University Press of New England. She is the recipient of residencies in fiction from Jentel Artist Residency Program and Vermont Studio Center. She lives on Cape Cod.